NILDA

NILDA

a novel by
NICHOLASA MOHR
with pictures by the author

HARPER & ROW, PUBLISHERS
New York   Evanston   San Francisco   London

Library of Congress Catalog Card Number: 73–8046
Trade Standard Book Number: 06–024331–7
Harpercrest Standard Book Number: 06–024332–5

FIRST EDITION

*Dedicated, with love, to the children of El Barrio—
and of the many barrios all over the world.*

THE CHILDREN
Why do you go so far
from the little square?

MYSELF
I go in search of magicians
and of princesses!

THE CHILDREN
Who showed you the path
of the poets?

MYSELF
The fountain and the stream
of the antique song.

THE CHILDREN
Do you go far, very far
from the sea and the earth?

MYSELF
My heart of silk
is filled with lights,
with lost bells,
with lilies and bees.
I will go very far,

farther than those hills,
farther than the seas,
close to the stars,
to beg Christ the Lord
to give back the soul I had
of old, when I was a child,
ripened with legends,
with a feathered cap
and a wooden sword.

THE CHILDREN
You leave us singing
in the little square,
clear streams,
serene fountain!

—Federico García Lorca

July, 1941

Summers in New York City's Barrio were unbearable. Even when there was a cool spell, it seemed a long time before the dry fresh air could find a way past the concrete and asphalt, into the crowded buildings which had become blazing furnaces. As Nilda played outside, she could smell the heat mingled with the odors coming from the tenements and sidewalks. Tiny beads of moisture settled in her nostrils, making it hard to breathe.

She was playing on the sidewalk where she had discovered a small patch of shadow. The side wall of the stoop steps of her building created this small island of comfort which now became her turf. With a small piece of white chalk, she began to draw pictures on the sidewalk. Getting even with her friends, she decided to scribble who loved who and which one stank. Pausing, she impulsively reached out to touch the unshaded concrete and jumped back, sticking her finger in her mouth to let the saliva take out the sting of the burn. She looked up and saw two of her friends.

"Man, it's hotter here than in my house," said Petra.

She was with her younger sister, Marge, who nodded in agreement. Nilda moved over and the two girls sat beside her, sharing the patch of shade.

1

"Paco is going to camp, lucky thing," said Petra.

"I wish I could go," said Marge.

"I'm going," said Nilda. "My mother got me a place in a camp someplace in the country."

"Is that the Catholic camp?" asked Petra. "Because if it is I sure won't go there. They beat you up there."

"They do not!" Nilda screamed. She had heard this before. Shrugging her shoulders, she said, "You never even been there."

"But I know some kids who did go and they told me some stories, you know. They said—"

"Don't tell me no lies," Nilda interrupted. "Where is the place they went to?"

"In the country," Petra answered. "Upstate or someplace like that."

"Well there! This place where I'm going is in New Jersey, very far away, so you don't even know what you're talking about!"

"Oh, I think it was New Jersey."

"Aw shut up, stupid. You are so dumb you don't know your ass from your elbow! Talking a lot of garbage." Nilda stopped talking and looked around her.

Up to that moment the block had been very quiet; people had been trying to keep off the hot street as much as possible. Now small groups of people were gathering about. The focus was on several men being led by Jacinto the grocer. For days everyone had been hoping that they would open up the fire hydrant. Jacinto was the only one who had the kind of wrench that could open the hydrant. He was afraid of the fine he might receive from the police, and he had refused to listen to everyone's pleas. "You

2

gonna pay the fine?" he had responded. "You know they're gonna get me because I got the store."

The intense heat had gone on for many days. Nilda knew now, just by looking at Jacinto and the group with him, that they were about to open the hydrant. All three girls jumped up in unison. Like an ant colony with antennae, it seemed, the entire block was informed immediately. People started to come out of the tenements or looked out of the windows asking, "Are they going to open it?" "Look, there's Jacinto; they're going to do it." "Mira! Mira! There they go!" Their sluggishness seemed to fade, and with renewed vigor people appeared in the street. Nilda turned and ran into her building. She was anxious to tell whoever was home what was about to happen and to get into her bathing suit. She climbed the four flights of stairs, racing all the way. Pushing open the door, she yelled, "They are doing it; they're going to open the hydrant! Hurry up before the cops come."

"I know. I see, I see," said her mother.

"Mama, I want my bathing suit."

"I got your bathing suit and a towel right there on the kitchen table. Now I'm going down," she said.

Her mother and Aunt Delia started out the door. Nilda ran after them.

"Mama, where's Paul and Frankie?"

"They're out, but they will probably be back soon enough to see the water," her mother said.

Downstairs everybody was waiting and watching as Jacinto and some of the other men started to turn the large wrench which gripped the round cap on the side of the hydrant. It got quieter and quieter with each turn. As

3

they removed the cap, complete stillness followed. A small stream of water dripped out of the round dark opening and a hushed sigh traveled the length and width of the onlooking crowd. Quickly, Jacinto turned the knob at the top of the hydrant with the wrench. Suddenly with a burst, tons of water came gushing forth, cascading onto the hot melting black tar of the street like a magical waterfall. People plunged right into the onrushing water with their clothes on, arms outstretched, mouths open, drinking in the cool liquid. Laughing and screaming, they pushed each other out of the way to get nearer the water, their clothes sticking to bosoms and bellies, buttocks, arms, and muscles all glistening with wetness.

Young women who were too shy to jump in were grabbed by the young men and pushed in. Their cries of protest resounded with happiness and relief as they ran laughing and jumping, covered completely with the cool water.

As automobiles turned into the street and passed in front of the hydrant, the young boys tried to get the drivers wet. When a driver forgot to close his windows and got soaked, the crowd would laugh and clap, ignoring his angry cursing and cries of protest.

The children skipped around, hopping and weaving in and around the adults. Some had bathing suits and some wore their clothes. The very small children had underpants or were naked. Except for the very old, who sat and watched with joy and amusement, everybody got drenched. Nilda yelled, "Come on!" and ran in and out of the spray with her friends. At times she would stay put in the water long enough to let the spray embrace her until she could feel the wonder of a chill traveling all over her body, a sensation she had forgotten in the long weeks of the heat. She was caught up in this mood of elation until she heard a low whining sound. In a few seconds everyone heard the clear sounds of the siren. The police patrol car turned the corner. She saw the car heading toward the hydrant. "La jara!" someone yelled. "La policía!" "The cops are here, man!" Swiftly, people began to scatter, backing up and running from the water.

Nilda stood among the people lined up against the steps of the tenements and in front of the small shops. The water gushed forth onto an empty street. She saw the two tall white men in uniform step out and look around. Everyone was silent, watching and waiting. One policeman held a large wrench, the other had one hand placed on his gun holster and the other hand wrapped around his nightstick. They looked menacingly at the groups of people that lined both sides of the street, and slowly walked over to the hydrant. "O.K. Now, who's responsible for this?" There was a dead silence. The two policemen shook their heads and began to close the hydrant. Round and round they turned the wrench and finally it was closed. Shut tight. Quiet grumbling and whispered protests emanated from the onlooking crowd.

"God damn you people," yelled one policeman. "You got no sense of responsibility. What if there's a fire?"

Someone responded from way back, "Coño, leave the water on, man. It's too hot here! Have a heart." Everybody clapped.

"Shit. God damn you bastards, coming here making trouble. Bunch of animals. Listen, don't pull that shit

5

again. You're acting against the law. If this happens again, one more time, I'm going to arrest all your asses! The whole God damned bunch of you spicks."

"Animals!" the other policeman added. Turning around and looking directly at the people, they waited, as if daring a response. Then the two policemen walked over to Jacinto's grocery. Some of the children followed. Nilda was with her friends.

"You coming, Nilda? Let's see what happens. Come on," said little Benji.

"No, I'm staying. I'll see you later, Benji." She did not want to be near the policemen; she wanted them to disappear.

A few minutes later they walked out of Jacinto's grocery. Each policeman had his own particular defiant swagger as he walked over to the patrol car and got in.

"Dirty bastard cops!" yelled a young man.

"Jacinto got another fine, man. Bendito."

"They know they can get him because he got the store, you know."

"That's a God damn shame."

Nilda saw the crowd dispersing. People reluctantly returned to their tenements, feeling the heat overtake them once more. She stayed in the street with her friends, enrapt in amazement at the river that flowed by the gutter. They were all fascinated by the things that floated along. The children waded in the cool stream, collecting lots of treasures. Nilda found a piece of comb and Petra found a paper cup. Marge and little Benji found some good bottle caps. They collected all these items with great interest. Little Benji put some water in the paper cup and drank it. "Ugh!" he yelled. "This tastes terrible!"

"Don't, Benji. Don't drink it; it's got shit and germs in it," said Nilda. "You'll get sick and it tastes awful." She knew because many times before she too had spit out the foul-tasting liquid.

The gutter river narrowed, slowly disappearing; and once again the dry hot concrete and black tar streets began to take command. Nilda looked down the street and saw the puddles of water begin to evaporate and the oppressive feeling of baking alive overtook her again. She turned to Petra who said, "Maybe it will rain," as if reading Nilda's thoughts. Benji picked up some of the bottle caps and said, "I'm cutting. See you."

Nilda looked from Petra to Marge. "I'm tired of this game. I'm going home. See you later."

She walked home, trying to step only on the areas where the pavement was wet. Nilda started thinking of camp and what it might be like with all kinds of trees and grass and maybe a lake. Like Central Park, she thought, or something like that. She tried to guess what might be ahead for her, maybe something better. These thoughts helped erase the image of the two big white policemen who loomed larger and more powerful than all the other people in her life.

August, 1941

Nilda had said good-bye to her mother at Grand Central Station and, now on board the train, she wondered what life would be like away from her family and the Barrio. The train was headed for Upstate New York, not New Jersey as she had told Petra. This was the first time she had ever been without her family and out of her neighborhood on her own. She looked around and up and down the train car and saw a bunch of kids, none of whom she recognized. The nuns sat in pairs, staring straight ahead and not speaking.

Slowly, then rapidly, the city began to fade from view as Nilda looked out the window. First, the Park Avenue Market began to disappear and she looked back at 110th Street where she went shopping with her mother almost every day; then all the buildings, tenements, streetlights, and traffic faded from view. Panic seized her and she swallowed, fighting a strong urge to cry as she longed to go back home that very second.

She saw large sections of trees and grass interspersed with small houses. Once in a while a group of cows behind barbed wire would come into view. "Look, cows!" "Wow, those are real cows!" some of the kids cried out. Nilda strained her neck, trying to get a good view of the animals as the train whizzed by. Once they saw some horses. The ride took them past many little houses, most painted white, some with picket fences surrounded by trees and grass. There were no tall buildings at all. Small white churches with pointed steeples. Large barns and weather vanes. Neat patches of grass and flowers. It reminded her of the movies. Like the Andy Hardy pictures, she almost said out loud. In those movies Mickey Rooney and his whole family were always so happy. They lived in a whole house all for themselves. She started thinking about all those houses that so swiftly passed by the train window. Families and kids, problems that always had happy endings. A whole mess of happiness, she thought, just laid out there before my eyes. It didn't seem real, yet here was the proof because people really lived in those little houses. Recalling a part of the movie where Mickey Rooney goes to his father the judge for advice, Nilda smiled, losing herself in the happy plot of the story.

"Don't pick your nose," snapped a nun. "You'll get worms." Nilda looked around her as if she had just awakened. "You! You! I'm talking to you." She realized that the nun was pointing to her and she could feel the embarrassment spreading all over her face as everyone laughed.

At the train depot they all boarded several buses and after a short ride arrived at their destination. The children were all lined up in different groups according to sex and age. Nilda stood in line with the rest of the girls in her group. She looked about her and saw several ugly grey buildings skirted by water. The day was gloomy, adding to the bleakness of the place, which looked like an abandoned factory.

The children stood about in their assigned groups as the nuns and brothers cautioned them to silence. Other children were walking about near the buildings; obviously there were some campers here already. Nilda thought, They don't look so happy to me. Someone blew a whistle. "All right now, let's march!" said a brother, waving his arm and pointing towards one of the buildings. He wore rimless glasses and his red hair was slicked down.

"Let's follow Brother Sean, everyone," said one of the nuns. There was a dank smell coming from the water. Nilda noticed a thin layer of oily film covering the water near the shoreline. She walked along with the other children towards one of the buildings. The gritty sand under her feet stank of oil.

They were led into a very large room with long wooden tables and benches. Everywhere Nilda looked there was a crucifix or a holy statue. Each group was assigned a table to sit at. A nervous chatter was beginning among the children. A large red-faced nun walked up and clapped her hands vigorously. "Silence, silence now, children. Let me introduce Father Shaw. He will explain everything you want to know. Now," she looked at the group seriously, "I expect complete quiet and your undivided attention when Father Shaw speaks." With that she stepped aside and an even larger red-faced priest with a pinkish bald head began to speak.

"Thank you, sister." He paused, looking at the rows of tables and benches filled with children, and said, "Now, I want to see all those lucky faces. Why lucky? I can tell you why! You have been fortunate enough to leave the hot city behind. How many kids do you know that can leave the city? We intend to have a good time, of course.

But every one of us is obligated to show our Savior Jesus Christ our thanks by living, behaving, and thinking like good Catholics. Not just at Mass. Here we carry it through every moment. Now, how many of you have made your First Communion?"

Most of the children eagerly picked up their hands. Nilda put her hands on her lap. Although she would be ten years old in a couple of months, she had never received Communion. "Well, that's wonderful!" Father Shaw said. "For those children who have not received Communion yet, we will have a special religious instruction group every day. They will have a chance to catch up on Catechism." His smile faded. "Rules are to be obeyed here. We deal with no nonsense. Let me warn everyone, especially the smart alecks, that any kind of misbehavior will be dealt with so that it doesn't happen a second time. We want no Judas or Jew!" Pausing, he then asked, smiling with humor, "Are there any here, by the way?" The large nun was the first to laugh, bringing giggles and cries of "Noooooo" from the children.

Nilda thought of her stepfather's constant blasphemy and his many arguments with her mother, as he attacked the Catholic Church. I wish I could tell Papa, she thought. He might just convince Mama to let me go back home right now, even before I have to open my suitcase.

In that same large room with the long wooden tables and benches, campers were fed their meals. Supper that night consisted of first, a clear soup, which was so tasteless that it took Nilda a while to recognize the flavor—it was chicken—then the main course, a sausage pie. The meat was wrapped in a soft dough having the consistency of oatmeal; it was served with creamed beets and grits, bread spread with jam, and a glass of powdered milk. Dessert was stewed plums and prunes in a heavy syrup. Nilda was not very hungry.

One of the sisters walked up and down between the tables, watching the children. "Here we eat what's put on our plates. We don't waste food. That's a sin! There are many less fortunate children who go hungry in Europe and all over the world." Nilda felt a sharp poke in her left shoulder blade. The nun was standing behind her. "You can do better than that, now." Before she could turn around to look, the nun had walked over to another girl. "Eat what you have on your plate, young lady, because that's all you get until breakfast. I don't want to hear that anybody's hungry tonight." Looking down at her food, Nilda put some of it on her fork and shoved it into her mouth. She tried not to think, as she chewed, of her mother and the good-tasting food she had at home.

A gong sounded. The sister clapped her hands. "All right, now just a minute, stay in your seats." She walked around inspecting the children's plates. "Well, we're going to overlook some of these full plates tonight because this is this group's first day here. Tomorrow we expect all the plates to be completely clean. Let's line up." The girls in Nilda's section left the tables and formed a line two abreast.

A young nun walked up to the group of girls. "I'm Sister Barbara," she said smiling. "Follow me, girls, and please no talking." She led them out of the building and over to the dormitory where Nilda had previously put her suitcase. The building was very much like the others, two stories high, the outside concrete and brick. Inside, the walls were painted a dark color; the paint was peeling and large cracks were visible on the walls and ceiling.

The group of children walked along into the dormitory, a very large room with rows of army cots all made up. Army khaki blankets were neatly tucked in the cots. Each cot had a pillow with a white pillowcase and at the end of the cot was a footlocker. Sister Barbara turned, still smiling, and said, "Shower time. Get your robes and towels, pajamas and toothbrushes. We have a nice full day tomorrow and it's time to get ready for bed." Nilda looked out; it was still light outside. She thought, Man, at home I could go outside and play with Petra and little Benji.

"Leave your clothes on, girls. We have to go to another building," said the smiling nun.

Sister Barbara led the group outside and into another similar building only one story high. Nilda looked at the long room with benches lined against one side of the wall and showers lining the other side. She could see the toilets in the next room; none of them had doors, just toilets lined up next to each other. The girls started to undress. Nilda felt a little embarrassed, naked with all those girls she hardly knew. Some of the others were already under the showers. "Oooooooh, it's cold." "Ayeeeee, it's freezing."

"Now, girls, we're a little short of hot water so just go in and come out quickly, that's all," said Sister Bar-

13

bara, all smiling and pleasant. Feeling the goose bumps all over her body, Nilda jumped in and out, drying herself and getting her pajamas and robe on. "Anyone who has to go to the john, go now." A few girls walked into the next room. "You cannot go later, now is the time, before we get to bed." Nilda was glad she had peed in the shower, and so she stayed put.

Back in the dormitory, Nilda noticed some food carts lined up against the side wall. They were all full of large bottles of Phillips' Milk of Magnesia. Set at the side of the bottles were tiny glasses that looked like the whiskey glasses they had at home for parties and Christmastime. Grabbing a cart by the handles, Sister Barbara started walking, pushing the cart over to the section where Nilda was. Still smiling and in a soft voice, she said to one of the girls, "It's time for our laxative." She handed the glass to the girl. The girl did not respond; she sat there looking at the nun.

"How is it going?" a loud voice said. Nilda saw the same large nun who had introduced Father Shaw earlier that day. "They are taking their laxative, aren't they? I hope no one here is a baby and has to be treated like one." Both women were now standing over the girl. Nilda watched as the older larger woman took the small glass out of the younger nun's hand and shoved it right up to the girl's face. The girl grabbed the glass and put it to her lips. "Hurry up now, quick, all at once! Let's go . . . the whole thing! No, no! Drink it all. There! That's it," said the large nun. "Now, let's not have any more fuss or I'll call Brother Sean. He has a very convincing friend, a good

14

whacking stick that will help anyone here drink their laxative." With that she turned and left, walking over to the other section of the dormitory.

Sister Barbara continued going to several cots and finally Nilda took a deep breath as she saw the smile on the nun's face directed at her. "You will take this, please. Time for our laxative."

"I already went to the bathroom," said Nilda.

"This is for tomorrow. This way you will be clean and pure when you greet God. Waking up, you will be ready to release everything in your bowels, getting a fresh start before Mass." Nilda looked and saw that Sister Barbara's smile never left her face. Like it was stuck on or something, she thought. Nilda reached out and took the small glass, holding it up to her lips. A wave of nausea hit her and she closed her eyes. As if anticipating what would happen, the young woman said, "None of that, now. I don't want to call Brother Sean. Nobody here has started this business so don't you be silly. Just drink it down."

Closing her eyes, Nilda began to drink the chalky sticky substance. "All of it, that's a good girl. Go on! Drink it all down. Good. A little bit more. Good. Ah!" Nilda made a heaving sound. "Uh, uh, just swallow and keep it down. Don't let it come up. In a couple of days when you get used to it, you won't even taste it." Smiling, she marched on to the next cot.

Nilda could feel the tears rushing out all at once. Pulling the covers over her head, she began to cry quietly. She licked the tears and welcomed the saltiness as it helped reduce the chalky taste in her mouth. She went on crying quietly until she fell asleep. During the night the sounds of sobbing and whimpering coming from the other cots woke her, but each time she closed her eyes, going back into a deep sleep.

The same large room that was used as the dining room and meeting hall was also used as a classroom. Nilda sat at one of the tables and daydreamed that she was back home. She missed her familiar world of noise, heat, and crowds, and she missed her family most of all. All the nuns, priests, and brothers were very white and had blue or light brown eyes. Only among the children were there dark faces. She wondered if Puerto Ricans were ever allowed to be nuns, fathers, or brothers.

"I hope we can work real hard, children," said the short nun, "so that when you return home you will be able to receive Holy Communion and make your families happy and proud." She walked around stiffly, stopping to ask the children if they had understood what she had said. She got very little response from anyone.

Papa wouldn't be proud. He would have a fit, thought Nilda, with a feeling of affection and warmth for her stepfather.

That night she looked around at the enormous dormitory with the many rows of army cots set side by side. The chalky taste of the milk of magnesia was still fresh in her mouth, making her feel nauseous.

The lights had been turned out already. She could hear a lot of quiet crying and whimpering. She started to think of home. Why am I here? Did Mama know about this place? She remembered her mother with her portable

16

altars for the Virgin Mary and all the different saints. Nilda's mother set these altars all over the apartment. Always lighting candles, saying prayers, visiting the spiritualist, who gave her all kinds of remedies and special prayers. Mama is always asking God or a saint for miracles. She is always talking about fate and that there is a divine reason for things. "A Destiny. Everything is written for you already up there!" That's what Mama says, she thought. We must not offend God. All of a sudden it all became perfectly clear to Nilda. Wow! I must have done something very bad to offend God! Something really really bad. She started to think about all the "bad" things she had done in her life. After a while she decided that it must be one special thing, or several things, or maybe everything!

Well, whatever it is, I'll repent. I'll repent it all. But now that it was time to repent she realized that she was in bed for the night. Once they put out the lights she could not leave her bunk. She had to do something right now, at that moment. Taking a deep breath, she said, "I promise you, oh Virgin Mary, to sleep all night with my hands folded across my chest just like you look in some of the statues I seen in church. I will recite all the prayers I know and some I just learned. And I promise to think only pure thoughts all night long." Shutting her eyes tightly and folding her arms, she said, "Please, oh please, let me go home tomorrow."

After breakfast the next day, there was a rumor that everyone was going to be sent home. As she heard the children talking, Nilda was both happy and frightened

17

at the same time. Everyone was whispering and talking about going home. In the early afternoon all the campers were called in, assembled in the big dining hall, and seated at the long tables. The large nun entered, walked over to the other nuns, and began whispering. Nilda heard the kids.

"We're gonna be sent home."

"Yeah, that's what I heard."

"Do you think it's true?"

"Maybe. I overheard some of the brothers and they said . . ."

Nilda was afraid to comment or respond lest she break the magic of the miracle that was about to happen. If they knew, it might spoil it all, she thought.

The large nun walked to the front of the hall and began speaking. "I am here for Father Shaw. He had to attend to some urgent business regarding the camp." Nilda's heart was pounding and she could hardly hear or understand what the large woman was saying. "Something has gone wrong with the plumbing and there is no water. Some of you will be sent home today and others will be sent home tomorrow." A huge cheer went up. The children were elated, jumping up and down on the benches. "Stop it! Stop the nonsense or I'll send for Brother Sean this minute," she said, clapping furiously. "Unfortunately," she continued, "we cannot fix the plumbing or the pipes. There is no water available. This is a major repair job which we cannot do this year." This brought giggles and happy sighs from some of the tables. "Quiet, quiet!" she clapped. "Now next year . . ." Closing her eyes with a sense of joy and relief that shook her body, Nilda stopped listening.

Back in her dormitory, packing away her things in her suitcase, Nilda was filled with happiness at her liberation and secretly guarded her miracle. "It worked!" she whispered. See, she said to herself, just like Mama always says, faith is very powerful! Looking about her and making sure nobody saw her, she made the sign of the cross and whispered, "I'll never doubt You again. I'll be a believer, dear Jesus and Virgin Mary." And so she made her solemn vow right there in the large dormitory, with the very best of intentions.

"You'll be late for Mass, Nilda. Hurry! Are you going alone?"

"I'm not gonna be late, Ma. I'm picking up Petra and maybe little Benji is coming."

Summer had gone by and school had started. Nilda still felt she ought to keep her promise to the Virgin, to believe. Since the "miracle" in camp she had attended Sunday Mass regularly. But it was getting harder and harder each Sunday morning, especially since her brothers never went to church and could sleep late. When she complained of unfairness, her mother would say, "They are boys, Nilda; what does it matter? But you, you are a girl. For you it is essential. Oh yes." This explanation did not make sense to Nilda, especially since her mother never went to Sunday Mass. She preferred instead to go to church during the week. "I have special prayers and novenas to say, Nilda. They are best dealt with during the week."

Now, Nilda could hear her stepfather grumbling in the bedroom. "Bunch of shit, filling her head with that phony stuff. Fairy tales in order to oppress the masses. Teaching them that to be good is not to fight back, is to take crap. . . ." He went on, "They're afraid of the revolution—"

20

"That's enough!" interrupted her mother. "What you say has nothing to do with God. One has to have faith. Faith is very powerful, especially faith in God. He will provide."

Nilda knew another one of those arguments between her mother and her stepfather was under way.

"I shit on the priest's bird, is what I do. Carajo! Bunch of impotent faggots oppressing the people," he shouted. "God feeds us? Clothes us? Mierda, I don't see him around talking to the bill collectors."

"God help us!" retaliated her mother, making the sign of the cross. "And may God forgive you, Emilio." She said this addressing one of the closest of the many portable altars set up around the apartment.

"I'd rather he sent me next month's rent first."

Nilda listened to the voices arguing and wondered at all the possibilities of truth set before her. Making a choice was a heavy responsibility, and for Nilda the choice would change as unpredictably as the weather.

At Mass in St. Cecilia's Church, she sat in the pew with the other children and watched intensely as the kids and adults received Holy Communion. Every Sunday Nilda tried to develop a closeness to the church.

On cold days after school last winter, Nilda remembered how she would go off to play in church all by herself. She did not want Petra or little Benji to go with her. Once she had almost got caught lighting rows of candles.

"Who's there?" someone asked loudly.

Recognizing Father Shea's voice, she ducked, quickly sneaking out. Most of the time nobody bothered her. Nilda found the church a warm place to play in and the fragrance of melted wax and incense had a comforting effect on her. She would spend a good deal of time looking at the statues, all the carving, and the tall stained-glass windows. She marveled at the idea that a mortal person could do all this. Surely somebody made out of flesh and blood must have done all this, she thought. Was it one person who did it all?

The snake beneath the Virgin's feet and the scenes on the Stations of the Cross captured her and she would extend her arm, touching the forms and curves with the tips of her fingers, feeling the shapes develop into recognizable objects. Sometimes, in an effort to feel "religious," she would look into the faces of the holy statues, and their expressionless eyes would stare back at her with a porcelain look, grotesque and unreal, making her think of the dummy figures in the wax museum at Coney Island of people who had committed horrible crimes.

She also recalled how when she got home from camp, she told little Benji about her miracle. He had listened wide-eyed, and respectfully nodded when she embellished the story. Nilda loved little Benji; he was a whole year younger than she and she could hover over him and protect him at times like a mother hen. He was solidly built, but short for his age. He had dark olive skin and straight black hair that fell in bangs just above dark brown eyes. There were eight children in little Benji's family: five sisters and three brothers. He was stacked somewhere in the middle. Benji's parents were of the Pentecostal faith, fundamentalists, strict in their religious beliefs. Little Benji and his brothers and sisters were not allowed to do a lot of things that other children in the neighborhood did. They could not play ball or participate in street games, or go to parties. Benji had to attend all the religious meetings that were held in the storefront church, "La Roca de San Sebastián, Inc.," on Lexington Avenue. Whenever she could, Nilda took little Benji to church for Sunday Mass. But his parents frowned at the idea, and it wasn't easy to convince them.

Nilda had shared her secret miracle with Benji and no one else. She was glad she didn't tell Petra or her brother Paul or anyone else; they might make fun of her.

Today she saw the people returning from the altar, walking up the center aisle, each with the little white wafer in his mouth. They seemed to have an aura of mystery and immeasurable importance. They have been changed, she thought, by the magic ritual. That will make me feel close to God, she almost said aloud. Turning to Petra she whispered, "I think I'm going to receive Holy Communion today."

"What?" Petra almost shrieked. "You're not supposed to. You never been to Confession yet."

"I can try it just once before I go to Confession," argued Nilda.

"Uh uh, that's a big sin. You're gonna have to confess it later on and do a lotta penance. You better not do it."

"What's going on?" asked Marge. Petra leaned over and whispered in Marge's ear. "That's a real bad sin," said Marge. "You wouldn't dare do that!"

"Yeah," said Petra, "you never dare do that!"

Nilda leaned forward, sitting at the edge of the pew, and in a moment sprang up, following the line of people walking up to the altar.

Looking straight ahead, she carefully strained to watch exactly what everyone did. When her turn came, she stepped up to the altar, kneeled down, and put the palms of her hands together, moving her lips as if in deep prayer, imitating the person who had just vacated that spot. Immediately the priest stood before her, tall and portly, in clean silk robes that shone brilliantly, reflecting the light overhead. He smelled so clean she was convinced he could not stink or go to the toilet like other people and he was indeed related to the statues in the church. She stuck out her tongue and waited. He began to pray in Latin, moving his hands back and forth before her, making the sign of the cross and quickly moving on to the next person, repeating the ritual once more. Tasteless at first, the wafer then felt sticky, like a postage stamp.

She got up feeling unsteady and overwhelmed by extreme fear. Walking back to her pew, she automatically began to scrape the sticky wafer from the roof of her mouth with her tongue. She sat down with a sense of relief to be back in her seat, thankful no one had struck her dead. As she began to relax a little, she heard the voice of an older girl from the pew behind say, "You're supposed to let it dissolve in your mouth; you're not allowed to chew the sacred body of Jesus."

The magic transformation that Nilda had anticipated developed instead into a panic. She felt nothing beyond the fear of retaliation for her unholy act. Now they won't listen any more, she thought. I've given up my right to any more miracles.

For three weeks Nilda's stepfather had been in the hospital. Her mother was packing a shopping bag of food and clothes for him.

"How long is Papa gonna stay there?" Nilda asked her.

"I don't know. Your Papa is very sick."

"What's wrong again?"

"He had a bad heart attack and he has to rest a long time."

"Ma, is Papa very old?"

"Old enough."

"He looks real old, Mama. The kids at school asked me once if he is my grandfather."

"Well, he's not and don't tell him that when he comes home, entiende?"

Nilda watched her mother. Her jet black hair was parted in the middle; she had not yet knotted it into a chignon and so it hung loosely down her back right to her waistline. Her mother's skin was very white. She worked very quickly, moving her hands, folding and putting things in the shopping bag. Her dark large eyes looked worried and she kept wetting her lips nervously.

"Am I gonna look like you when I grow up?"

"You're going to look like yourself, Nilda."

"Frankie looks like you."

"You look like me, too."

"Not as much as him."

"Ay, chica. Don't start that nonsense, Nilda; I'm too busy now."

Nilda sat sulking. She knew she looked like her real father. This morning when she looked in the mirror and saw herself, studying her eyes, skin, and hair very carefully, she had to accept the obvious. Her straight brown hair and Oriental features were just like Leo's. Even the dark tone of her skin was just like his.

Frankie walked in. "Ma, when's lunch?"

"Frankie, you just had breakfast."

"I'm hungry."

"Well, you can have one piece of bread and that's it. The food will be ready when I come back from the hospital. I have to see Papa. O.K.?"

He looks just like Mama, Nilda thought.

"I'm waiting for Jimmy to pick me up. He promised to come today with me and Victor to see Papa." Her mother went on, "Victor is still in the library and I don't want to be late. Papa looks forward to my visits and the food from home. He says the meals in the hospital are terrible."

Jimmy, Nilda's oldest brother, had left home about six months ago. Her mother and stepfather had pleaded with him to stay, but he quit high school and left. Nilda's mother lit candles for him every day.

Aunt Delia walked in holding her copies of the *Daily News* and *La Prensa*, the Spanish newspaper. Everybody else shared one copy of the newspaper, but the old woman

27

always had her own copy of both newspapers. "Number 205 came out and I played 286," she sighed. "Monday I'm going to bet it again but in combination this time." Betting the numbers and reading the papers absorbed 90 per cent of her life. "Look at that!" she said emphatically in Spanish. "They did it again!" The only time the old woman ever spoke English was when she read the *Daily News* out loud. Opening up her copy of the *Daily News*, she said, "Somebody's been cutting up bodies and putting them in the garbage cans. They're finding the parts of a body all over the city. The head in one place and . . . listen to this. . . ."

"Not again," said Frankie. "I heard that story eight times already this morning."

The old lady was almost deaf and went right on reading aloud in English. "In Queens they found two legs wrapped up . . ."

Nilda looked at the old, small, thin woman and wondered how her tiny face could hold so many wrinkles. She's really old looking, way older looking than Papa, she thought.

"And in Brooklyn, sanitation men discovered part of a torso wrapped up in a cardboard box."

"Please, Delia, that's enough," her mother said loudly in Spanish.

"What?"

"Have something to eat, Delia," her mother went on, changing the subject.

"I'm not hungry," said the old woman.

"If you would wear your teeth you could chew better and you would eat more."

28

"None of them fit."

Nilda's mother shook her head and sighed. Aunt Delia had five pairs of false teeth. Two had been gotten through the public health service, and three had been given to her by well-meaning neighbors after relatives had died. She would not consider the possibility of wearing a hearing aid, insisting she wasn't hard of hearing. "Some woman was found raped and beaten after being robbed."

"I wonder what's keeping Victor and Jimmy," her mother said aloud to herself.

Nilda got up and walked out of the kitchen and into the living room. Sitting down next to Paul, who was reading the comics, she said, "Don't you wish Aunt Delia would shut up sometimes? Always talking about some creepy thing."

"Even when it's not in the paper she makes them up," said Paul.

All her brothers were older than Nilda, and Paul was third from the oldest; Frankie was the youngest. Paul was the dark one. His skin was the color of cinnamon and his eyes were large and dark like her mother's. Secretly she loved Paul the best and sometimes felt guilty about it. "Paul, how old you think Aunt Delia is?"

"I don't know. She must be real old, I guess."

"The kids asked me if she was over one hundred years old."

"Go on," said Paul, "if she were one hundred years old she couldn't even move."

"That's what I told them. I said she only looks like that 'cause she got no teeth and she don't eat, so she gets shriveled."

The front door opened and Jimmy and Victor came in together. Victor was carrying his books.

"Where's Mama?" Jimmy asked.

"In the kitchen. She's waiting for you; she don't want to be late," she replied.

"Hey, baby! What you doing, ugly?" Jimmy went towards Nilda, who jumped up, giving him a big hug. "I got a new car downstairs; you wanna ride?"

"Wow, Jimmy, a car! Take me for a ride, please, please!"

"O.K. When I get back from the hospital with Mama."

"Do it now, just for a minute."

"Come on now, you can wait," he said.

"You'll forget, Jimmy, you will."

"No I won't, I promise."

"All right," she said, smiling. Jimmy went into the kitchen. "Paul, did you hear? Jimmy's got a car," she went on. "I'm gonna go down to see it."

"Hey yeah, I'll go with you. Let's find out what color it is first, Nilda."

Nilda and Paul could hear the argument as they started to go into the kitchen.

"Where you get the car? What's going on, Jimmy? Job? What kind of job pays such money to a kid like you, eh? What are you doing? God, I got enough grief with Papa sick," her mother was saying. "Keep away from the drugs, Jimmy."

"Aw, Mama, stop it. It's this guy I'm working for. He's got a lot of money and I'm his assistant, you know, drive him around like, and stuff like that. That's all."

Nilda saw her mother wiping her eyes and shaking her head.

"What color is your car, Jimmy?" Paul asked. "We're gonna go down to look at it."

"It's a dark green Cadillac convertible. Here's the key. Open the door and sit down inside till we get downstairs." He flipped the keys over to Paul, adding, "Here's a quarter for you and Nilda. You can mind it and make sure nobody sits on it, O.K.?"

"Half of that is mine, Paul," Nilda yelled after him as they both sped downstairs.

Downstairs, they looked around and saw a brand-new green car. "This must be it, Nilda."

"Let's get in. Hurry up, open it."

"Just a minute, I gotta get the key in the lock." Paul put the key in the lock, opened the door, and jumped in the driver's seat. Nilda hopped in beside him. They opened the windows.

"Wow! Man, look at all this shiny silver."

"That's called chrome," said Paul.

"Well, it's really beautiful. Let's turn on the radio."

"O.K." Paul turned a knob and waited. Nothing happened. He then turned a few more buttons and waited. Nothing happened.

"What's the matter, Paul?"

"I don't know. I guess Jimmy knows how to do it a special way."

"I guess so," said Nilda. She was excited sitting there in the great big new car. She had been for a car ride twice, but that was in old cars. She remembered that once

31

Jacinto the grocer had taken some of the neighborhood kids to Coney Island in his old car. Another time a friend of her stepfather had taken her family to a faraway place called Long Island. It was so crowded and hot during the ride that she had been glad to get out.

"I think you have to start the car, maybe," said Paul, "before you can turn on the radio, and we better not do that."

"Let's just sit here," said Nilda. "This is real cool. Boy, I'll bet you Jimmy is rich, huh Paul? He got all them new clothes all the time and everything. I wonder where he lives."

"I don't know, but it must be real nice."

"Hey, man!" A group of kids came over. "What's happening, baby?"

"This is my brother Jimmy's car, man."

"No shit!" said one of the boys sitting on the fender.

"Hey, man, get off!" said Paul. "Coño, don't sit on the car. Can't you see it's new?"

Another boy said, "You bullshitting us, Paul. This ain't your brother's car."

"He's not bullshitting. This is our brother Jimmy's car and he's right upstairs in my house. He's coming down any minute. He told us to mind it and gave us a quarter."

By this time there was a larger group of kids standing around the car looking at the brand-new shiny vehicle.

"Wow, this is a really nice car," said a young girl Nilda recognized. "Can I sit inside with you?"

"No, I can't do that," said Nilda emphatically. "Besides, I'm getting paid to mind it."

"How much?"

"A whole quarter."

"Nilda, stop telling everybody we got money, stupid," said Paul, nudging Nilda.

"Let me see it," said one of the boys.

"I don't have to show it to you, man. I got the money."

"I don't believe you."

"Show him, Paul, go on." Paul gave Nilda a look of exasperation, reached in his pocket, and held the shiny coin up. "See!" said Nilda.

"I didn't see," said a boy in back.

"Don't jive me. I already showed you it and I'm not gonna show it again."

"Let me in," they heard a voice say. It was Frankie. Paul opened the back door.

"I want to sit in front, Nilda. Move to the back."

"I will not, Frankie. I was here first and I'm minding the car for Jimmy."

"Who said?"

"It's true, Frankie," said Paul. "Now leave her alone and sit in back." He looked at Frankie, exercising his authority as the older of the two boys. Frankie slipped in back, leaning against Nilda with his elbow.

"Ouch!" she said. "Don't give him one penny of our quarter, Paul."

"What quarter?" asked Frankie.

Oh boy, thought Nilda, I can't do anything right sometimes.

"Paul, what quarter?"

"Jimmy gave Nilda and me a quarter to mind the car for him."

"You gonna split it with me, too!"

"Jimmy didn't say nothing about that."

"Aw man, come on," Frankie went on arguing.

Nilda looked up and saw her mother, Victor, and Jimmy all coming towards the car. Jimmy had on brand-new clothes. Like he's going to a party, thought Nilda. Victor was wearing his same old suit and Mama had on her good dress and shoes.

Jimmy came over, leading the way. "O.K., come on out now; we have to go. Paul, give me the key." The group of children surrounding the car backed away as the adults approached them. Nilda opened the door and jumped out. Frankie and Paul followed.

"Can I come along, Mama?"

"No, you stay, Nilda. We'll be back soon."

"Hey, Jimmy, can I have some of that quarter that you gave Paul and Nilda?"

"Sure, Frankie," said Jimmy, turning on the motor.

"He didn't even mind the car. It's not fair," Nilda protested. The three adults were seated in the car, talking to one another, and no one answered her.

"So long. See you kids later," said Jimmy as the car pulled out and disappeared.

Paul turned to go to the candy store. He said, "Now I'm gonna get change. Nilda, you get five cents and Frankie, you get five cents."

"Hey, that means you get fifteen cents!" cried Nilda.

Paul said, "That's right, Nilda. You were gonna get twelve cents and me thirteen cents, but your big mouth just cost you a whole seven cents."

Nilda looked at him angrily, but said nothing because she knew Paul was right.

Nilda followed along as Leo and her mother walked on ahead. They had gone early in the evening to see a man who knew something about her brother Jimmy. It had been weeks now since her mother had heard from him. No one knew where Jimmy was or what he was doing. Recently they had heard that he was wanted by the police.

Leo had accompanied her mother because her step-father was still in the hospital. Her mother, Leo, and the man had spent a long time talking, mostly in whispers. Nilda had overheard phrases like "he's hooked on drugs . . . mainlining . . . could be a seller and a user . . . tecatos . . . the police are after the gang. . . ." and other confused talk. She knew it had to do with Jimmy and the police, but exactly what she could not completely understand. Several times, Nilda had been sent down for treats to the corner candy store. That was the best part, she thought.

The man lived on East 126th Street and Nilda began to get tired as she thought of the long walk home. It was a warm night and Nilda began to play her sidewalk game. She loved to play that game, especially on different streets where the sidewalks were new to her. It was a game of discovery in which she uncovered many worlds of wonder. The diagonal, horizontal, and vertical cracks in the sidewalks became dividing regions, stimulating her imagination. The different shapes of the worn-out surfaces of concrete and asphalt developed before her eyes into dragons, animals, oceans, and planets of the universe. She continued looking for new and wonderful worlds that lay hidden underneath the concrete.

Nilda was completely absorbed when she saw tiny red dots all about the size of a dime. She bent down to examine the shiny surface and as she touched the dot with her shoe, it spread. It's liquid, like paint or something, she thought. As she walked on, the sidewalk was covered with these dots of shiny liquid leading somewhere. Intrigued, she traced the dots as she would a number picture puzzle, trying to connect them so that she could solve this new mystery. The red dots led Nilda to a doorway and beyond, into a pool of glistening red liquid inside the hallway of a building. "Ay, ayyyy," someone moaned. Nilda heard heavy breathing. She went in farther and heard the moan again above her. Looking up and into a corner, she saw a man clutching his stomach. His light blue shirt was streaked with crimson and his hands were drenched in blood. His face twisted in pain, he looked at Nilda, his dark eyes pleading for help. Whimpering, he rocked his head, and his black hair, wet with sweat, fell down over his forehead.

Nilda felt her own stomach turn cold as ice. Running out of the building to find her mother and Leo, she saw them coming towards her. "Mama, there's a man. He's all full of blood, in that building in there." Her voice was shaking. Swiftly they went past her into the hallway.

"Oh my God, Virgen María Madre de Dios, he's been stabbed."

Nilda could hear her mother screaming. Leo was out in a second.

"Police! Police! Help! Ayuda! Somebody's been hurt," Leo was shouting. He ran into a bar next door. People began to open windows and gather about.

"He's been hurt, poor man, we need help, bendito! Se muere! He's bleeding very badly," her mother went on, pleading for help.

The superintendent of the building came out, and by this time many people were shouting and asking questions.

Nilda waited outside in front of the building. Two small boys came by. They looked at her. "Hey, what happened, man?" they asked.

"Somebody got stabbed, I think in the stomach, and he's bleeding all over." She pointed to the blood on the sidewalk. People had stepped in it, leaving red shoe-prints.

"Does he live here?" asked one of the boys.

"I don't know. I don't live here myself. I was just walking by and I saw—"

"Hey, maybe I know him," interrupted the other boy. "Let me see."

They tried to get in the hallway but the entrance was crowded with people. Nilda watched them disappear into the crowd of adults as she waited nervously for sight of her mother or Leo who were inside the building. She heard the siren sound and a patrol car pulled up, followed by a white ambulance.

"O.K., break it up. Come on now, step aside, break it up. Stretcher coming through."

After a few minutes, Nilda heaved a sigh of relief as she saw her mother first, and then Leo, step out into the street. The wounded man was carried out on the stretcher and taken away in the ambulance. Slowly people began to disappear and the street got quiet again. Her mother and Leo exchanged good-byes with some of the people who lived in the building. "Muchas gracias por todo."

"De nada."

"Adiós."

"Hasta luego."

Nilda walked alongside her mother and looked back at the sidewalk which was still streaked and blotted with blood. The red was beginning to bury itself in the concrete. The rain will wash it away, she thought.

They decided to turn into one of the streets leading to the Madison Avenue bus. "After that we better ride back," said Leo. The street they came to was noisy and crowded with people. Most of the shops and bars on the street were open and brightly lit, busy with activity. Nilda saw groups of women, some standing against the tenements and in front of the shops, others sitting on the stoops of the buildings. As they walked past the women, Nilda saw that some were very young, with cheeks painted bright red, crimson lips, and false flowers pinned in their hair.

"Hey, good looking! Want a good time?" said a young girl who had come forward, almost blocking the way.

Some others followed saying, "Daddy, leave Mama and relax with me."

Nilda looked at them and realized they were talking to Leo. Calling out to him, yelling endearments.

"You're a sweet papa and it don't cost much. Vámonos adentro, come inside for a minute, lemme talk to you." They were beckoning him to come with them. Some had sweet voices, others almost commanding.

"Come on now! Papi dulce, right in here in this building you'll have the best time of your life!"

Nilda stared in amazement at the very young ones who seemed about the same age as the older girls on her block.

"Ten dollars the whole night and a good bed."

"Bueno. Five for me and everything nice and clean."

Some of the women outstretched their arms with sweeping gestures, as if to gather Leo and take him away. Calling out different prices and conditions to him, they completely ignored Nilda and her mother. The same sense of urgency in the voices somehow reminded Nilda of the Marketa on Park Avenue. The sounds were familiar, like the sounds of the vendors calling out, promising to give the people the cheapest but best product, outbidding each other for a sale. Both Leo and her mother had remained completely silent during the entire promenade. Once out of the block, her mother said, "What a shame and a pity, they are so young, bendito."

"I thought one could be no more than fourteen," said Leo.

"What are those women doing?" Nilda waited for an answer. "Leo, what did they want?"

After a pause her mother said, "They are salesladies, that's all. They wanted us to come in and buy some of the products."

"What kind of products? I didn't hear them mention no products. Weren't they talking to Leo?" She saw Leo and her mother exchange glances. "Are they bad, Mama?"

"No, they're not bad, Nilda, las pobrecitas, just unfortunate."

"What do you mean unfortunate? What is that?"

"Some of them don't have parents or a family to care for them and so they have to do certain things in order to live and eat, that's all."

"What things?"

"Ay, Nilda! Things! That's all."

"Tell me what things?"

"Ya basta, Nilda. Now I told you and that's all!"

Nilda looked sulkily at them. Why doesn't she tell me? I know what things. She always does that, like I'm a baby or something. Boy! she said to herself. She knew better than to pursue it any further or to try to ask Leo.

The three of them walked quickly down the street and onto the avenue. The Madison Avenue bus was speeding towards them. They got to the bus stop in time and got inside. It was quite late by now and Nilda was very sleepy. As the bus began to move on downtown, her eyelids grew heavy. She looked around her at the people on the bus. They were all mostly dark, Puerto Rican and black people. Pressing her head against Leo's arm and closing her eyes, she thought, Before the white people start getting on, we'll be long gone off the bus.

Early November, 1941

"Nilda, you have to go this morning to the welfare food
station with Sophie. I have to get ready to go see your
papa in the hospital."

Nilda's stepfather had been home, had a relapse, and
had returned to the hospital about a week ago. "Can I
open the food when we get back home?"

"Let Sophie do it and you can help her put things
away, O.K.?"

Nilda made a face. "All right," she said.

Sophie had been living with them for a week, arriving
the day after her stepfather had taken ill again. There
had been a timid knock on the door and Frankie had
opened it up.

"There's some lady here to see Mama," he said.

Nilda went to see who it was and there stood a tall
young woman with a suitcase by her side. "Hello, you
wanna see my mother?" asked Nilda.

"Does Jimmy live here? Is this his house?" she asked.

"Yeah, this is his house, but he don't live here. He's
gone someplace else. He's—"

"Who is it?" Nilda heard her mother's voice and turned

41

to see the look of surprise and then shock on her mother's face. "Yes?" her mother asked.

"Does Jimmy live here? Are you Jimmy's mother?"

"Yes, I am. You want to come inside?"

The young woman shyly picked up her suitcase and walked in. She looked at the older woman and burst into tears. Putting her hand over her face, she said, "I'm sorry but I have no place to go. My mother put me out. She won't let me stay there any longer. I'm pregnant. I'm gonna have Jimmy's baby!"

Victor walked out of the bedroom and stood there looking at Sophie and his mother. "Hi, Sophie," he said.

"You know this girl?" her mother asked.

"Yes, she's Jimmy's girl from 102nd Street."

Nodding her head and half closing her eyes, Nilda's mother said, "Dios mío. All right. Sophie? That's your name? Come on in, Sophie, over to the kitchen. You want some tea, sí?" She turned to look at the children who, by now, were absolutely fascinated by the turn of events. "That's enough. Now go on about what you were doing. I'm going to talk to Sophie."

"Somebody raped that girl?" Aunt Delia asked Victor. "No!"

"Then what happened? What's she doing here? She looks pregnant. She's got a suitcase!"

Victor bent over to talk in Aunt Delia's ear, trying not to shout so that they could not hear him in the kitchen. Nilda watched as Aunt Delia sucked her gums and looked at Victor incredulously.

"Is she Spanish? Puerto Rican?"

"Russian parents but she was born here."

42

"What? She what?" the old lady asked.

"No, she's not. She's American."

"Well," the old woman said, shrugging her shoulders, "it happens all the time in the newspapers." Victor turned and went back into the bedroom. Aunt Delia looked around her and, seeing that no one was going to listen, walked away with her newspapers tucked under her arm.

Sophie had moved in that night, sharing a room with Frankie and Nilda, and had been living there since. No one knew where Jimmy was.

Nilda resented Sophie. "Try not to fight with her," she heard her mother say. "She's older and you have to show her respeto."

"I don't like her sometimes, Mama; she can be mean."

"You have to try to make an effort because she's a guest and after all you live here. Esta es tu casa."

"She calls me brat and ugly. She always finds something I do wrong. She says I eat too much and I'm too spoiled and that if I had her mother I'd really learn how to behave and . . ."

"She's probably teasing you and you take it too seriously."

"Does she have to . . . is she gonna stay here all the time? With us?"

"Right now she does; she has no place to go. Pobre infeliz, she's pregnant and maybe she's a little nervous."

"All right, Mama," she said, putting her arms around her mother's waist, giving her a big hug.

Returning the hug, her mother rocked her and stroked her hair. "I love you," her mother said.

"When is Papa coming home, Mama?"

43

"Quién sabe? Soon, I hope. I don't know how much longer we can hold out without his working."

Nilda walked along with Sophie and held her hand tightly. Now and then she would give her hand a squeeze. When she thought Sophie wasn't looking, Nilda would turn her head slightly to glance at Sophie's swollen belly. Every once in a while Sophie would slow down and stop, bringing her hand around to rub the small of her back, arching and pulling her shoulders back. Her belly would thrust upward, looking even larger. Nilda wondered if Jimmy knew about Sophie and if they were going to get married and have a wedding. Her mother had warned Nilda not to ask anything, so she said nothing. Sophie's mother must be real mean to throw her out, she thought. She remembered a part of the conversation that she had overheard between her own mother and Sophie.

"My mother don't like Puerto Ricans. She warned me to keep away from that spick Jimmy. Now she told me she no longer has got a daughter, that her daughter is dead." Nilda had heard her mother mumble an answer, and then Sophie crying.

It was a long walk to the welfare food station. They went past rows of tenements and crossed many streets. She had walked this route with her mother time and time again, going to pick up surplus food early in the morning. She never knew what they would give in the big shopping bag. Usually it was mostly canned goods, cereal, and flour. Sometimes they gave clothes and shoes that were very ugly and didn't fit right. Once they gave canned

44

dessert, big cans of plums. Nilda closed her eyes wishing that today they would give something good. Like those good red cherries, sweet and syrupy, that come in a glass bottle.

It was a warm day, the last spell of Indian summer, and she was thirsty and tired when they got to the food station. There was a long line of people already waiting and they took their places at the end of the line. "Do you think we'll get something good?" she asked Sophie.

The young woman looked down at Nilda, shrugged and turned away. Nilda felt uneasy. Sophie had been very quiet and moody this morning and she did not quite know how to approach her. They waited and waited. She knew it was going to be a long time before their turn would come.

As they approached the counter Sophie looked down at Nilda. "We are going to get ice cream today," she said in a quiet voice.

Nilda couldn't believe her ears. Almost afraid to ask, she did. "What flavor?"

"Vanilla."

Nilda jumped and turned around. "Vanilla? Vanilla!"

"Shhhhh . . . don't make a fuss and scream, now. Be quiet or we won't get any."

"Are you sure, Sophie? They never did that before."

Sophie looked down at her and with a look of annoyance brought her forefinger up to her lips. "Look now, see?" She pointed over to the back of the counter. Nilda stretched up on her toes trying to see in back, beyond the long high counter. "See," Sophie said, "they are putting it into those white containers."

Sure enough, she could see the women in white uniforms transferring the soft velvety white substance with large ladles into white cardboard containers, sealing them, and putting thin wire handles on them. "Just like the candy store," Nilda half whispered. She turned to look at the rest of the people in line who had come after them, wanting to shout, Vanilla ice cream for everybody! Instead she smiled a knowing smile at the lady in back of them who smiled back at her briefly. She's not very excited, thought Nilda. Wait till she finds out.

She wanted to carry the ice cream home, but it was packed away with the other things in the large shopping bag. All the way home she wondered if there would be enough for everyone. She hoped the ice cream wouldn't melt before they got home.

"I'm getting thirsty. How about you?" Sophie asked.

"Uh huh!" nodded Nilda.

"I can just imagine what it tastes like, sweet, creamy, and cold," Sophie said. She went on, becoming talkative all the way home.

As they climbed up the stairs after the long walk, Nilda's head throbbed and her throat was unbearably dry, but she was happy to be the bearer of good news. Once she entered the apartment she went to find her mother, then remembered that she was visiting her stepfather in the hospital. "We got ice cream, vanilla ice cream!" she said.

No one answered. Except for Aunt Delia, who was studying her newspaper, the apartment was empty.

"We got ice cream today, Titi Delia." The old woman looked up. "We got vanilla ice cream at the food station."

"Did you read what happened to that couple? They were stupid enough to open the door to . . ."

Nilda looked at her and said, "Never mind." She went back to the kitchen.

"Sit down, Nilda. I'll serve you a little bit now," said Sophie.

"Maybe we better wait for Mama."

"She's not gonna mind. After all, we went to get it. Right? Sit down; go on. I've already got the plate. Go on, now."

"O.K. then."

"Hurry up now before it melts." Sophie put the plate in front of Nilda.

Nilda noticed it looked different from regular ice cream, but scooped a spoonful into her mouth anyway. Something horrible was happening to her. She could not swallow what was in her mouth. A lumpy liquid began to drip down the sides of her mouth down to her chin. Gagging and coughing, she spit out the sticky oily substance. Lard! God, that's what it was. It was lard! she thought, closing her eyes. She could hear cackles of laughter behind her. Turning around to look, she saw Sophie. Sophie's eyes were wet and her cheeks streaked with tears as she held on to the sink to balance herself. Her large belly swayed and shook with uncontrollable laughter.

Nilda waited in her room. "I hate her and I wish she would drop dead! When Mama comes home I'll tell her and she'll throw her out." She had been crying in her bed with her back to the door in case Sophie walked in. "When she asks for forgiveness she'll have to eat a whole big plateful of lard. All of it! She can't leave nothing over or she can't stay. I'm gonna tell Paul so he won't think she's so nice any more." In spite of her anger she felt ashamed that she could be so easily and completely fooled. "Maybe I'll only tell Mama. They might tease me, especially that Frankie; he thinks he's so smart." A sinking feeling somewhere inside was beginning to interfere with her anger.

Nilda heard the front door shut, and voices. Taking a deep breath, she sat up. She wasn't crying any more but she was afraid she would burst into tears again, so she waited a little while, looking out the window. The clotheslines were full of towels, sheets, underwear, and all kinds of clothes. They were moving, flapping, swaying as the wind blew. Living on the top floor of the tenement, she could see down the alleyway in back. She could see the clotheslines going crisscross and zigzag all the way down to the bottom floors. After waiting a little while, she got up and walked to the kitchen.

Her mother was sitting with her elbows on the table, her face buried in her hands, supporting her head as she bent slightly forward. Aunt Delia was sitting on one side of her and Sophie was sitting on the other side. Her mother lifted her head. Her eyes were red from crying. "He might be home in about ten to fourteen days. . . . God, I don't know what I'm going to do. María Purísima."

"Mama, what happened?"

"Your papa is still very sick and he has to come home, but he can't work. Complete rest for God knows how long."

"Mama, I gotta tell you something, Ma." Her mother did not answer. "Mama, I gotta tell you something!"

"What is it? Go on, tell me!"

"No, I gotta tell you alone."

"What alone! You have something to say, Nilda, say it. Por Dios, what do you want from me, eh!"

Nilda could see her mother was angry, but she went on anyway. "Well, it's what Sophie did."

"Well, what did she do?"

"She told me we were getting ice cream at the food station instead of lard, and then . . . well, when we came home from the food station she gave me some lard to eat."

"She gave you lard to eat, and you don't know the difference between ice cream and lard?"

"Mama, she said it was ice cream and . . ."

"It was just a little joke, Mom," Sophie said. "I was just kidding."

"Some joke, you mean witch!"

"Nilda, you are too sensitive. You can't live in this world being that sensitive," Sophie added.

"And you are too awful and you get out of my room!"

"Nilda! Basta! Stop that right now!"

"But, Mama, she was laughing at me." Nilda could feel the tears swelling in her eyes.

"With all my problems and all the things I have to do, I have to worry that you don't know the difference between ice cream and lard." Her mother shouted, "Go to your room! Go on, get out of my sight!"

As Nilda ran out she could still hear her mother. "Ten years old; when I was ten I had no mother and . . ."

"I hate them all, I just hate them all!" Nilda whispered

49

to herself as she lay face down on her bed.

As she often did when she was upset, she took her "box of things" out from under the bed. Nilda loved to draw; it was the thing that gave her the most pleasure. She sat looking at her cardboard box affectionately. Carefully she began to stack her cardboard cutouts. Her stepfather would give her the light grey cardboard that was in his shirts whenever they came back from the Chinese laundry. She cut these into different shapes, making people dolls, animals, cars, buildings, or whatever she fancied. Then she would draw on them, filling in the form and color of whatever she wanted. She had no more cardboard but she had some white, lined paper that Victor had given her. Drawing a line and then another, she had a sense of happiness. Slowly working, she began to divide the space, adding color and making different size forms. Her picture began to take shape and she lost herself in a world of magic achieved with some forms, lines, and color.

She finished her picture feeling that she had completed a voyage all by herself, far away but in a place that she knew quite well. "At last," she said. "All finished." Sticking out her tongue, she thought, I'm not showing this to Mama. She put her things away under the bed. Glancing in the mirror, she looked at herself with some interest. She was going out now; she wasn't so angry any more.

Mid-November, 1941

Nilda heard the bell ring as she walked into her classroom
and sat down at her desk. The teacher, Miss Elizabeth
Langhorn, was already there opening the supply cabinet.
She was a short plumpish woman close to sixty years of
age. Her thinning grey hair was cut short and done up in
a tight permanent wave. She had a sallow complexion and
small eyes surrounded by puffy skin. Because her voice
had a loud sandpaper tone, the kids nicknamed her "Fog-
horn." The loose-fitting dresses she wore were made of a
crepe material, usually dark in color, and most of them
had stains that years of dry cleaning had permanently set
into the fabric. Her bosom caved in and her stomach extended out. She always wore low-heeled shoes in need of
a shine.

Every day Miss Langhorn opened her supply closet
first thing in the morning and closed it after milk-and-
cookies time. She would reopen it after that for "emergen-
cies only," quickly locking it up again. "Don't tempt a
thief," she would say to the class in a knowing tone.
"That's how it all starts; first it's just a pencil, then perhaps a fountain pen. It's all so easy, why not open somebody's purse? Oh, no! Start right from the beginning and

you'll get into the habit of being honest. H-O-N-E-S-T-Y," she said, spelling out the word. "Brave people they were, our forefathers, going into the unknown where man had never ventured. They were not going to permit the Indians to stop them. This nation was developed from a wild primitive forest into a civilized nation. Where would we all be today if not for brave people? We would have murder, thievery, and no belief in God."

It was always more or less the same speech that preceded the Pledge of Allegiance. Nilda remembered that yesterday it had been a speech on Abraham Lincoln and the rights of slaves to become citizens.

Miss Langhorn picked up a piece of chalk and wrote the morning's assignment on the blackboard. On her desk sat the long, thick wooden ruler for all to see. Everyone knew that today someone would get rapped on the knuckles with that ruler. The lucky students only got threatened; however, real luck meant you didn't get caught. Miss Langhorn had a strict set of rules everyone in the class knew by heart. One of her most strict rules was that no Spanish was allowed in her classroom. Anybody caught speaking or even saying one word of Spanish had to put out both arms and clench his hands into fists. "None of that," she would say, "if you are ever going to be good Americans. You will never amount to anything worthwhile unless you learn English. You'll stay just like your parents. Is that what you people want? Eh?" she would ask earnestly, waiting for an answer.

"No."

"No, who?"

"No, Miss Langhorn."

Nilda looked at the ruler on the desk, recalling that feeling she got when she had to hold her arms outstretched. She always shut her eyes because she knew she would run away or cry out if she saw the ruler coming down to strike her. She hated when the skin broke and the knuckles swelled; her hands stayed sore all day and hurt for a long time. This was especially upsetting to Nilda when she looked forward to working on her cutouts and drawings for her "box of things" at home.

Miss Langhorn had a high stool placed in the back of the classroom, off to one side, and a large white cone-shaped cap made of cardboard. On this cardboard cap was written the word "dunce" in large black letters. Any student who refused to take the punishment had to wear the dunce cap. Nilda had worn the cap three times this term.

Students were hit for talking, lateness, and coming into class unwashed. Sometimes it just depended on Miss Langhorn's mood.

"Well, class, are we ready to work hard this morning?"

"Yes, Miss Langhorn."

She walked over to the side of the room and opened up some of the windows from the top, letting in the cold, crisp late-autumn air.

Nilda felt the cold breeze. Soon it's going to be winter, she thought. I hope it snows a whole lot.

"Now, let's see if we can be really good today, eh?" Miss Langhorn went on smiling. Her teeth were discolored from heavy smoking. "No need to use this," she said, picking up her wooden ruler. "I have nothing to do with it. You are responsible for what happens and you bring it down upon yourselves. Good behavior and progress go hand in hand indeed. It all stems from the home. Why, I hear them on the Madison Avenue bus coming to work, and sometimes going home. . . . Yapity yap yap. How are they ever going to learn to speak English? When I was a child we could look up to our parents. Why, my father . . ."

A similar version of the same story concerning Miss Langhorn's childhood had been told every day now, at least once a day, since the beginning of the school term.

"It was a happy family we had as children. At dinner time we would all sit around the large, old oak table. Father would say grace."

Nilda began to daydream. This year me and little Benji and the other kids are going to build a neat fortress of snow in Central Park, she was thinking.

". . . a family of modest means but honest, hardworking. Mother had to make do with little or no servant help. Store-bought dresses were a luxury; Mother had to buy material herself and bring it to the seamstress," she went on.

Maybe, Nilda thought, we could build an igloo house like I seen in them pictures about Eskimos.

". . . we knew the value of a dollar. Nobody gave you anything free in those days. Father was a splendid man. He and Mother would . . ."

Miss Langhorn's voice was far, far away.

Nilda was bent over her English reader when she heard Miss Langhorn say, "Milk-and-cookies time, children." Her stomach turned. I hate milk-and-cookies time,

54

damn! she thought. She finished writing out her name and heading in the assignment book:

> *Nilda Ramírez*   *Class 5B-2*
> *P.S. 72 Manh.*   *November 19, 1941.*

Looking up to the front, she felt her stomach turn again. Every morning the small containers of milk were lined up on Miss Langhorn's desk. For three cents any student could buy one. Next to the milk, the teacher had set out a box of chocolate-covered graham crackers. Miss Langhorn sold these personally. They cost two cents apiece or three for a nickel.

"All right, children, let us line up."

About half the class could afford to buy milk every morning. A much smaller percentage could afford to buy both milk and cookies. Very rarely did Nilda join the line for milk; most of the time she had no money at all. Every morning Nilda longed to have milk and one of those cookies.

"Here, Nilda, you can have one of mine," Mildred, the girl who sat next to her, had offered once.

It was so delicious, she remembered. Another time Leo had given her money and she could buy both the milk and cookies. That was great! she recalled. All that sweet chocolatey taste on the outside, but when you bit the inside it was real good and crunchy, slowly melting in your mouth. A few times when she had money for milk, Nilda tried to buy just the graham crackers but Miss Langhorn had said, "No, it's against school rules. You can buy the cookies only to have with your milk." At the beginning, some of the kids would share their cookies, but now Miss Langhorn had set a class rule that no sharing or offering of milk and cookies was allowed.

As she did almost every morning, Nilda just sat and stared with the other children who weren't eating. They all waited for the milk break to be over, which took about twenty minutes. It seems to get longer all the time, thought Nilda. Someday I'm gonna come in and buy a whole nickel's worth of cookies. And when I grow up I'm gonna buy a whole box, sit down, and eat them all up. If Miss Langhorn happens to come around and ask for a cookie—she'll be real old by then—I'll see her probably strolling down Central Park and I'll be sitting on a bench holding the box and eating. When she asks me for a cookie I'll say, "I'm sooooo sorry, my dear Miss Langhorn, but I don't think it's polite to ask. Do you? Eh?" I'll chew loud and make sure I smile at her.

The morning dragged on until Nilda heard the lunch bell. She was going home for lunch this term. After the experience at camp this past summer, she had convinced her mother to let her come home for lunch. She hated the free lunches given at school. "All that awful soup, Mama. It tastes like water. The bread is hard, and the milk tastes funny, and you always get prunes for dessert. The food tastes just like at the camp. I know I'm gonna be sick. I just know it."

It had taken a lot of talking, but at last her mother had agreed to let her come home. She, in turn, had also agreed to the condition that she eat whatever her mother could spare. "No complaining, Nilda," her mother had said. "If you start with the bobería that you don't like this or you don't like that, you go right back to eat at school! Se acabó! Understand?"

This whole week it had been chocolate pudding and tea with milk. At first she had been overjoyed at the idea of chocolate pudding for lunch. Her mother served it cold sometimes and hot sometimes, like cereal. But after several days, the thought of chocolate pudding again sent a feeling of disappointment right down to the bottom of her stomach. Oh well, it's still better than eating in this place, she thought, and headed for home.

To get home Nilda had to pass through the dark tunnels on Park Avenue. That was the worst part; even worse than the short lunch hour. It seemed that no sooner was she up the steps and in the apartment than she had to leave in order to arrive back at school before the late bell rang.

Nilda reached her corner of Park Avenue and 104th Street and looked carefully into the tunnels. There were three tunnels; one set in the middle for traffic, and one at either side for pedestrians. The tops curved into archways; inside each tunnel a single small bulb shone, giving off very little light. Nilda squinted her eyes as she stood at the entrance trying to see inside. Lately, some of the older children had come around at this time of day, asking for money, and she recalled how she got shoved around when she told them she had none.

"Don't be a sucketa, stupid," her brother Paul had told her, "put your money in your shoe," which is what she did whenever she had any.

Sometimes she walked through the middle tunnel when she felt she would run into trouble, but the large trucks and cars coming through frightened her. She saw the tunnel was empty and quickly stepped inside. People were coming in from the other side; they were adults, two men and a woman. They were talking in loud tones and Nilda heard their voices and footsteps echoing the length of the tunnel. When she was with a group of friends they would all scream just to hear their voices echo. Sometimes when she was alone she would sing, enjoying the resonance of her voice as it filled the dark chamber; but she was afraid someone would hear her so she very rarely indulged herself. As she went past the middle of the tunnel, she side-stepped the puddles that filled up and seeped through the cracks and holes in the concrete. Holding her breath, she tried to avoid the smell of stagnant water and urine. At the other side, she stepped out and looked quickly to see if there was any traffic coming, and then, almost running, she went towards her building.

Nilda started to climb the first flight of steps leading up to the fourth floor where her apartment was. A strong odor of fried pork permeated the hallway and, as she moved up the steps, the odor got stronger. It was almost overwhelming. She could tell that the meat was spiced with garlic and herbs, just like her mother prepared pork-chops. With it was mixed the odor of cooked rice. Nilda could smell the saffron, olives, and sausage that were mixed in the rice. Somebody's sure lucky, she thought. Her stomach growled and her mouth salivated as she climbed up the steps, and the mixed odors of the many flavors cooking went right through her. It must be some-body on our floor, she thought, and they're gonna have a party or something. Funny, I didn't hear nothing about it. She stood in front of her doorway and paused before opening the door. Stepping inside, she could still smell the food.

"Mami, are you cooking rice and porkchops?" she asked with disbelief, rushing toward the kitchen.

"Nilda?" her mother called.

She stepped into the kitchen and saw her mother's wide smile and the large cast-iron pot she used for making rice sitting on the stove puffing away. Her mother held a long fork in her hand and was standing over the frying pan. Nilda heard the pork sizzling in the hot oil.

"We hit the bolita, Nilda!" her mother said, jubilant. "Night before last I dreamed I looked in the sky and in the form of clouds was the número 305. So, yesterday morning I sent Paul on his way to school over to Jacinto's bodega and told him to leave my bet for número 305 combinación for the bolitero. I put thirty cents on it, and sure enough 530 came out! I was going to play it straight, but then I remembered that in my dream there was another small cloud and it was almost shaped like a C, so I said, O.K., that means I have to bet combination! That way no matter how 305 came out as long as it was those three numbers I would make a hit. It was a message from heaven, Nilda. My prayers were answered."

"Oh boy, Mama, how much is that? A lotta money?"

"Enough to see us through for a little while. Come on, sit down and eat. I got chuletas and arroz con gandules."

"It smells like a party, Mama."

"All right now, hurry up and wash so you won't be late for school."

"Can I stay home to celebrate?"

"Never mind. You go back to school. You can celebrate at three."

"I hate that teacher; she's mean and she's always giving lectures and saying she's gonna do this and that and . . ."

"Good, you could use some lectures. You do as the teacher says and learn, so you can be somebody someday. Amount to something. I don't want to hear no complaints, because it'll be much worse for you here with me. Comprende? I only got to the fourth grade; I never had the advantages you got here in this country. You want to be a jíbara when you grow up? Working in a factoría? Cleaning houses? Being a sucketa for other people?"

Nilda went to the bathroom to wash and could still hear her mother talking. She doesn't even care about my side of it, thought Nilda. But she was too happy about the lunch to brood and came out smiling and ready to eat.

Her mother set out a plate filled with food and she sat down. She chewed each mouthful with enormous pleasure, eating vigorously.

"Papa is coming home this weekend. Gracias a Dios, we will be able to have a nice dinner and a few things for him when he gets home. Nilda, that reminds me, you have to accompany me next week to the welfare office to see about Home Relief." Turning her head away, she continued in a half whisper, "Papa can't work no more. Thank God for the number," she said, making the sign of the cross.

Aunt Delia walked in with a brand-new housedress on. It was yellow and the fabric was covered with a tiny red-and-white flower print.

"You look pretty, Titi," said Nilda, pointing to her

dress. Aunt Delia smiled, showing her gums. "Your mother bought it for me; she hit the numbers." The old woman sat down and opened her paper. Slowly and intently she began to study its contents. Nilda could hear her reading quietly to herself. Looking at Aunt Delia, she wondered how the old woman could read every word in English and yet not speak one word of English in a regular conversation.

"We'll be able to get some new things for the baby, Nilda." Her mother smiled and went on, "It will be my first grandchild."

The clinic had told them that Sophie was due to have the baby any day now. All attempts to locate Jimmy had failed and no one had heard from him. Nilda was used to sharing her room with Sophie now, and sometimes almost liked her.

"It's getting late. Hurry, you'll be late for school."

"Mami, can I have money for milk and cookies tomorrow? Please?"

"Sí, but only for tomorrow, because we have to stretch what money we have."

"Bendición, Mama," said Nilda.

"Dios te bendiga. Hurry up now and be careful."

She ran down the steps two and three at a time, bouncing up when she hit the ground. Outside she felt buoyant as the cold sharp air filled her lungs. Skipping, she ran towards the tunnels, rushing to make it back to school before the late bell rang.

Late November, 1941

Nilda looked at the big round clock on the wall facing the rows of benches in the large rectangular waiting room. They had left the apartment early that morning, taking the bus downtown to be at the Welfare Department by nine A.M., and it was now a quarter past eleven. The hands on the clock looked so still, as if they were never going to move on to the next number. She concentrated on the red second hand that jumped sporadically from black dot to black dot until it finally reached a number. Shutting her eyes, Nilda would open them quickly, hoping to catch the red second hand in action. At the beginning, she had lost almost every time, but after a while she was able to catch the second hand just as it landed on a dot. She began to figure out just how long it took the second hand to reach the next number, thereby causing the large black hand to move ever so slightly. The game was beginning to bore her and she lost interest. She leaned against her mother, who was shifting her weight from side to side, trying to find a more comfortable position on the hard bench.

"Mami," Nilda whispered, nudging her mother, "I'm tired. How much longer we gonna be?"

"Be still, Nilda," her mother answered quietly.

"I'm thirsty. Can I get another drink of water?"

"You been up to get water at least five times. Just be still; they'll call us soon. Everybody here is also waiting. You are not the only one that's tired, you know." Her voice was almost a whisper, but Nilda knew she was annoyed. Nilda hated to come to places like this where she felt she had to wait forever. It's always the same, she thought, wait, wait, wait! She remembered the long wait they'd had at the clinic last time. It was over five hours.

"Stop leaning on me, Nilda; you are not a baby. Ya basta! Sit up and be still!" This time her mother had turned to look at her and she knew she had better be still.

The only good thing is that I don't have to go to school, she thought. Her mother would give her an excuse note tomorrow, so she did not have to worry.

Nilda looked around the large room again; each long row of benches was filled with people sitting silently. There were no other children her age. Now and then someone new came in from the outside, walked up to the front desk and handed the clerk a card, then sat down on a bench, joining the silent group.

She looked at the grey-green walls: except for two posters, placed a few feet apart, and the big round clock, the walls were bare. She began to study the posters again; she knew them almost by heart. They were full of instructions. The one nearest Nilda had a lifelike drawing of a young, smiling white woman, showing how well she was dressed when she went to look for employment. The reader was carefully informed about proper clothing, using this figure as the perfect model. Her brown hat sat on her short brown hair. Her smiling face had been scrubbed clean, her white teeth brushed, and she wore very little makeup. Her brown suit was clean and her skirt was just about six inches below the knee. She carried a brown handbag, wore clean gloves and nicely polished shoes as she strolled along a treelined street, confident about her interview. She sure looks happy, thought Nilda. She must be a teacher or something like that.

The second poster was a large faded color photograph of a proper breakfast. The photograph showed fresh oranges, cereal, milk, a bowl of sugar, a plate of bacon and eggs, toast with butter and jelly. The reader was warned that it was not good to leave the house without having had such a breakfast first. Looking at the food, Nilda began to remember that she was hungry. She had eaten her usual breakfast of coffee with boiled milk, sugar, and a roll. It seemed to her that she had eaten a long, long time ago, and her stomach annoyed her when she looked at the bacon and eggs. I hope they call us soon, she said to herself.

The lady clerk at the front desk looked up and read a name aloud from a card. "Mrs. Lydia Ramírez," she called out.

"Come on," her mother said as she stood up and walked past the benches full of waiting people. Nilda followed her up to the front.

The lady clerk pointed and said, "Into the next room. You will see Miss Heinz." She then handed her mother a card. Nilda walked with her mother into another large room lined with rows of desks. A woman, seated at a desk across the room, raised her arm and waved to them.

"Over here, please." They walked quickly up to the woman and waited. The social worker, without lifting her head, pointed to the empty chair at the side of her desk. Her mother sat down. The woman continued to write something on a form sheet. Nilda stood next to her mother and looked down at the social worker as she went on writing. Her head was bent over and Nilda could see that her hair was very white and fine, with tiny waves and ringlets neatly arranged under a thin grey hair net. The tiny grey hairpins, which were carefully placed to hold each little lump of ringlets together, were barely visible. Her pink scalp shone through the sparse hair. Nilda had never seen such a brilliant pink scalp before. I wonder what would happen if I touched her head, she thought; maybe it would burn my finger. Finally, after a while, the woman lifted her head, nodded, and, still holding the pencil she had been writing with, asked, "Mrs. Lydia Ramírez?" Before her mother could answer, the social worker turned to Nilda and said, "My name is Miss Heinz. Does your mother understand or speak English?" Nilda turned to her mother with a look of confusion.

"I speak English," her mother replied quickly. "Maybe not so good, but I manage to get by all right."

"Let me have your card, please," Miss Heinz said, holding out her hand. Nilda's mother bent forward and gave Miss Heinz the card she had been holding. "Well, that's a help. At least you can speak English. But then," pointing to Nilda she continued, "why is she here? Why isn't she in school? This is a school day, isn't it?"

Nilda could see her mother turning red. Her mother never liked to go to these places alone; she always brought Nilda with her. Ever since Nilda could remember, she had always tagged along with her mother.

"She wasn't feeling too well so I kept her with me. She goes to school of course," her mother said. Surprised, Nilda looked at her mother. She had not been sick at all.

"Well, she should be home in bed, not here! Or are you alone?"

"No, I am not alone," her mother bit her lips and went on, "but there was no one at home this morning." Nilda knew Aunt Delia was home with her stepfather, and so were Sophie and the baby. Pausing, her mother went on, "My husband is resting; he is sick. So, I just thought—"

"This is not going to do her any good," interrupted Miss Heinz. Looking at Nilda, she asked, "What's wrong with you?" Nilda looked at her mother wide-eyed.

"She had an upset stomach," her mother answered.

Miss Heinz, blinking her eyes, heaved a sigh and picked up a folder with the name *Ramírez, Lydia.* "Now let's get on with this. I'm way behind schedule as it is, you know. Plenty of other people to see. Mrs. Ramírez, you have one married son and four children in school, three boys and a daughter. Your husband suffered two heart attacks, his second leaving him incapacitated, and you want us to give you public assistance. Am I correct?"

"Yes," her mother said in a voice barely audible. "He can't work no more."

"Well then, we'll have to ask you some questions. Now, are you legally married?"

"Yes."

66

"How long? I see that your boys have a different last name. They are named Ortega."

"I been married twelve years." Her mother wet her lips.

"Were you legally married the first time and, if so, are you a widow or a divorcée?"

"Divorce."

"In Puerto Rico or in this country?"

"I married in Puerto Rico, but I got divorced here."

"That was twelve years ago? Then is this your second husband's child?"

Her mother sat up straight and answered, "Yes." Nilda glanced at her mother. Surprised and confused, she knew that she had been almost three years old when her mother married her stepfather.

"Your oldest son, Victor, can he help out?"

"He goes to high school, but he gets something after, like a delivery boy sometimes, and he gives us what he can."

"You also have an aunt living with you. Does she help?"

"No, she's an older woman and she has a relief check, but it's very little, and she can only spare for food and medicine. You see, she's also hard of hearing and—"

"O.K.," she interrupted. "How is your health, Mrs. Ramírez?"

"I'm fine. O.K."

"Can't you find some employment?"

"I got a lot of people to care for and small children I cannot leave."

Nilda realized that she was tired of standing. Looking at the woman, Nilda saw her write something each time she asked another question. Her fine grey mesh hair net came down over her forehead and stopped abruptly at the spot where her eyebrows should be. Nilda carefully strained her eyes, focusing on that spot, looking for her eyebrows, but the woman didn't seem to have any. Her skin was very pink, with a variety of brownish freckles that traveled on her hands, arms, and neck, giving her skin the look of a discolored fabric. She wore a light beige dress with a starched white collar. On her right hand she wore a silver wristwatch and two silver rings. Nilda thought, She looks tightly sealed up. Like a package, only you can't see the wrapping because it's like see-through cellophane.

"How many rooms in your apartment?"

"We got six rooms." They went on talking and Nilda felt her legs getting heavy under her and a sleepiness begin to overtake her.

"Let me see your hands! Wake up, young lady! Let me see your hands!" Startled, Nilda saw that Miss Heinz was speaking to her. Extending her arms and spreading out her fingers, she showed the woman her palms.

"Turn your hands over. Over, turn them over. Let me see your nails." Nilda slowly turned over her hands. "You have got filthy nails. Look at that, Mrs. Ramírez. She's how old? Ten years old? Filthy." Impulsively, Nilda quickly pushed her hands behind her back and looked down at the floor.

"Why don't you clean your nails, young lady?" Nilda kept silent. "How often do you bathe?" Still silent, Nilda looked at her mother. She wanted to tell her to make the woman stop, but she saw that her mother was not look-ing her way; instead she was staring straight ahead.

"Cat got your tongue?" Miss Heinz asked. "Why doesn't she answer me, Mrs. Ramírez?"

Without turning her head, her mother said, "Nilda, answer the lady."

"I take a bath when I need it! And I clean my nails whenever I feel like it!" Nilda exploded in a loud voice.

"No need to be impertinent and show your bad manners, young lady."

"Nilda!" Her mother turned around and looked at her. "Don't be fresh! Stop it!" Looking at Miss Heinz she said, "I'm sorry."

"That's quite all right, Mrs. Ramírez, I understand. Children today are not what they used to be. Young lady, you are no help to your mother. I hope you're proud of yourself."

Bending over, Miss Heinz moved her head, shaking the lumps of ringlets as she opened the center drawer of her desk. She searched around, moving paper clips, pencils, index cards wrapped in a rubber band, and finally pulled out a small shiny metal nail file. Holding it up in front of Nilda, she said, "Now Miss, this is for you. I want you to take this home with you so that you have no more excuse for dirty nails. This," and she shook the small shiny silver file, "is a nail file. Have you ever seen one before?"

Still sulking, Nilda answered, "Yes, I know what it is."

"Good! Here, you may take it," she said, smiling as she handed the nail file to Nilda, who did not move.

"Take it!" her mother said. Nilda reached over and took the metal file. Miss Heinz looked at Nilda, who said nothing. "Nilda! What do you say?" her mother asked.

"Thank you," Nilda said in an irritated tone.

Miss Heinz turned away and, closing the folder, she said, "Before we can make any definite decision, we will have to have an investigator come out to your home for a visit. Since you have had public assistance before, you know the procedure I'm sure. It will take a little while, but we will let you know."

"Good-bye, Miss Heinz, and thank you very much."

"Not at all. Good-bye now," and she bent over her desk again. Nilda and her mother walked out of the room and out of the building.

Walking alongside her mother, Nilda could feel the cold sharp air of winter. She held the shiny cold metal nail file in her hand. That mean old witch, she thought. And Mama, she's mean too. Nilda felt her mother put her arm around her and she pulled away.

"What's the matter? You got a problem maybe, Nilda?"

"I don't have an upset stomach, Mama. Why did you let her talk like that to me? Why didn't you stop her?" Nilda felt the angry tears beginning to come down her face. "You should have done something. You don't care anything about me. You don't care."

"Nilda, stop it! I had to say what I did, that's all. I have to do what I do. How do you think we're gonna eat? We have no money, Nilda. If I make that woman angry, God knows what she'll put down on the application. We have to have that money in order to live."

"I don't care. I don't care at all!" Nilda screamed. Without warning, she felt a sharp pain going across the left side of her face, followed by a stinging feeling. Her mother was in front of her, looking at her furiously.

"I'll slap you again, only harder, if you don't shut up." Nilda began to cry quietly. They walked along silently to the bus stop.

Still holding the nail file, Nilda thought about Miss Heinz. Oh how I hate her. She's horrible, she said to herself. I would like to stick her with this stupid nail file, that's what. When no one was looking I would sneak up behind her and stick her with the nail file. Then she would begin to die. No blood would come out because she hasn't any. But just like that . . . poof! She would begin to empty out into a large mess of cellophane. Everybody in that big office would be looking for her. "Oh, where is Miss Heinz?" they would all say. They would be searching for her all over. Poor Miss Heinz. Oh, poor Miss Heinz. First her eyebrows disappeared. Did you know that? She had no eyebrows. And now she's all gone. Disappeared, just like that! Poor thing. My, what a pity.

The bus pulled up. As Nilda climbed inside she felt the nail file slipping between her fingers and heard a faint clink when it hit the pavement.

December 6, 1941

Nilda held on to the metal bar at the top of the crib and, leaning forward, looked down at the baby as he moved his hands and kicked his feet. She was fascinated by the fingernails, which were as delicate as tissue paper, set on the perfectly formed little fingers. He is just wonderful, she thought. So small and yet all the parts are there; nothing is missing. Wow! His head was covered by lots of jet black hair that was soft and silky, and his face had the tiniest mouth and nose. "James Ortega, Junior," she whispered.

The baby had been home for two weeks. Nilda's mother had shifted things in the apartment so that Sophie and the baby could have a room to themselves. Frankie now shared a bedroom with Victor and Paul, but slept on the sofa in the living room. Nilda had Frankie's cot in her parents' bedroom. She missed her bed and her room, especially her window. Her own bed used to be by the window and she could look out and see the sky anytime she wanted. She missed the privacy she had been used to because her stepfather had been home for a while now and still had to rest in bed most of the time. Nilda was constantly aware of the fact that she could not make any noise. The only good part of this moving-everybody-around business is the baby, she thought. Smiling, she extended her forefinger and put it up against the tiny hand. The baby, grabbing it, made a little fist and gripped on tightly. Nilda giggled and moved her finger back and forth as little Jimmy held on. "Hey, who do you think you are anyway?" she laughed. "So strong and so tough, eh!" The baby responded by turning his head toward her. Sophie walked in with a baby bottle in her hand.

"You wanna give him his bottle, Nilda?"

"Can I? Oh please, yes!"

Sophie put the bottle down on the bureau and picked up the baby. "Take that blanket and put it over your shoulder," she said, handing the baby to Nilda. With the baby in her arms, Nilda settled down on the bed. Sophie handed her the bottle. "Now, when he stops drinking just pick him up and pat him on the back like I showed you. Wait till he burps and then you can give him the bottle again. O.K.?"

"Yes, I know. I can do it, I can do it."

Nilda bent her head over slightly and took a deep breath, inhaling the sweet warm fragrance of the baby's hair. Pressing the baby close to her, Nilda felt warmth and pleasure. She disliked her dolls; the hard cold plastic surface was unappealing, so she usually put them away where she did not have to touch them. He's so beautiful, not at all like those dumb dolls, she thought, and laughed when she remembered what her mother had said about the baby. "Little Jimmy is not much bigger than a loaf of bread." Her stepfather had been upset at the idea of two more people living in the apartment. When he returned home from the hospital, there had been a big argument.

"Where is your Communism now? Your love of the people, Emilio?" Her mother's eyes flashed with anger. "Your love of the common people is that you deny my grandchild a home? Like our Virgen María and Niño Jesús they will have no place to go. Well, they stay and this is their home right here! That's final! Ya basta! Dios mío sagrado," and she made the sign of the cross.

"And where is your son? Where is your Jimmy? Mr. Big Shot with the cars and the clothes, eh?" her stepfather yelled. "We were not good enough for him so he had to be dishonest, and now we have to clean up his mess. And who will thank us? Not your son, that's the truth!"

Her mother replied quietly, "God. God will thank us and He will provide as He always does. And we will find Jimmy and he will do right by this young woman and his son. Yes, he will settle down."

"Bullshit," interrupted her stepfather. "Plain mierda, that's what that talk is. What will happen is what always happens. Your son is making us into a bunch of sucketas."

In the long run, however, her mother had won and Sophie came home with the baby. When Nilda had complained about her room, her mother had told her it was only temporary, that as soon as Jimmy returned, he would get an apartment for his new family. "Why can't somebody else get changed? Why does it have to be me?" she had insisted.

74

"Nilda, we cannot take Aunt Delia's room away because she is an old woman and we must respect her privacy. It is up to you and your brothers to make some sacrifices. A new life is now part of our family, so we must all take care and protect the baby. It is our duty as his family." Nilda had responded to this by sulking until the baby had come home, and then, after his arrival, she had become ecstatic.

Little Jimmy had finished the bottle and Nilda picked him up, leaning him very carefully against her shoulder and patting him on the back. She gently patted and rubbed her hand in a circular movement until she heard the baby utter a loud belch. "Good boy!" She started to walk out of the room with the baby in her arms and almost bumped into Sophie, who was entering the room. "He just finished his whole bottle at once, Sophie. He made a big burp. He's so good—"

"Just put him down now and leave," interrupted Sophie. Nilda could see she was upset.

"Can I take him inside to the living room with me, just for a little while, Sophie?"

"Just leave him. Put him back."

"Aw please, let me take him for a little while."

"Nilda, get out!" she snapped.

Nilda quietly put the baby back in the crib and walked out of the room. Whew, what a crab, she thought. Her mother was sitting in the living room with Aunt Delia. She wanted to complain about Sophie, but she knew her mother was nervous and worried about the investigator who was supposed to visit them soon. Instead, she asked,

"Mami, what's the matter with Sophie? She is such a cranky thing. She won't even let me bring the baby in here for a little while."

"You fuss too much over the baby anyway, Nilda. Besides, didn't you just give him his bottle? Well now, that's enough. Just go play with something else and let the baby rest."

"Is supper ready yet?"

"In a little while we are all gonna eat. Why don't you take a rest, eh? I'll call you when the food is ready." Her mother smiled and coaxed her, "Go on now. Go on, rest a bit. I'll call you."

Shrugging, Nilda walked into her parents' bedroom and sat down on her cot. Her stepfather was sleeping and she could hear his soft snoring and the ticking of the clock on the little night table. Next to the clock sat a glass filled with water, and in it were his false teeth. Nilda stared at them and, after a while, they seemed to be floating. She half expected them to speak, and she shuddered.

Turning away, she lay back on the cot and looked up at the ceiling. Very carefully, she started to search in between and around the cracks, discolorations, and peeling paint, that took on different shapes and dimensions, for her favorite scenes. This was a game she loved to play. By using her eyes she discovered that, if she concentrated carefully, she actually began to see all kinds of different shapes and forms and exciting events taking place on the ceiling. One of those scenes was a group of horses running wildly in the woods. Mounted on the horses were men dressed just like in the movies of the

Count of Monte Cristo. They wore plumed hats and capes, and the horses had saddles covered with tassels and fringes. After a little while, Nilda finally saw the riders and galloping horses in the cluster of woods. It was all so exciting that she concentrated on the adventure.

She was completely engrossed when she heard her stepfather saying softly, "Nilda, is that you?"

"Yes, Papa."

"What are you doing, nena?"

"Just resting for a little while. I was feeding the baby, but then Sophie wouldn't let me play with him any more."

"You are gonna wear him out, Nilda. He is not a toy, you know." Lighting a cigarette, he inhaled and blew out the smoke. Nilda turned over onto her stomach and propped her head on her arms as she watched her stepfather.

Smiling, he said, "You want me to make some rings?"

"Oh yes, go ahead, Papa, make them."

Inhaling from the cigarette deeply, her stepfather began pursing his lips and forming them into the shape of an O, rapidly expanding and contracting them as he exhaled. He kept repeating this, and each puff of smoke took on a circular shape. Nilda laughed as she looked at the circles of smoke and her stepfather.

"You look like a fish," she giggled.

"Oh, yeah? But I bet you a fish can't do this trick with a cigarette," he laughed.

"Tell me a story, Papa, all about where you come from again, and the war and all that. Please."

Smiling, her stepfather began to talk. "Well, my town is a small village on the northern coast of Spain. The people there are poor and hardworking. They all live in little houses."

"Everybody has a little house?"

"Yes, there are no big buildings, or subways, or department stores. Everybody lives in a little house of their own." Pausing, he went on, "Today, of course, the people are not free. Fascism has taken the land and is destroying the people."

"Even the children?"

"Of course the children! What do you think war is? Hitler, Mussolini, aiding that pig Franco. That's how he won, you know. Oh, yes! Look at that, Nilda." With a look of disgust he pointed to the small altar set upon a shelf in a corner of the bedroom. On the altar a small red candle burned, emitting the scent of incense. In a small white vase were paper flowers. Some holy pictures had been placed alongside. Above the shelf hung a framed drawing, in color, of a saint as he walked down a street, clad in rags, his body full of bleeding sores, and all the dogs in the town eagerly licking his wounds. "The Catholic Church helped Franco as well, with that kind of shit that your mama believes." Looking irritated at the altar, he went on, "Garbage to enslave the masses."

Nilda loved to hear her stepfather talk, he carried on so. Especially when her mother was not around, he did a lot of cursing. She already knew most of what he said, and was about to say, since she had heard it for as long as she could remember. Before her stepfather, she had only a vague memory of scattered moments in her life. She had been not quite three years old when her mother had married him. Now she had his last name and called him Papa. No one talked about what happened before. In fact, it was never mentioned at all. This had not bothered her at all until recently, when her mother had spoken to the lady social worker at the welfare station. She knew that her real father, Leo, and her mother had never married. Many times when she thought of Leo she had a close feeling for him, but she also knew she could not talk about it.

". . . so your mother had to send you to a Catholic camp. Well, look what happened. The place was falling apart, eh? What do they do with the money? Spend it on themselves. Well, no more. And even when I go back to work and I make extra money, I will not give it to your mama to send you to no Catholic school for bullshit propaganda."

"Papa, next time you go to a meeting, will you take me?"

"You better ask your mama. She told me she doesn't want you to come along any more, so if you want to come, you better ask. I'm tired of arguments. She says my friends don't believe in God, so you can't go no more."

"Do they believe in God?"

"What God? Nilda, did you ever see Him? I never talk to Him. I never see Him. I don't believe in nothing I can't see or talk to."

"Mama says faith is a very powerful thing, and that if you have faith, you can feel Him."

"Is that so? Well now, I know what I feel. I only feel tired, happy, sad, an urge to make a caca, sometimes constipated, and, too many times, hungry." Pausing and looking at his captured audience, he asked, "And what do you feel?"

"Hungry too." Nilda broke into a big smile. "I wonder if supper is ready." Jumping up she said, "I'll go see." She heard her stepfather chuckle as she left the room.

In the living room Nilda saw Aunt Delia seated in the large armchair, talking in Spanish to Sophie. Sophie was seated on a small chair next to the old woman. The *Daily News* was spread out on Aunt Delia's lap and she was pointing to a picture in the middle section of the paper. She was speaking rapidly to Sophie, who agreed with everything Aunt Delia said by nodding her head, since she did not understand a word of Spanish.

"Mira, mira," said the old woman, and she began to read in English, "Two masked gunmen entered the bank and at gunpoint made everyone keep still while they forced the bank tellers to give them the ready cash." Pausing, she added, "Qué barbaridad!" and sucked in her lips. "They fled, only to be pursued by a patrol car. In a shoot-out battle a few blocks from the bank, the police killed one man and seriously wounded the other." Shaking her head and smacking her lips, she went on, "One policeman was also wounded and taken to Bellevue Hospital where he is reported to be in good condition. The men have been identified as Howard . . ."

Nilda walked into the kitchen. "Mama, is the food ready?"

"Yes, Nilda, you can eat in just a few minutes with Frankie, Paul, and Victor. Then I'll serve Sophie, Aunt Delia, and Papa. I'll eat with them." In the small kitchen they ate in shifts, usually four at a time. "Nilda, you have to go with Sophie tomorrow, after Mass, to see her mother."

"Her mother?" Nilda asked. Surprised, she went on, "Are you coming too?"

"No. Victor will take you and Sophie and the baby to the building where her mother lives. She has agreed to make up with her mama. It's the right thing to do. Baby Jimmy is her grandchild too, and she should know about it. It's wrong to keep it from her. Sophie is her only child and this woman is a widow, so it's only right."

"Does she want to go?"

"She agreed."

"I'll bet you she doesn't want to go, the way she says her mother is."

"Well, it's already settled, so that's that."

Nilda sat down on a chair uneasily and said, "I don't wanna go, Mama. Besides, remember? I'm supposed to go to Benji's church tomorrow. Petra and Marge are coming too. They are gonna have a big service with music and food and a whole big thing. I won't have time."

"You will be back in time to go with your friends. You will have plenty of time."

"Why do I have to go? Send Frankie. Why me? It's always me. Anyway, if Victor is coming, why do I have to go?"

"You have to go because you are Jimmy's sister and another girl. It's right that you go."

"Can't you come too?"

"No."

"Why?"

"Never mind. Nilda, you are going to accompany

81

Sophie to see her mother and that's all. You have to go. After, I will meet her too."

After a short silence, Nilda asked, "Is Baby Jimmy gonna leave and go live there?"

Her mother, busy stirring a large steaming pot with a long wooden ladle, said, "Maybe. But only for a little while, until after the investigator comes. We are not supposed to have Sophie and the baby living here."

"Can't Sophie go and we keep the baby, Mama?"

"Nilda, don't be foolish; he's Sophie's baby. Anyway, Jimmy will come home soon and they will have their own apartment." Her mother turned and saw that Nilda was brooding. She asked, "Don't you want your old room back, with your bed by the window? First you were mad and now you don't know what it is you want."

"I know that I don't want the baby to leave!" she said, almost at the point of tears.

"Stop being silly; nobody's going to leave so soon anyway."

Nilda continued to sit, feeling miserable. The thought of Sophie's mother scared her. Sophie had said her mother hated her and would never forgive her. When she kicked Sophie out, she had told her never to come back. Oh boy, Nilda thought, I'm not going to stand too close to that lady. She looked out the window. It was a cold and dreary grey day. She remembered that it might snow tonight.

"If I get Paul to take us, can I go to the park tonight?"

"We'll see how late it is. I don't want a bunch of kids in the park alone at night."

Screwing up her nose, sucking in her cheeks, and

crossing her eyes, Nilda made a horrible face. Her mother looked at her and said, "Nilda, you are a nice-looking girl, but if you keep making those ugly faces, one day your face is gonna freeze and you will grow up as ugly as a toad."

"If I can go to the park, I promise I will not make any more faces, Mama."

Smiling, her mother said, "Suit yourself, but I don't change my mind. Now go get your brothers; it's time to eat."

"All right." Nilda reluctantly stood up and slowly walked out. As she went through the living room, Aunt Delia was still reading the paper. This time she was alone. She moved her lips, shaking her head and uttering sounds of shock and outrage.

December 7, 1941

The wind was strong, sharp, and cold as they walked toward First Avenue near the East River. Sophie held Baby Jimmy; he was wrapped up in several blankets. At first Nilda thought he would suffocate, but now, with the cold sharp wind on her face, she wished she had a few blankets herself. Victor walked alongside Sophie and the baby.

"How many more blocks, Victor?"

"Just about two. We're almost there."

"Are you gonna come up with us, Victor?"

"Will you stop asking so many questions, Nilda!" he snapped. Oh boy, he's not too happy about going either, she thought. Her brother Victor was quiet and serious by nature. Even though Jimmy was the oldest, they all looked to Victor for advice. He very often made decisions and was respected as the older brother. Her mother would say, "I can always count on my Victor. Thank God for such a son." He was in his senior year in high school and was a very good student. Nilda would brag about him to her friends. "He's real smart," she'd say, "always reading books and always in the library. He got the highest mark in his whole class. When he graduates, he's going to go to college someplace and be something big, like a lawyer or even a bookkeeper. You know, something like that. Mami says he's not going to be a sucketa working in no factory."

Nilda walked along, too cold to worry about the visit and anxious to reach there and get warm. At last they approached a grey tenement. The building was narrow, four stories high, and old and worn looking, resembling all the other buildings in the area. They walked up the stoop steps and into the small foyer. Nilda felt the warmth as she trembled, shaking off the coldness from the outside. "Man, it's cold out," she said.

Sophie stood there holding the baby. Nilda began reading the names on the mailboxes on both sides of the walls. She read silently, Zapatoki, Stasik, Jahelka, Brozyna, Lapinski. . . . Some of the names were hard to read. Not one Spanish name, she thought. The hallway was as empty as the cold streets outside.

"I guess you better wait down here, Victor. My mother might think you are Jimmy and get real angry," Sophie said, looking at Victor. "But once I'm inside, I'll send Nilda down to come get you," she added with embarrassment and looked away. She stood still awhile and began to bite the corners of her lips, first biting the right corner and then the left. "O.K., we might as well go on up," she said, smiling despite a frightened look in her eyes.

Nilda followed Sophie through the hallway and up the stairs. A strong odor of cooked cabbage permeated the hallway. She could hear the hall radiator hissing as the warm steam escaped into the stale air.

"Is it a long way up?" whispered Nilda.

"It's the top floor, three more flights," Sophie answered, also in a whisper. They continued to climb the narrow stairway. The floor was covered with dark green linoleum that had just been washed clean. A slight odor of disinfectant, mingled with the odor of cooked cabbage, made Nilda a little faint.

"One more, Nilda, then we'll be there." Sophie stopped and rested against the wall, holding little Jimmy who slept soundly. Catching her breath, she started up again. They reached the last landing and walked up to a narrow, dark brown door with the number 15 printed in black. Standing in front of the door for a second, she handed the baby to Nilda and said in a barely audible whisper, "Here, take him for a minute." She smoothed out her coat and straightened her hair. Reaching down, she picked up the infant again. Holding the baby, she pushed the small bell on the right-hand side of the door.

Nilda heard a short ring sound at the other side of the door and then a dog bark. The dog, jumping at the door, began to bark loudly. Nilda ran back toward the stairway.

"Don't be scared, Nilda; that's Queenie, my dog." Smiling, she seemed to gain confidence as the dog continued to bark, and rang the bell again, this time more forcefully. "Queenie, it's Sophie. How's the girl? Queenie?" The dog began to yelp, cry, and whine. Sophie laughed nervously and handed the baby back to Nilda. "Take him, Nilda. He's sleeping, so hold him still."

They heard footsteps on the other side of the wall; the footsteps came all the way up to the door and stopped. A voice from inside said, "Who is it? Who's there?" The

86

dog stopped her whining and it got quiet. "Who is it? Anybody out there?"

"Mama? Mama, it's me, Sophie." Silence followed. "Mama?" The dog started a low crying and whining. "Mama, it's me, Sophie. Can I come in?" After a short silence they heard the footsteps disappearing somewhere inside the locked apartment. Nilda was beginning to tire and the baby was stirring, so she carefully leaned against the wall, trying to ease the weight.

They heard a noise; the door next to them, with the number 16, opened. For an instant Nilda could see a face on the other side of the door chain. Then someone slammed it shut. Sophie put her finger to the bell and pressed it for a long time. The dog began to bark loudly once again. They heard the footsteps coming back towards the door. Getting very close to the door, Sophie placed her mouth over the lock and said, "Mama, it's me, Sophie, and my baby. Mama? I have a baby, your grandson. It's a boy. His name is James. I brought him to meet you, to meet his grandmother. Can we come in? Mama?"

"Who is there? What do you want?" the voice from inside asked.

"Mama. . . ." Nilda heard Sophie talking in another language. Her voice was steady at first, then it began to crack. She was crying but she continued to speak. "Mama" was all Nilda could make out. Sophie seemed to be pleading. She stopped and waited for a response, then continued to speak, crying and pleading. Nilda could not understand a word of what she said. Sophie stopped talking and waited, quietly sobbing.

The voice inside answered loudly in English. It was a woman's voice, strong, and with an accent. She pronounced the words very clearly. "Who is this? Sophie, you say. I don't know anybody by that name. My Sophie, my daughter, is dead. She died. She run off with a nigger and now she's dead. He poisoned her. You are mistaken. I don't have no daughter no more. You got the wrong house. Go away to another place; maybe they know you there."

"Mama! Maaamaaa!"

Startled, Nilda heard a shriek as Sophie lifted both her hands and began to hit the door, shoving her weight against it. "Maaama! Maaama!" Sophie kept screaming between sobs, almost choking as she shrieked out to her mother. "Maaaaama!"

Nilda felt little Jimmy jump up in her arms and begin to cry. People opened doors, muttering, then slammed them shut again. The baby was crying steadily now.

They heard the woman from inside the apartment shouting, "Get out! I'll call the police. Go away. Go someplace with those people who killed my daughter. The niggers. Go there. My daughter is dead, gone, finished. No more. I call the police!"

Sophie had her face buried in her hands, sobbing. Lifting her head she looked at Nilda, her face streaked with tears and her nose wet with mucus. Wiping her nose on her sleeve, she said, "Let's go." Baby Jimmy was still crying. She took him from Nilda. Turning around just before going down the steps, Sophie yelled, "Remember, Mama, remember I'm dead, dead, dead!" She went down the stairs swiftly. Nilda followed, almost running, frightened, her heart pounding as she thought of the lady in the apartment. She wanted to run all the way home and back to her own mother. She was glad the lady had not opened the door.

Victor was waiting, standing in the outside doorway, rubbing his hands together to keep warm. He looked uneasy. Nilda noticed the look of shock and concern on her brother's face as he looked at Sophie and the baby. "What happened?" he asked. "I heard some shouting." Sophie was absentmindedly rocking the baby, who had stopped crying. She opened her mouth to speak but began to cry. "Here, Sophie," said Victor, "I'll take him. I'll carry him home." He reached over and took the baby from her. She cried quietly, continuing to cover her face with her hands. They walked out of the building and began to walk home. Victor handed her a handkerchief and she held it up to her face. He looked at Nilda inquiringly.

Shrugging her shoulders, she whispered to her brother, "Her mother wouldn't open up the door."

The three of them walked back briskly. This time the wind was going with them so that it hit their backs instead of their faces and seemed to help them walk a little faster.

What does she mean her daughter is dead? Didn't she know that was Sophie? What does she mean her daughter was poisoned? Nilda walked home asking herself these questions. I wonder what Sophie told her in that other language. Maybe that's what got that lady so mad, what Sophie said to her in that language. Well, whatever she said, I didn't understand one word except when she said "Mama." My mother would never throw me out, and she would certainly know who I am. She would recognize me right away. Of course, unless I had some sort of accident and had to get my face changed. Like in that movie where that woman had a real bad scar on her face and wore a big hat that could hide her. Then she meets a doctor and he fixes it and makes her so beautiful that no one knows who she is any more. But she still got the same voice. Didn't that lady know Sophie's voice? That couldn't have gotten different, she said to herself. She knew Sophie's mother did not like Puerto Ricans, and that was why she didn't like Jimmy. I guess when she told her to go back to the niggers, she meant us, Nilda thought, getting angry. Well, I hope that Jimmy and Sophie have a big wedding and get a nice apartment like Mama says, and when that lady knocks on the door, I hope they don't let her in neither. Nilda went on thinking. The whole business made no sense to her. She walked along, now no longer frightened, and glanced at Sophie, who still held the handkerchief to her face. She felt really sorry for her, wishing deeply that there were something she could do.

They reached Lexington Avenue and Nilda remembered the party and began to worry about being late for the church service. It was supposed to start at about five P.M. She was going to meet Benji at four o'clock and get together with Petra and Marge; they had to plan where they were going to sit at the service and what they were going to do.

"What time is it?" she asked her brother.

"I don't know. I don't have a watch."

90

"What time do you think it is? Is it four o'clock?"

"No, it can't be. We left at one; it didn't take us that long. It can't be more than about three o'clock."

They soon reached their building and started up the stairway. As they walked into the apartment, Sophie said in a quiet voice, "I'll take the baby, Victor." Taking Baby Jimmy, she disappeared into the long hallway. Nilda heard the door to her room slam shut.

"Victor? Is that you? You are back so soon?" Nilda heard her mother's voice. Her mother walked into the living room with a worried look on her face. "Qué pasó, chico? What happened? Didn't I just hear Sophie? Did you get there all right?"

"We got there all right, Mom." Victor looked seriously at his mother. "All I know is I waited downstairs. Nilda went up with Sophie and the baby. I heard some shouting, but I was standing in the outside hall and nothing sounded clear."

Looking directly at Nilda, her mother asked, "Well, what happened? Did she get to see her mother? Was there anyone home? Was she in?"

"We got up there, but the lady wouldn't open the door."

"What do you mean she wouldn't open the door?" her mother asked, her voice getting louder.

"She said that her daughter is dead. That somebody poisoned her. That Sophie should go back to the . . ." Nilda hesitated.

"The what?" her mother asked urgently. "The what?"

"She said the niggers. To go back to the niggers because they poisoned her, I think." She paused and then

91

went on, "Mama, is the food ready? I'm really hungry; can I eat? I have to meet Benji, remember?"

"Did she open the door at all, Nilda?"

"No, not at all. We only heard her talking and a dog barking. Sophie said it was her dog. Can I eat? Mami, I have to go soon."

"Did Sophie tell her about the baby?" her mother asked.

"Yes, she told her. She even told her his name too. Please, Mama, can I—"

"O.K.," her mother interrupted. "Wait a second now!" Picking up her hand, she covered her eyes. For a moment Nilda watched her mother silently, afraid she was going to burst into tears. But then her mother lowered her hand and Nilda saw that even though she looked upset, she was not going to cry. Turning to Victor she said, "Victor, feed yourself and Nilda. I'm going in to speak with Sophie. Everything is on the stove. We can't have no seconds today, so just fill the plates once. And Nilda, you don't go without telling me. I have to know the time you'll come back. You hear?" There was a tenseness in her voice. "Wash up first."

Nilda ran into the bathroom and washed. She was hungry, and anxious to meet her friends. There was going to be food tonight at the church, so she didn't mind not having seconds. Her thoughts were filled with going to the party, listening to the music, the speeches, and making plans with her friends.

December 7, 1941
Late Afternoon

Nilda hurried over to Benji's building. It was grey out and getting dark. Still no snow, she thought. Walking up the stoop steps she could see inside the hallway. Benji was waiting next to the hall radiator, trying to keep warm. She pushed open the inside door and said, "Hi, Benji. Did you hear the news on the radio? All the radio stations were talking about what happened."

"Yeah. Man, everybody up in my house was talking and my mother and abuelita was crying—"

"The Japanese bombed the whole United States Navy in Pearl Harbor. That's what some of the news said, and now we are gonna be at war," Nilda interrupted excitedly.

"Papa made us all get down on our knees and pray. As soon as everybody got up again and started to talk, I grabbed my coat and split." With a worried look he asked, "Nilda? Do you think they will bomb us here?"

"No," she answered reassuringly. "My brother Victor says we are too far away, that they don't got planes to fly that far. You don't have to worry."

"Good," he said, smiling at Nilda. "What a surprise, huh Nilda?"

"Not to my papa," Nilda said. "He knew we would have to get into the war because of Franco. You know, Hitler and Mussolini helping him all the time. My papa said sooner or later it would happen. He was not surprised at all." She paused and saw that Benji was looking at her confusedly. She wanted to explain it further to Benji but remembered about the service tonight. "Hey Benji, are we still gonna have the meeting and the party at your church?"

"Oh yes, Papa said that it is a good thing. We need the meeting because it is sin and the devil that causes war and we got to pray and fight evil."

"Good," sighed Nilda with relief. Looking out toward the street, she said, "I wonder where Petra and Marge are. They better not be late."

"They're listening to the radio, I bet you." Leaning against the wall next to the hot radiator, he moved closer to Nilda. Smiling up at her he said, "I'm glad you're coming with us, Nilda." Nilda smiled back at him and nodded her head. Benji went on, "Sometimes, though, I wish Petra wouldn't have to bring that Marge with her all the time. We can't do anything without worrying about her, and she can be such a pest."

"Petra don't like it neither, but you know how strict her parents are, especially her father. She can't go no place without her little sister. That Marge is worser now that she got them Shirley Temple dolls, and the way her mother combs her hair, too. You know what? She wants me and Petra to call her Shirley. She told me she's going to change her name and—"

"Not me! Never happen!" interrupted Benji. "I'm not

gonna call her Shirley. Her name is Marge López and that's just what I'm going to call her. I don't care."

"Me neither!" Nilda said emphatically. "And I don't care if she does get mad and cries. She's such a crybaby and she only does it so we can feel sorry for her and give in." After a short pause Nilda jumped up quickly. "Benji. Did you tell her about that man Justicio? Doña Amalia's husband? Or about our plan?"

"No, of course not. Nilda, do you think I'm stupid? Petra wouldn't tell her neither; you know what a tattle-tale Marge is. If she knew, she would rat on us, man! And their father is so strict, they could never be allowed to play with us again. I know that she doesn't know nothing about it."

"Listen, what do you think? Will he do it tonight?"

"Well, at the last meeting he almost did it. He says next time he's going in and getting his wife out and ain't nobody going to stop him. You know, my papi says that when Don Justicio gets drunk, the devil gets into him so that nobody can control him."

"But Don Justicio's still gonna try tonight, ain't he?" asked Nilda anxiously. Benji nodded his head. "Did you ever see it? I mean the whole thing, Benji?"

"Well, once I almost did, but they grabbed him right away and his wife, Amalia, fainted. All the ladies were screaming. I only saw a little."

"Hey, where should we sit? What do you think?"

"Well," Benji said seriously, "I know just where to sit so we can see the whole thing. But you and Petra have to follow me fast, or somebody else will sit there. Now, when Don Justicio makes his speech, he says the same

95

thing every time and then he does it. Well, when he makes his speech, I'll tap you and you tap Petra, because they grab him fast since everybody is usually ready for Don Justicio. O.K.?"

"Right! I'll be ready, Benji," Nilda nodded.

"Hey, how are we gonna tell Petra in front of Marge?"

"Let's have a game of hide-and-go-seek, Benji. You be It. I'll watch where Petra hides and tell you, then I'll go with Marge. You can find Petra and tell her our plan. O.K.?"

"Sounds good. Only, you know how Papi feels about my playing games. What if he sees us? Man, then I'll be in trouble for sure."

"Don't worry, Benji. I'll look out for them; I won't hide far. When I see them coming out of the building, I'll yell 'Ungawa Ungawa,' like in the Tarzan movies. That's what Tarzan yells all the time when he's in trouble. All right, Benji?"

"O.K., Nilda."

The door flung open; Petra and Marge walked in. Nilda saw that they had on their good Sunday clothes, almost brand-new. She had not gotten anything this year and wore the same coat for school and Sunday. Remembering she had a torn pocket where the lining was showing, Nilda slowly covered the spot with her hand.

Marge had dozens of curls that looked like tiny bedsprings all over her head; several came down over her forehead, partially covering her eyes. Small red bows were pinned at either side of her head to match her red knee socks. Petra wore her hair in two neat braids tied with blue ribbons. Both sisters had fair complexions and blonde hair; however, Marge had an abundance of thick hair, very golden in color. Her family was very proud of Marge's hair and looks. "She's the picture of Shirley Temple," their mother would say. Marge always wore the latest Shirley-Temple-style clothes. Nilda had heard their mother discussing Marge with a neighbor once. "She even has dimples like Shirley Temple," she had said. "People mistake her for Shirley Temple sometimes. They just stare at her." Nilda remembered waiting for the two girls one day to go out to play. She had watched as Marge was getting her hair combed. With painstaking effort, their mother undid one of the many lumps of hair that had been wrapped up and knotted in a long thin piece of white rag. Then, taking the lump of hair and wetting it with a green sticky solution, she twisted it around her finger with a comb, jerking it loose. It would separate into one tiny, short blonde curl. With a smile and a chuckle of satisfaction, their mother would continue to make another curl. Boy, Nilda thought, it seemed to take forever to get out to play that day. She had been grateful that Petra always wore two plain braids. Petra was two years older than Marge and one year older than Nilda. She was easygoing by nature, never asserting her authority as the oldest in the group.

"Hi!" said Petra. "Is there going to be a party and a service tonight, Benji?"

"Oh, yeah. Papi said now we need it so that we can fight the devil and sin that cause wars."

"My papa knew we were going to have the war," Nilda announced. "You see, they are just puppets of Hitler and Mussolini and Fascism."

97

All three children turned and, with confused expressions, looked at Nilda. After a short silence, Petra asked, "Fascism? What is that?"

"Well," Nilda said, "that's when they kill people. Like they don't let you be free. And they also kill little kids."

"Oh," Marge said, "that's their religion."

"No!" answered Nilda. "It's not a religion."

"Well, I never heard of it. My father never mentioned it to us," Marge said.

Nilda looked around her. All three of them were waiting for her to speak. "Look," she went on, "when you want to be free, O.K.? And you do what they want, or else!"

"My father says we do what he wants, or else!" Marge said quickly. Petra and Benji giggled.

"Your father is not gonna kill you and drop bombs and destroy whole villages, now is he?" Nilda yelled furiously. "Just like Hitler and the Japs who bombed the whole U.S. Navy? You gotta know that, I hope, for your own sakes!"

A door opened from the back of the hallway, and a voice yelled, "Hey, shut up. Get out of the hall and go play outside. Stop that God damn racket." They all heard a loud slam as the door shut.

Benji looked at Nilda and whispered, "I get it now."

"Me too," said Petra.

"Let's play a game of hide-and-go-seek," Benji said. No one answered him or moved. "Come on, Nilda, let's play." Going over to her, he whispered in her ear, "Our plan, Nilda, remember?"

"Oh yeah, let's get out of this dumb hallway. Let's go

out and choose who's gonna be It," Nilda said, and ran out of the building with the other children following her. Outside, they gathered in a circle. "Eeny meeny miney moe, catch a monkey by the toe. My teacher said to pick this one." Nilda did this very quickly, pointing to Benji. "You're It, Benji," Nilda yelled. "Come on, let's hide."

"Remember Papi, Nilda," Benji said nervously.

"Oh yeah. We have to stay close to the lamppost because Benji's father might catch him playing," Nilda explained. "Now, when I yell 'Ungawa' like Tarzan in the movies, you have to come out fast and act like we were just talking. Let's go. Go on, Benji, start counting."

Benji started counting and, as everyone ran, Nilda waited, whispering to Benji, "Benji, Petra went behind that big black car across the street. I'm gonna follow Marge. You tell Petra our plan."

The game continued until Nilda was It. As she leaned forward against the lamppost, her hands covering her eyes, counting, ". . . fourteen, fifteen, sixt . . ." she heard voices; people were coming out of the building. Quickly she yelled, "Ungaawaa, Ungaawaa!" Benji came running; Marge and Petra followed. Breathless, they walked up to the stoop steps to join the people who were assembling.

All of Benji's brothers and sisters were there with his grandmother, his mother, his mother's younger sister, who held on to two small children, and her husband, who carried an infant in his arms. The men all wore dark suits and coats. The women had on very plain clothes and, except for Benji's mother, no makeup. Benji's mother was dark-skinned, and Nilda noticed that whenever his mother went to church she covered her face with powder. The powder was very light in tone; bits of it settled in the creases and wrinkles of her face, giving her an ashen look. Nilda thought, She looks like she's got a mask on, and remembered the white flour she put on her own face for Halloween.

The older kids and grown-ups held small black Bibles. Whenever Nilda asked a question about their religion, they always quoted from the Bible.

"When are we leaving?" someone asked.

"We have to wait for Don Wilfredo to come down," someone else answered.

After a short while Benji's father came down. He was dressed in a black suit, black coat, and wore a wide-brimmed black fedora on his head. He was a small man, fair in complexion, so thin that the brim of his fedora was as wide as his shoulders. Slowly raising his arms, he said, "This day when our Lord has sent us fire, doom, and destruction . . . let us go directly to the house of God." Looking around him, he continued solemnly, "Let us pray as we walk, and think of Him. El Señor nos protege."

"Aleluya!" people responded.

"Amen."

"El Señor es poderoso."

Don Wilfredo slowly dropped his arms and started to walk. The large group of people followed as he led the way. Nilda walked close to Benji with Petra and Marge. Man! This looks like a parade, she thought.

December 7, 1941
Evening

As they marched to the storefront church, Nilda saw the people they passed on the street point and stare at the group. They continued marching silently. Nilda wanted to say something, but since no one spoke, she remained silent. They finally arrived at the church. The large storefront window had the words

LA ROCA DE SAN SEBASTIÁN, INC.

printed on it in large black letters. Just below them, in smaller black print, were the words

IGLESIA PENTECOSTAL

Underneath the words was a painted scene of St. Sebastián in a white tunic, with long blond hair down to his shoulders, a blond beard, and a golden halo painted over his head. He stood barefoot on top of a large boulder on a mountain of green grass. He looks just like the statue of Jesus in St. Cecilia's, thought Nilda.

The entire window was covered by the painted scene, so that it was not possible to see inside the church too clearly. The large room was brightly lit and some people were already seated. As they entered, Benji whispered to Nilda, "Follow me; hurry up." Nilda, Petra, and Marge trailed along as Benji went over to the second row. He sat in the first seat near the aisle. Then Nilda, Petra, and Marge sat down next to each other. Benji looked at Nilda and nudged her with his elbow. "This is just right," he said, laughing. Nilda laughed and nudged Petra who began to giggle.

"What's so funny, everybody?" asked Marge.

"Nothing," said Petra, laughing.

"If nothing is funny, then why are you all laughing? Let me know too," she insisted.

"Shh," Nilda said, raising her finger and frowning at Marge. "Be quiet." Marge settled back, sulking. Some of Benji's family began to seat themselves next to the children.

More people came into the church, greeting one another. "Buenos días. What a sad day today."

"Amen."

"Good day. Aleluya!"

"What a tragedy."

All the seats were beginning to fill up. "Hi, Benji," said one boy. "What are you doing sitting way up here? Wanna sit back with us?"

"No, it's O.K. I gotta stay here," Benji answered, looking away, avoiding the boy.

"What's your father do in the church again, Benji?" Nilda asked. She knew his father had an important position.

"He's the sexton. He takes care of seeing that the

103

church is taken care of; like it should have enough chairs and tables, lights and all that. He was working here all day for the service tonight."

"Oh," said Nilda, impressed.

Women carrying shopping bags walked up to a long table which was to the right of the small center platform. They began to take out bowls and pots of food, setting them on the table. There were jars of juice and maví. Nilda loved maví; it had a tangy taste. Paper plates, cups, and napkins were set down next to metal forks and knives.

On the other side of the platform was a piano, a drum set, maracas, two tambourines, the back of a banjo head, rhythm sticks, and a güiro. There were rows of wooden folding chairs, going from the back of the room right up to the pulpit on the platform. An open space was left in the center, creating an aisle.

The minister walked up to the pulpit. He was a short plump man with a dark brown complexion. He wore his tight curly hair short; it was greying at the temples and thinning at the top. One of his front teeth was capped in shiny gold and reflected the lights as he smiled, greeting the people. "Aleluya, brother," he said. "Amen."

The musicians appeared and walked up to the platform, taking their places by the instruments. A very fat woman sat down at the piano. She had a fair pink complexion and looked flushed as she thumbed through the music sheets. The rest of the musicians were men, and each one took up an instrument. Another man followed, holding a guitar, and took his place next to the drums.

Raising his arms, the minister looked at the con-

104

gregation. He looked to the left and to the right with his arms outstretched. The church was full; every seat was occupied and there were some latecomers standing in the rear. It got very quiet. He then raised his right hand, holding it above his head and pointing up with his forefinger. The minister began the sermon, speaking in Spanish. "What is the message? Eh? Today we have a sign from the Lord. Our Savior, El Señor."

"Amen," people called out.

"Aleluya."

"Oh yes."

"I was gonna talk about sin and the devil and little things like that. Oh yeah! I say little things like that because . . . NOW! . . . I say NOW! The Lord Jesus has spoken to us of war and enemies. God is patient with His children. Until finally, we go too far! Our country is in danger. And we? What do we do? Live in sin. Tomorrow I'll think about Jesus. Today I'll gamble and drink; tomorrow I'll think about Jesus. Today I'll covet my neighbor's wife; tomorrow I'll think about Jesus." With that the minister leaped out from behind the pulpit and pointed to one of the congregation. "You!" Then he pointed to another. "You!" And another. "You!" . . . "You! What have you done? Come on now. Have you thought of Jesus every moment? Have you thought of our country and God?"

"Amen!"

"Aleluya."

"Help me, oh Lord."

"El Señor, help me!" people began to shout.

The minister waited a moment and went on. "What

have you been thinking, brothers and sisters? Commit yourselves to Jesus. The Bible tells us, the Bible warns us. Oh yes it does. Devastation! Destruction! Fire, doom, and damnation. That's no news. No sir. Are we gonna be surprised?"

"No. Jesus help us sinners."

"Aleluya." Everyone was yelling out.

Walking back to the pulpit, the minister looked at the congregation and said in a softer tone, "Let me read from the Bible, from Jeremiah, chapter twenty-one." Pausing, he began to read from the large Bible placed in front of him. "The word which came unto Jeremiah from the Lord, when King Zedekiah sent unto him. . . ."

Nilda listened as the minister spoke, enjoying the way he preached. She liked their services. This was more fun than Mass at St. Cecilia's. Nilda wondered when that man Don Justicio was coming. She wanted to ask Benji about it, but she looked at Benji and saw he was quietly concentrating on what the minister said.

". . . But I will punish you according to the fruit of your doings, saith the Lord, and I will kindle a fire in the forest thereof, and it shall devour all things round about it." Closing the book and picking up his arms, he paused awhile, then shouted, "Oh Lord, save us. Have pity on us. We commit ourselves to You, dear Master, Jesus." Turning to the musicians, he clapped his hands briskly and said, "Let's have a chorus."

Immediately, Nilda heard the drums and all the percussion start. A Latin beat sounded, quick in tempo, with a loud African rhythm. Then the piano and the guitar began playing the melody.

The minister began to sing, "Adore, adore Jesus. We shall be saved." Everybody joined in singing, and they clapped their hands. People were swaying in their seats, clapping and singing on, "Be not afraid. We will go to heaven."

Nilda started tapping her feet, following the rhythm. This is great, she thought. Except for the words, it sounds just like regular music. It was the same kind of music she heard on the Spanish radio stations, at parties in her own home, and in her neighborhood. She began to rock back and forth in her seat, tapping her feet with the rhythm.

The minister was on the platform, clapping his hands, and singing.

"Amen, Jesus loves me." People were standing, rocking and swaying as they sang chorus after chorus.

"Save me, Jesus."

"I love You, Lord," voices called out.

"Come on. Come on," the minister shouted. "Let Him enter into our bodies. Sisters, brothers, we shall be saved!"

Nilda heard a shriek. A woman stood up; she was shaking all over. The minister raised his hand towards the musicians and they lowered the sound of the music, slowly stopping altogether.

"Ayyyyyy! Ay . . . ayyyyyy!" the woman shouted. The minister rushed over to her. Benji's father took the woman by one arm and the minister held her by the other arm. "Eeeeeeeee," the woman yelled. They brought her up to the platform. She swooned and shrieked.

"He is entering her body," the minister said. "Kneel,

sister, kneel. Let Him in, sister, let Him in. Amen."

The woman was crying and shaking. "No more, Jesus. I will sin no more. I was a sinner; drinking, and going to bed with any man who asked me. Oh Lord! Now I don't need men. I don't need sin. I got You, Jesus."

"Aleluya, sister."

The woman was kneeling, and every few seconds she would jerk her body and scream.

"The Lord is in her body," the minister said. "Look. Look at her, everyone. He is sending His message through her body! He has penetrated her soul!"

Another scream was heard and several people in back were jumping around. "Come on up here. Brothers, sisters. Let the Lord get into your bodies. Commit yourselves to Jesus."

"Kneel, children of God, brother, sister, kneel." Some kneeled, others fell on the floor shaking, crying. Everyone was shouting.

Nilda watched wide-eyed and began to giggle softly. Benji looked at her and whispered, "That's when the Lord gets into them," covering his mouth and suppressing laughter. Nilda and Benji were trying hard not to laugh out loud.

Petra looked at them and said, "They all look like they're having fits." Benji tried to tell her something but kept giggling instead.

"The Lord is supposed to be in their bodies," Nilda said, looking at Petra and Marge, trying not to giggle. Marge looked terrified; she had never been inside this church before. Petra had attended only a short service

108

once last year. Nilda had gotten used to the ceremony; she had come often with Benji. They usually sat in the back by the door with the other kids, sneaking out to play during the service. Today, however, they sat up front, looking forward to something else.

The music started again; this time they played a slow bolero rhythm with a soft melody that sounded familiar to Nilda. After a while she recognized it. It was a marching tune they played in school. The congregation had composed themselves and stood up with their hands over their hearts, singing in English, "Three cheers for the red, white, and blue. . . ." They sang the second chorus in Spanish.

The music stopped and everyone sat down. The minister began to speak. "Today we have been blessed by the Lord. He is here in our house, entering our bodies, welcoming us to . . ."

"Shit!"

They heard a shout at the door. "Amalia, come on out!"

Benji whispered to Nilda, "That's him; that's Don Justicio."

Nilda's heart jumped. She turned to Petra and said softly in her ear, "It's Don Justicio, that man."

The church was completely silent. "Come on out! Carajo! Condená!" Several men followed as Don Wilfredo walked to the back where the man was standing by the door.

"Welcome, Don Justicio, to the house of God!"

"Amen."

"Come in, brother."

"Join us," said Don Wilfredo.

"I want my wife. Amalia? Come on out, God damn it!" Don Justicio shouted angrily.

"Shhhh. Now, none of that, sir," said one of the men. "Calm down, or you will have to leave."

Nilda watched several men escorting a tall thin man up the center aisle to the platform. As they passed, Nilda could smell alcohol. "Phew!" she whispered to herself, and thought, Boy is he drunk.

The tall skinny man stood by the platform, glaring at everyone. He wore a brown leather jacket, baggy pants, and worn-out dirty shoes.

The minister smiled and, looking up at Don Justicio, said, "Welcome, Brother Justicio. You are blessed when you come to the house of the Lord."

"Look!" the man said, swaying unsteadily on his feet, "I came here to get my old lady. That's all. I'm gonna take her out of here. I'm the macho in my house. I wear the pants. I'm gonna take her out. We don't believe in this here religion. I forbid her to come here."

"Now now, brother, pray with us. Give Jesus a chance," said the minister, putting his hand on Don Justicio's shoulder.

Pushing away, Don Justicio said, "Shit, don't you understand? I want my wife the hell out of here. What the hell are you doing to her anyway? Amalia? Where are you, coño! Amalia? Condená!"

A short plump woman came running down the aisle. "Justicio, please behave yourself," she cried.

Don Justicio saw his wife and ran towards her, raising his arm to strike her. She jumped back. Two men grabbed him, pinning his hands behind his back. "Stop it now, none of that," the minister said

"O.K., all right, let me go. I won't hit her," Don Justicio said. "I won't." They released him. Looking at his wife, he made a fist. "Amalia, you're going to pay. You hear?"

"Ay, Justicio, have faith. The good Lord will show you the way if you open your heart," his wife pleaded.

"Praise the Lord," people called out.

Jumping back, Don Justicio shouted, "You are coming out, Amalia. I don't believe in this shit. Hypocrites! I shit and pee on this place."

Benji tapped Nilda. "Here he goes." Nilda was too shocked to move. She watched Don Justicio quickly jump up on the far end of the small platform, open up his fly, and let loose a long stream of pee.

"Ay, Dios mío, stop him," yelled his wife. The men jumped up on the platform and grabbed Don Justicio, pushing him down, almost knocking over the table full of food. Some, angrier than others, began to punch him.

"No! Ay, no! Don't kill him, please. Don't kill him," yelled his wife.

The minister shouted, "That's enough. Enough! Take him outside." Don Justicio got to his feet. Disheveled, with his nose bleeding, he was dragged out the door.

"Pig."

"Animal desgraciado."

"Disgusting."

"We shouldn't let him in here no more."

"Bestia."

111

People shouted as he walked by. Some people fixed the table and rearranged things. Some others were wiping up juice that had spilled; others were cleaning up where Don Justicio had urinated.

Off in a corner, Doña Amalia sat swaying and crying. Some of the women were consoling her. "Poor dear, what a cross you have to bear." "Never mind, all the more to give yourself to Jesus." There was a noise and scuffling outside the church door.

Nilda turned to Benji. "Man, what a mess!"

"Well, he really did it this time. He never really peed before," said Benji, impressed.

"Did you get to see it, Petra?" asked Nilda. Although Nilda had seen Don Justicio urinate, she had not actually seen very much of his penis.

"Well, I saw some of it," Petra said timidly.

"How about you, Marge?" Nilda asked.

"I was too shocked to look," Marge said, looking annoyed at them.

Ignoring her, Nilda said, "I saw the whole thing. Right, Benji? From right here we could see it all. It was very big. Right, Benji?"

"That's right," agreed Benji. He looked at Nilda and Petra and the three of them began to laugh. Marge sat sulking. Making a face, she turned away.

People returned, taking their seats once more. The minister went up to the pulpit. "Brothers and sisters, we must all pray for Don Justicio. We must learn to forgive as God forgives. He is a sick man, possessed by the devil. God save our Sister Amalia, and let us pray that the Lord gets into Don Justicio's body and drives

112

out the devil that makes him behave in such an evil, disgusting way. Amen."

"Aleluya."

"Jesus save his soul," people echoed.

The band played and a few hymns were sung.

"Now let us end our service with a new duty in mind, to serve our country against the enemy and turn more than ever to Jesus. Let us be free from sin. Lord be praised! Now we shall eat and drink of God's food and thank Him as we realize how fortunate we are." Lifting up his arms he said, "Amen."

"Amen."

"Aleluya."

"Amen, oh Lord."

Everyone stood and began to chat with one another, folding the chairs and lining them up against the wall.

At last! thought Nilda. I'm starving; I hope that man didn't spill the maví. Groups of people were lining up for food. She went to the table with her friends. Looking toward the food, she saw pots of rice with chicken, a codfish stew with peppers, onions, and tomatoes, and a large platter of tropical vegetables, steaming hot, sprinkled with oil and garlic. "Ummmm," she said to the kids. "This looks just delicious."

"Yeah," they all agreed.

It was time for the social worker to come to investigate. Everybody was jittery. Nilda had been coming home from school each day asking her mother if the investigator had come. It was already the middle of the week and they were still waiting. Nilda would look at her mother, searching for some reassurance that everything would come out all right, but the worried look on her mother's face seemed almost permanently fixed. All week her mother had been saying to Nilda, "Don't make noise; your papa is resting! Stop playing with the baby so much; he might throw up. Go on! Play someplace else. Stop being a nuisance."

Her mother had been telling everyone what to say to the investigator in case they were asked questions. Every day she would repeat herself, telling Sophie what to say about her situation and why she was living here. Nilda and her brothers were instructed to answer with polite yes-and-no answers and, when asked about personal family matters, to say only "I don't know" and not another word.

Nilda had just arrived from school and was quietly putting her things away so she could go play with Baby

Jimmy. She heard her mother telling her to be quiet. Oh, I just wish she wouldn't tell me the same things every day, she thought. Always the same story. I know I have to be quiet. Washing up, she went over to Sophie's room and knocked softly on the door.

"Come in," said Sophie.

"Hi, Sophie. How's the baby?"

"All right. You wanna feed him?"

"Oh thanks, Sophie." She must be in a good mood, thought Nilda. Sophie very often gave the bottle to the baby herself or offered to let Frankie feed little Jimmy, even though she knew Nilda loved to feed him. Taking the blanket and the baby, Nilda settled down as Sophie handed her the bottle. "Hi, handsome! You are gonna get your bottle. Oh, I love you," Nilda said, hugging the baby. "You know what, Sophie? He got bigger in one day. Look, he's starving! Guess what? He smiled at me yesterday. He really did."

Sophie began to hum. Nilda looked at her, surprised to see her so happy.

Looking at Nilda, Sophie said, "Jimmy's coming."

"Really?"

"Yes. One of his friends came to us this morning. Jimmy is living in another state, in New Jersey. But he will be coming back to New York to get me and the baby."

"Are you gonna leave right away?" asked Nilda.

"Well, as soon as he gets here, I guess."

"Are you gonna live far away, Sophie?"

"I don't know, Nilda; it all depends on what Jimmy wants to do, or where he is. His friend said New Jersey so I guess that's where we'll go." Nilda felt a lump in her throat as she looked at the baby. She did not want Baby Jimmy to leave and wanted to say something, but she felt too miserable to speak. Sophie picked up a nail file and, humming, began to file her nails.

Nilda swallowed and finally asked, "Can I come to visit you and the baby?"

"Of course you can. All of you can come and, if we have an extra bed, you can stay overnight and baby-sit."

"Oh wow! Sophie, thanks! That's great," Nilda said, feeling happier.

The door opened and Frankie walked into the room. "Hi . . . oh, Nilda, you're feeding him. I'll take him when you finish."

"Get out! I'm going to hold him for a while. Right, Sophie?"

"Let her hold him for a while; then you can play with him, Frankie."

"All right," he said. "Mama told me about Jimmy. That's great, Sophie."

"I can't wait. I want him to see the baby; it looks just like an Ortega," Sophie said.

"Yeah, man. He sure looks like a spick!" Frankie said. They all laughed. He went on, "Aunt Delia calls him 'la mancha de plátano.' Man! Was she ever crying when you came home from the hospital." Sophie and Nilda began to laugh.

"He finished his whole bottle!" Nilda said proudly. Holding up the empty baby bottle, she went on, "See? He always finishes it with me. Don't he, Sophie?"

"He finished it with me too," said Frankie.

"He does it more with me," Nilda said, sticking out her tongue.

"Show-off!" said Frankie.

"Come on now. Stop it," said Sophie.

They heard the doorbell ring and all three of them quietly looked at each other. Soon muffled voices sounded and they knew a stranger was in the apartment.

"Frankie, go see who it is," Sophie said. Quickly, Frankie left the bedroom. "Give me the baby, Nilda." Nilda handed Sophie the baby and walked out into the living room.

There was a tall woman standing with her mother in the living room. She had sandy brown hair, cut very short, a tan camel's-hair coat, belted in back, and brown oxford shoes. She carried a brown briefcase and handbag; both were almost the exact color of her shoes. "It certainly is a help that you can speak English," the woman smiled. "You would be surprised how hard it is to understand some of these people. How long have you been in this country, Mrs. Ramírez?"

"I been here about twelve years," her mother said. "Won't you please sit down? I'll hang up your coat. Would you like a cup of coffee? I just made some fresh."

"Oh well, no, that's all right. I'll just put my coat right here on this chair and sit right down."

Her mother hesitated and then said, "How about some nice hot coffee? Yes?"

"Oh no, don't bother."

"No trouble, Mrs. Wood. I got it all ready."

"No, thank you. I really have to get on with it, you know. I have many families to visit." She pulled out a manila folder. Then she took out a brown fountain pen and began to write something on a white sheet of paper. Nilda watched her and wondered if the ink was going to come out brown. She was disappointed when she saw that it was coming out blue, just like ordinary ink.

"How many rooms do you have?"

"Six."

"How many people living here?"

Her mother wet her lips and said, "Well, I got a married son . . . but, living here . . . we got three boys and my daughter, my husband, and my aunt. She's alone. She's a widow many years."

"Then that's seven people. Three adults and four children. Correct? How old are they? Are they all in school?"

"My older boy, Victor, is seventeen years old; Paul is fifteen, and Frankie, my youngest boy, is almost thirteen. My daughter, Nilda, is ten. They are all in school. My son Victor will be graduating high school this June," she said proudly.

"Does your aunt have children?"

"No, she married when she was very young and her husband died after they were married a short time; she never had no children."

"Does she do any sort of work?"

"No. She's sick and old. She has a small check from the Home Relief, but it's very little and just enough for food and medicine."

"Can't she help out?"

"Well, she gives if she got something, but she barely has anything for herself."

"You know we cannot pay rent for you if you have other people living here," the woman said, and jotted something down on the paper. "Does your aunt have her own room?"

"Yes," her mother said. "We don't use the dining room because we eat in the kitchen, and that way we can have an extra bedroom."

"Well, Mrs. Ramírez, she will have to pay, you know. Something, even if it's minimal."

"All right, she will give something, don't worry," her mother said anxiously. "She will."

Nilda thought, Wait till that lady sees Sophie and the baby. The two women went on talking. The social worker continued to ask questions.

Aunt Delia walked in with her newspapers folded and tucked neatly under her arm. Smiling, she looked at the woman and nodded her head courteously. Mrs. Wood looked up at Aunt Delia and returned the greeting with a slight nod.

"Oh, this here is my aunt, Mrs. Wood. She's a little hard of hearing and she don't speak English. She understands just very little." Her mother looked at Aunt Delia and said to her loudly in Spanish, "Delia, this is the investigator. Understand?" Then turning to Mrs. Wood, she said, "This is my aunt—Mrs. Rivera." Pausing, she went on, "Delia, this is Mrs. Wood."

"Who?" Aunt Delia asked.

"Mrs. Wood," her mother answered loudly.

"Nice to meet you, Mrs. Rivera," Mrs. Wood said pleasantly.

Aunt Delia gave her a broad friendly smile, exposing

119

her gums. Then, with a serious expression, she said in Spanish, "It's a crime what's happening to the world today. Somebody is always getting raped. Listen," she went on rapidly, "it's a daily occurrence with the sex maniacs always attacking innocent women. They are the ones responsible for the war. Oh yes. They are! Would you like to see it right here in the paper? Let me—"

"Delia!" her mother interrupted. "This lady is not interested. She's the investigator! Not now. That's enough!"

"What did she say? What did you say, Mrs. Ramírez?" Mrs. Wood asked.

Before her mother could reply, Aunt Delia said, "She can read, can't she? She looked like an educated person. Lydia, let me show her here right here in this article. There's a picture even. Wait!" and the old woman started to open up the *Daily News*.

"What's that, Mrs. Ramírez? What is she saying in Spanish? What is she trying to tell me?" Mrs. Wood asked, perplexed.

Her mother smiled at Mrs. Wood. Making an effort to sound matter-of-fact, she said, "It's nothing, Mrs. Wood. My aunt can't hear too good." Walking over to Aunt Delia, her mother slowly picked up the *Daily News* and folded the paper, giving it to Aunt Delia. "Not now. Dear God!" She went on quietly but firmly in Spanish, "I have to talk to this woman. Please, Delia, go inside." Reluctantly Aunt Delia accepted the newspaper.

"Is she trying to tell me something, Mrs. Ramírez?" Mrs. Wood asked, very curious by this time. "I think I should know what it is."

"She's just nervous about the things she reads in the

newspapers, that's all," her mother said softly to Mrs. Wood. Aunt Delia was still standing, holding the newspaper in her hand and frowning at the two women.

Turning toward Aunt Delia, so that Mrs. Wood could not see her face, her mother looked at Aunt Delia, opened her eyes wide, gritted her teeth, and said in Spanish, "Delia, get the hell outta here right now!" Turning back to Mrs. Wood, she said, "You see, Mrs. Wood, she's just a little nervous. You know how the newspapers are full of crime these days and all that. She's old and she worries about things like that."

Aunt Delia started to walk briskly out, but turned back just before leaving. Looking suspiciously at Mrs. Wood for a moment, she winked and said, pointing, "I'll bet you knew about it all the time, but wouldn't let on." Chuckling and mumbling to herself, Aunt Delia left the room.

"What's that?" Mrs. Wood asked.

"She just said it was nice meeting you, Mrs. Wood, and you should be careful in the streets."

"Oh yes, well, how sweet. You can't be too careful these days." There was a short pause and Mrs. Wood said, "Well now, you know, I have to see the apartment and look around. Just routine, I'm sure you understand."

Nilda looked at her mother, who didn't say anything, and wondered, When is she going to tell her about Sophie and Baby Jimmy?

"Mrs. Wood, this here is my daughter, Nilda. Nilda, this is Mrs. Wood, the lady from the Welfare Department."

"How are you, young lady?"

"Fine, thank you," Nilda said timidly.

"How old are you?"

121

"Ten."

"Oh, a nice big girl. Well. I'm sure you are a big help to Mother. Well. How do you like school? What grade are you in?"

"Yes. I am in the fifth grade. I go to P.S. 72 on 103rd Street."

"How nice. . . . Do you like it there?"

"Yes."

"Isn't that nice, and you speak English so well."

"She's born here, Mrs. Wood," her mother said, offended.

"Oh . . . yes, that's right. Well I mean . . . that is, sometimes . . ."

Her stepfather walked into the room. Nilda noticed he had put on his good suit and his teeth, but did not have time to shave.

"This is my husband, Emilio Ramírez. This is Mrs. Wood."

"How are you?" he said, shaking her hand. "You know, Mrs. Wood . . . Mrs. Wood? That's the right name? O.K. Well, you know, this is only a temporary assistance. I have a good job, and we just got a union in my place, so that as soon as I get my ticker," he smiled and pointed to his heart, "in good shape again, I'll be able to go back to work."

Her mother looked at Mrs. Wood with a desperate expression; she had put down on the report that her husband would not be going back to work.

"Yes," the social worker said. "Well now, I have to look around and just fill out a few forms. If you don't mind, I really have to get on."

122

"Lydia, did you offer Mrs. Wood something?" her stepfather asked.

"Oh never mind, Mr. Ramírez; I really have to get going. It's all right."

"No," he said, "have something. Coffee? Tea maybe?"

"No. Really I couldn't, but thank you anyway." Looking at her wristwatch, she added, "I must be getting on, you know; there are many other people on the list." Standing, she said to Nilda's mother, "Please, may I . . . ?"

"Oh sure, yes . . . this way please. . . . Listen, Mrs. Wood," she walked out into the hallway, "my daughter-in-law is just spending a few days here with my grandson. . . . You see my married son, James, is working in New Jersey, and he just sent them here, you know, to be here with me a little. . . . That way I can see my first grandson. . . . But they will be going back this week, by Friday." She knocked on Sophie's door. "Sophie? May we please come in?" Sophie opened the door, looking very worried. "This here is Mrs. Wood. She's come down from Welfare. . . . This is my daughter-in-law, Sophie Ortega."

"How do you do," Mrs. Wood said, and walked into the room. The baby was in the crib on his back, kicking, and chewing on a pacifier. "Isn't he adorable!" Mrs. Wood looked down at him. "Hi there. My, he has a lot of hair, and so black." Looking up at Sophie, who was fair and had light brown hair, she added, "He must look like his daddy."

"Oh yes! He looks just like Jimmy," Sophie said, and smiled proudly.

"How old is the baby?" She went on asking questions.

123

Nilda had been walking behind the women and now stepped around them and went up to the crib. Looking at the baby, Nilda leaned over and began to play with him, touching his hands and shaking his feet. Baby Jimmy began to coo and make noises.

"Nilda, that's enough!" her mother snapped.

"Mrs. Ramírez, you have a lovely grandson. Good-bye, Sophie," Mrs. Wood said.

Nilda followed as her mother showed Mrs. Wood the other bedrooms, the bathroom, and the kitchen. Frankie had been doing homework, and answered a few questions briefly and quickly. They walked back into the living room.

"Well, Mrs. Ramírez, you know we cannot pay rent for all these people."

"No people, just my aunt and my daughter-in-law who is leaving by Friday," her mother said, almost pleading.

"All right, I'll put that down. And we'll see. Now, we may be able to assist you with . . ."

They went on talking and Nilda heard her stepfather again. He walked into the room and said loudly, "You sure you won't have something, Mrs. Wood?"

"No thank you, Mr. Ramírez. I'm late as it is," she said.

"So late you can't have a glass of water? Have something!" he said, almost commanding.

"Emilio . . . por favor," her mother said.

"Capitalism puts us in this position. You know that, lady? I worked all my life; why do I have to ask for charity?"

"Please, Emilio . . ." her mother said. Mrs. Wood turned beet red and tried to smile.

"What are you going to give us, Mrs.? Gold perhaps? That you have to inspect everything here?" he said, raising his voice.

"Emilio! This lady is only doing her job. Now let us be," her mother said anxiously. "Please, Emilio . . . cállate!"

"All right, all right," he said, and sat down, glaring at Mrs. Wood.

Mrs. Wood stood up, quickly putting on her tan camel's-hair coat. "Well," she said smiling.

The front door opened and Paul came running in. "Hi, Ma. . . . Oh, hello," he said. Mrs. Wood looked at the boy.

"Mrs. Wood, this is my son Paul. Paul, this is Mrs. Wood, the lady from Welfare." Mrs. Wood opened her eyes wide, surprised as she looked at Paul.

"Hello," he said.

"This is your son?" she asked.

"Yes, this is my third child," her mother answered. Nilda had seen this happen many times before; Paul was so much darker than everyone else that people were always surprised. She hated it when they stared at Paul like this woman was doing. Mrs. Wood asked Paul the same questions she had asked Nilda and Frankie. Nilda couldn't wait for her to stop talking and leave. Leave Paul alone! she thought.

She stayed in the living room as her mother and Mrs. Wood went towards the door, and heard their voices.

"Good-bye and thank you, Mrs. Wood. You been very nice, and I appreciate whatever you can do for us. . . . You see, anything would be a help and . . ."

"Good-bye." Mrs. Wood's voice was far away.

"Good-bye. Thank you so much again," her mother called out.

"Shit! Bunch of capitalist bastards." She heard her stepfather as he marched down the hallway.

She looked at Paul and smiled. "Boy, Paul. I'm glad that's over. Now Mama won't be so cranky no more."

"Yeah, me too. That lady seemed nice. Didn't she, Nilda?" asked Paul. Nilda looked at Paul and wondered, Didn't you see her looking at you that way? Maybe it's just me, she thought. "Don't you think she was nice, Nilda? Maybe she'll help us out."

"Yeah," she said, "maybe." They heard voices; her mother and stepfather were arguing.

"Emilio, por Dios . . . how could you? You think it's easy?"

"I'll go back to work . . . tomorrow! You think I can't support my family? What kind of shit does a man have to put up with?"

"You have to rest. . . . Please . . . you want me to go crazy?"

"Never mind. I'm calling the union right now, Lydia."

"Ay . . . Emilio, please just stop it."

Nilda heard the voices still arguing. "Jimmy is gonna come and get Sophie and the baby. I don't want the baby to leave, Paul," she said, almost crying.

"Don't be silly, Nilda. He gotta leave. He's gotta be with his mother, right? You gotta be with your mother, don't you?" Nilda nodded and swallowed, trying not to cry. "You'll visit them. Wait, you'll see. Probably see him more than if they were still staying here."

126

"Do you really think so, Paul?" she asked hopefully. "Sophie did say I could visit, and maybe stay over if they got room. You know, like to baby-sit and all that, since I know just how to take care of Baby Jimmy and he loves me so much. You know, he recognizes me already."

"You see? So there! What did I tell you?" Paul said, smiling at Nilda. She smiled back at Paul with a sense of reassurance. The voices had stopped arguing and it was quiet.

"Hey, we missed the radio programs. I'll bet 'The Lone Ranger' is over. What time is it?" She turned on the radio. The news was on. "Yes, this is a massive war effort by the entire nation. Americans are rallying to the call. Fathers, brothers, sons, uncles, and cousins, Americans and patriots all! These brave men are getting ready to leave their loved ones as the draft call gets under way. Young men are showing their patriotism by enlisting, and volunteer stations are being set up in each and every small town in the U.S.A. In Gillespie, Illinois . . ."

Nilda shut the radio off. "Oh shucks, we missed it."

"Look for something else, Nilda," said Paul.

"Naw, I'm going out to play," she said. Getting up, she added, "Come on, Paul. Come out and let's play a game of tag."

"Go on, man. Nilda, I'm too old for that," he said indignantly.

"I'm cutting out. See you, Paul." Nilda left and got her coat. Running into the kitchen, she said to her mother, "Mama, I'm going out to play. Bendición."

"Dios te bendiga. Nilda, get home in time for supper and homework."

127

She jumped down the steps, taking them two at a time. Outside it was cold. Cars and buses sped by the avenue. She looked around her. Now, she thought, who's around for a game of tag?

Late January, 1942

She heard voices; waking up, Nilda opened her eyes.
What time is it? she wondered. Dazed from sleep, she
turned to look at the clock on the night table next to her
parents' bed. It said quarter to eleven. It was still dark
outside. She realized it was nighttime. Confused, she sat
up. People were talking; it sounded like everybody was
up. It was cold in the apartment, so she slipped on her
shoes and threw a blanket around her body. She followed
the sound of the voices; they were all in the kitchen, and
she could smell fresh coffee. As she entered the brightly
lit kitchen, she squinted her eyes and inhaled the mixed
aroma of freshly made coffee and cigarette smoke.

"Oh, look who's here. Ugly!" Looking up at the voice,
she saw it was Jimmy and broke into a smile. "Man, look
at that! She gets bigger all the time. A regular young
lady. Come here and gimme a kiss," he said. Nilda
walked over and embraced Jimmy; they hugged and
kissed each other. "I just saw the runt. Man, he's even
uglier than you are," he said to Nilda.

"He's beautiful!" Nilda protested, half smiling. Everyone laughed.

"Nilda, you want some milk and coffee? Jimmy

brought some ham, hot bread, and coffeecake. I'll make you a nice sandwich and some boiled milk with coffee? Sí?" Nilda nodded her head, still slightly drowsy, and sat on Jimmy's lap.

"Gimme some cake too, Mami."

"O.K., nena," her mother smiled.

Sophie was sitting on a chair, holding Baby Jimmy. Nilda's stepfather sat drinking a cup of coffee and puffing away at a cigarette. Victor was sitting on another chair, eating some coffeecake. Frankie and Paul were standing, each munching on a piece of the coffeecake. Aunt Delia stood next to Sophie, smiling, with her papers tucked under her arm. Everyone was looking at Jimmy, who spoke.

"Like I was saying, this is a swell job in New Jersey. It's around Hoboken and I got a small place, but it's enough room for Sophie and the baby. We got a real modern kitchen, a tile bath, a living room, and a private bedroom. The rent is cheap, man, a lot cheaper than in New York." Jimmy paused and smiled at Sophie.

"You gotta union in this place, Jimmy?" her stepfather asked.

"Don't need no union, Emilio," Jimmy said. He was the only one who called the old man Emilio. The other children called him Papa.

"That's what you think now. But you see, you need a pension. Rights for the worker that include disability benefits, like in my place. We haven't got all that yet, but we are working towards it. Look, let me give you the name of our . . ."

"We don't need it there," Jimmy interrupted.

130

"Let me give you the name anyway."

"I ain't promising nothing, O.K.?" said Jimmy.

"Fair enough!"

"I don't believe in Communism," Jimmy said.

"Getting help and decent wages, that's Communism! That's not good? Helping the poor, the masses, that's Communism! That's bad? Getting what you deserve instead of charity, that's—"

"O.K.," her mother interrupted. "Everybody knows that, Emilio."

"No! . . . not in this house, everybody does not know that!"

Ignoring her stepfather, her mother went on talking. "What about the draft? Eh, Jimmy, will they call you?"

"Well, if I can work for defense I may not have to go. Anyway, I'm not going to worry about that."

"Now, where is this place again, Jimmy? What do you do there?" asked her mother.

"Mama, I told you it hasn't got a name yet. They just started it. I told you it's in Hoboken, New Jersey. I'll take you there as soon as we get settled."

Her mother turned around and looked at her son Jimmy for a moment and asked, "What's the exact address?"

"Look, I told you everything now, O.K.?" he said, almost shouting. "I have to go anyway. Sophie, you ready?" he said, annoyed. Sophie nodded and smiled at him.

"You don't have to rush out, Jimmy," her mother said. "Just because I wanna know where you are going and what you do. You know you got a young wife and baby

131

now, my son. They are a great responsibility. You gotta do right by them, eh? You know that, don't you?" she said affectionately. No one spoke and it got very quiet in the room.

"I'm joining the Army when I graduate," said Victor. "I've already made up my mind." Everyone turned to look at him; he had been very quiet. "I'm going to volunteer. I won't wait to be drafted."

"What?" her mother said, shocked. "Since when?"

"Since . . ." Victor looked at everyone. "I just told you," he said softly.

"Man, Victor, don't be a sucketa. What the hell are you joining up for?" Jimmy asked.

Victor, looking at Jimmy, said in a firm tone, "Because I believe in my country and I believe we should defend it."

"Man, you wasn't even born here; you was born in Puerto Rico. What country? What country you talking about?"

"Puerto Rico is part of the United States. And anyway, what if I was born there! I've been here since I was six years old and I am an American," Victor answered.

"Oh yeah?" Jimmy said, getting angry. "You're a spick. You can call yourself an American, all right. But they are gonna call you a spick!"

"If that's the way you want to think about things, Jimmy, then I really feel sorry for you. You got no feelings for your own country. In this country, if you work hard you can be somebody, get an education and accomplish something!"

"First of all I was brought here, man. I didn't ask to

come! And in the second place, I don't believe in that sucker stuff, Victor. You wanna believe that, O.K.! Go ahead. It is more blessed to take, baby, than to receive leftovers. That's my motto. I don't want for them to give me no shit. I take and I get."

"What kind of talk is that?" her mother asked. Ignoring her, the two brothers went on arguing.

"You call taking what doesn't belong to you honest? What isn't yours, right?" Victor asked.

"I take it so it's mine! What am I gonna do? Wait until I'm an old man, have nothing! Work all my life, like a slave, and then be nothing! Like him?" Jimmy shouted and pointed to her stepfather. Nilda had left Jimmy's lap when the arguing started and now stood next to her two younger brothers.

"It's better than shooting up that dope. And hanging around with hoods and criminals!" Victor said angrily.

"Stop it!" her mother said.

Jimmy started towards Victor. "Don't talk like that to me, you fucking punk!"

Victor jumped up out of his chair. Nilda felt frightened and heard herself whimpering. Her mother stood between the two brothers. "Stop . . . stop! . . . Now look . . . a little peace in this house. For God's sake! Virgen María!" her mother shouted, almost in tears. Victor and Jimmy both stared at each other, not speaking or moving.

Aunt Delia, looking confused and worried, asked, "What is it? What? What is everybody saying? Why are the boys fighting?" Everyone ignored her.

"I musn't have this. You hear? You musn't do this. My children cannot fight like this. You are a family, brothers!" her mother said, standing firmly between them. The room was silent.

Nilda's stepfather had his hand on Victor's shoulder. "Calm down, son, you are gonna aggravate your mother," he said.

Jimmy turned away from Victor, looked at his step-father, and made a gesture of disgust. "Let's go, Sophie. Move it." Sophie jumped up quickly and left the room. Jimmy followed her. Everyone was very quiet.

"Let him go. I'm glad he's going. He's up to no good. He's not my brother," Victor said.

"Don't you ever say that!" her mother shrieked. "Never, never! He will always be your brother. You don't say that in my house!" Nilda saw her mother was trembling with rage. Victor looked at his mother for a moment, then lowered his eyes and walked out of the room.

"What?" Aunt Delia asked. "Whose house? Listen, what's going on here? What did Victor say? I have to show him where the trouble is. It happened this morning again, to a family who opened the door to a stranger. You mustn't let in strangers." Going over to Nilda's mother, she said, "Lydia, what do you think? I should show him. No? Lydia, where it all happened, right here in the paper."

"Delia, go to sleep; it's all over now. Everybody has to get up tomorrow. Go on to bed." She spoke into Aunt Delia's ear.

"Go on to bed, kids. Go on," her mother said. "Emilio, you finished? Why don't you go to sleep."

"No, it's all right, Lydia," her stepfather said, sounding very tired. "I'll wait for you."

Nilda waited until Aunt Delia, Frankie, and Paul

had left, then said to her mother, "Mami, please let me say good-bye to the baby. Please."

"Sure, but don't stay long; tomorrow is school," her mother said. Nilda was relieved that her mother was not so angry any more. Picking up her blanket, she carried it to Sophie's room. The door was shut. She waited a bit, then knocked very gently.

"Who's there?" asked Jimmy.

"Me. Can I say good-bye to the baby?"

The door opened and Jimmy stood before her. "Look, Nilda, it's late and we have to get going . . . and anyway, he's asleep."

"I know . . . but . . . just let me see him . . . to say good-bye, that's all."

Turning to Sophie he said, "Sophie, show Nilda the baby and let's split. Finish packing; don't worry about taking all that crap, will you? I'll buy more." Nilda walked in timidly, feeling somehow that it was not the same room any more, and that she was in the wrong place. The baby was all bundled up in mountains of blankets.

"Come on, Nilda. Here he is," said Sophie, "but don't wake him now or I'll murder you. I just gave him a bottle and I want him to sleep through the night." Nilda looked but could hardly see his face. She did not know what to say or do.

"O.K., you took a look?" Jimmy said.

"O.K.," Nilda said. She paused for a moment and then went on, "Good-bye, Jimmy and Sophie . . . and . . . maybe I can . . . like you said, come to see you or something."

"Sure, Nilda, sure. Good-bye, honey." Reaching into

his pocket, Jimmy took out a quarter. "Here, you get yourself something."

"Gee, thank you, Jimmy." She took the money and just stood there. They turned and started putting things into several suitcases that were open on the bed.

"Let's go, Sophie. I haven't got all night!"

Nilda left the room and walked back to bed. Her parents were still in the kitchen talking. She put her shoes under the cot and climbed in, covering herself, trying to shake off the chill of the cold apartment. She could hear the Madison Avenue bus stop at the corner, and go again quickly. It's gonna feel funny not to see the baby no more, she thought. I wonder if he'll remember me when I go to visit him. Her thoughts started to wander and she became very drowsy. Turning over, she felt something in her hand; it was the money Jimmy had given her. Oh, she thought, I better put this away. Bending down, she slipped the coin into her shoe and, closing her eyes, fell asleep to the rhythm of the traffic whizzing along Madison Avenue and the ticking of the clock on the night table.

May, 1942

Nilda had been waiting with her mother a good part of the morning. They sat on a bench at the health station. Finally she heard her name. "Nilda Ramírez, next." A young nurse held a manila envelope. "Mrs. Ramírez? Give me the pink card. You have to wait here."

Nilda followed the young nurse through a door into a long room with many partitions dividing the space into eight small units and a narrow corridor. Each unit was about four and a half feet wide and a heavy green curtain closed off each entrance for privacy. Nilda followed the nurse into one of the tiny rooms. There was a small light-green metal table set with a clean white towel and some medical instruments. A metal stool was set right next to the table and a wooden chair was placed opposite. The nurse took the manila folder and put it on the table with the pink card. "Take off your clothes, honey, and put them on the chair. Leave your shoes and panties on," the nurse said and left.

Nilda started to undress. She heard someone being examined in the next cubbyhole. "Say ahh," a man's voice said. "That's good. Now breathe deep."

A man dressed in white walked in and sat down on the

stool. Nilda knew he was the doctor. "Well now, young lady, let me see," he said, and picked up the folder. "Mmmm . . . ah ha . . . ah ha . . . ummm . . . O.K.! Now, we're just going to give you a checkup; don't be scared. No needles today," he smiled. "Now say ahh. Open your mouth." He put a wooden depressor on her tongue.

"Ahhh," said Nilda.

"Good," he said. "Now you are doing just fine." He examined her eyes, ears, and chest. "Haven't menstruated yet, have you?" he asked. Nilda looked at him blankly, then became confused as he waited for an answer. "Your period. You haven't gotten it yet, have you?"

"No." It was the first word she had said and she felt embarrassed.

The doctor asked her a few more questions. "O.K. You are in good health. Now get dressed and the nurse will take you outside and examine your hair for lice." He got up quickly and left. Nilda began to get dressed.

The nurse walked in and picked up the manila folder with the pink card. "Come on, you have to get examined for lice." Nilda hurried and followed her back outside where her mother was. Nilda started towards her mother. "No . . . hey, come here. Over here first! You are not through yet," the nurse said, looking annoyed. She led Nilda into a partitioned area on the far right side of the room. Pointing to a bench that was placed in front of the partition, she said, "Sit there until your turn comes," and then walked behind the partition.

There were three girls sitting on the bench ahead of Nilda. She sat down next to them. She could see right into the room where another nurse, an older heavyset woman, was examining a little girl's head very carefully. The young nurse walked out and disappeared.

"I wonder if she's gonna make it," said the girl sitting next to Nilda. "They caught some nits on a girl before. Man, was that nurse hollering and calling her a pig."

Nilda felt her heart jump. Her mother had thoroughly cleaned her head with kerosene yesterday and had inspected it very carefully this morning. Nilda had protested and carried on, but her mother had insisted. "You are not going in with a trace of anything in your hair. That's all there is to it! They are not going to call us cochinos." All last night she had secretly prayed again and again that she would have lice in her hair, because she dreaded the idea of going to camp. Now, as she looked at the nurse, she hoped her head was clean; at this moment she was more frightened of the nurse than she was of camp. The girl who was being examined left the room smiling.

"Julia Díaz, you're next," said the nurse. One of the girls jumped up and went into the room. After a while, the girl came out of the room with a look of relief on her face. "Carmen-María Quin . . . Quintera? Next!"

"What camp you going to?" Nilda heard the girl next to her ask.

"I don't know exactly. That is, they didn't tell me the name yet," Nilda replied.

"You never been there?" asked the girl.

"No . . . but I been to camp before," Nilda said.

"How did you like it?"

"I didn't like it at all. It stunk," said Nilda.

139

"Why you going again?" asked the girl.

"I gotta go, man; my mother says I gotta go," Nilda said.

"Me too," said the girl. "I have to go to a Catholic camp. They are too strict. I don't like it. I hate it. The sisters are mean, you know."

Nilda's eyes widened. "Hey, is that camp by any chance called 'Saint Anselm's Camp for Catholic Youth'? That's where I was."

"No," the girl said. "This one is named 'Our Sacred Lady of Refuge.' "

"Do you got boys there?" asked Nilda.

"You kidding? With my mother? No, it's only for girls. I been going there since I was a little kid. I try to talk my mother out of it, you know, but now," she lowered her voice, "I got my period and Mami said I gotta be away from boys. She's worser and stricter now. And my papi he . . ."

"Luisa de Jesús, next!" the nurse called.

A few moments later Nilda heard the nurse saying loudly, "OH . . . oh no . . . no no, young lady. What's this? Honestly! Don't these people know that they are going to be examined? Ugh!" She pushed the girl's head away in disgust. Walking over to a small table, she picked up a pad and began writing. Then she picked up a manila folder and continued writing, filling in a form.

Nilda saw the girl, who looked down at the floor, her face flushed with embarrassment. Oh man, thought Nilda, she looks like she's gonna cry.

"Didn't your mother clean your hair?" the nurse yelled. The girl did not answer. "Well? I'm talking to you."

"Yes," she answered.

"It's full of nits; you know that? You've got a filthy head. Shame on a big girl like you. Look, you're developing already! I'll bet you're menstruating! Walking around with a filthy head. Honestly! Some people!" She looked at the girl and went on, "Who brought you here today? Your mother?" The girl nodded her head. "Well go on, go get her; I have to speak to her." Quickly, the girl jumped off the stool and ran out towards the other side of the large room. Nilda watched as the nurse walked around, busy putting things here and there.

The girl came back with her mother, a small thin woman, her hair tied in a kerchief. She carried a paper shopping bag and a worn-out pocketbook. She entered the room smiling at the nurse and nodding her head. One of her front teeth was missing and she kept putting her hand up to her mouth.

"You know she's got a dirty head," the nurse said to the woman. The girl translated what she said into Spanish, speaking to her mother.

"No," the mother shook her head and said to the nurse, "she clean."

"She's got a head full of nits. I just saw it. You want me to find one for you?" The girl translated what the woman had said. The mother looked at the nurse. She began to speak to the nurse quietly and intensely.

"What did she say?" the nurse asked.

"She says that she cleaned my head good with the kerosene and everything and maybe there are one or two nits but they could not be alive. Like they are left over from what she cleaned—"

141

"I found nits!" the nurse shouted, interrupting her. "Doesn't matter if they are old or new, dead or alive, or left over. You, my dear, have a dirty head." Looking at the mother impatiently, the nurse said, "Now here is what you do. Take this prescription and follow the instructions. Use it! It's already very late; it's almost June. I don't think she can get to camp this summer. I doubt it this year." The mother looked at her daughter, waiting for the translation. The girl spoke to her mother.

"No . . . no es posible! No," the mother began to protest loudly in Spanish, shaking her head and waving her arms.

The nurse interrupted, "Look, now stop arguing! That's what she's got in her head. Look." The nurse pointed to something on the wall and then pointed to the girl's head. Nilda could see it was some sort of poster, but she could not make out what was on it. The girl and her mother walked out.

"Nilda Ramírez, next!"

As she sat down on the high stool Nilda heard the mother quietly protesting. The nurse quickly washed and dried her hands. Nilda tried to keep calm and not move, although nervous and anxious, as she felt the woman's cold fingers parting her hair and digging into her scalp.

"Don't fidget and keep still. Put your head down," the nurse said.

Nilda looked around the room for the poster the nurse had shown that girl's mother. She could see it quite clearly. In the center of the poster was a carefully detailed drawing of a head louse. It was brown in color with a

142

small round head attached to a large oval-shaped body. Two eyes bulged out of its head, antennae jutted out above each eye, and three feet sprouted out symmetrically on either side of the fat scaly body. Nilda was both fascinated and revolted at the idea that this was the same tiny creature that traveled in her hair by the dozens, leaving the tiny white nits, each smaller than a pinhead. It looks like one of them prehistoric monsters from the movies, she thought. She thought of the "Flash Gordon" chapters and all the weird things he had to fight in outer space.

"Go on now," she heard the nurse say. "You're clean. Here's your card."

Nilda ran outside to her mother, smiling. Her mother smiled back at her. She sat down, giving her mother the card, and said with a sense of relief, "Mami, I passed."

From Grand Central Station, like the first time, along
with many other children, Nilda went off to camp again.
It was an all-girls camp, nonsectarian, taking children
from all areas of the Eastern states. Her mother told
her that it would be different this time. Reassuring her,
she had said, "Look, Nilda, I had to pay something for
the camp. It's not a free camp like the last time. I had to
buy two pink jumpsuits for uniforms; everybody wears
the same thing there. Everybody is the same. You see?
Nobody is going to hit you, Nilda. There is not gonna be
no nuns and none of that. I promise. O.K.?"

She was going for a whole month. That's like forever,
she thought, feeling miserable. As the train sped out of
New York City, leaving the Barrio and the tall buildings
behind, Nilda became frightened, not knowing what was
going to happen to her. Looking around her in the train
car, she noticed that there were no dark children. Except
for a couple of olive-skinned, dark-haired girls, she did
not see any Puerto Rican or black children. She wondered
if the two girls were Spanish.

Nilda thought about last summer and the nuns, and
felt a sense of relief as she looked at one of the women
counselors who was dressed in a light pink cotton suit.

144

The woman caught Nilda's glance and smiled at her. Nilda quickly looked away, hoping that the woman would not ask her any questions. She did not want to speak to anyone. She began to think of home and her family, making an effort to keep from crying.

She knew her brothers had gone to camp. Paul was big enough to work at his camp and make some money. Lucky thing! she thought. She remembered Victor was not going to be at home any more. Determined, despite his mother's protests, he had joined the Army right after graduation. He had been gone two weeks already. She just couldn't imagine not having Victor at home any more. She had been very proud that her brother was going to be a soldier and had told Miss Langhorn all about it at school. "He is a good American," Miss Langhorn had said. "You and your family should be proud."

She remembered Victor's graduation party. Her mother had managed a small dinner for the family, and a cake. Aunt Rosario had come down from the Bronx with her husband, Willie, and her two children, Roberto and Claudia. Her mother and Aunt Rosario had been brought up together in Puerto Rico; they were first cousins. She was her mother's only relative in this country. Nilda saw Aunt Rosario and her cousins during holidays every year and on special occasions. She would travel with her family to the Bronx or Aunt Rosario would come to the Barrio to visit with them. Nilda didn't much like Roberto, but she enjoyed playing with Claudia.

Nilda smiled, thinking about all her family and Baby Jimmy. She remembered it had been a long time since she had seen him. He won't even know me any more when I see him again, she thought. Last winter they had re-

ceived a card from Jimmy and Sophie postmarked somewhere in New York, not New Jersey, with no return
address. She went on drifting into mental images.

A loud whistle sounded and the train began to slow
down. "Bard Manor . . . Bard Manor . . . fifteen-minute
stop," she heard a man's voice calling.

Outside they all lined up and marched over to several
buses that were parked near the small railroad station.
After a short ride, Nilda got off the bus with the rest of
the girls. Nilda looked about her and saw no buildings;
there were large areas of grass and trees. Off at a distance
from the road she saw a group of cottages set among
green hills.

They approached the cottages, which were made of
unfinished logs with a dark rough bark. Nilda entered a
cottage with her group; it was a large dormitory, simply
furnished. There was a total of eight beds, four at either
side of the room. A wooden bureau was placed next to
each bed, with a small wooden bench at the foot. Each
child automatically took a bunk.

"Hello, girls," said one counselor. "Let me introduce
myself. I'm Miss Rachel Hammerman, and you can all
call me Miss Rachel." Looking at the other counselor, she
said, "Jeanette?"

"Yes," answered the other counselor. "Hi. I'm Miss
Jeanette Pisacano. You can all call me Miss Jeanette."

Miss Rachel said, "Has everyone got a bunk? O.K.
Then that will be your bunk for the rest of the time you
are going to be here. In this section of Bard Manor Camp
for Girls we have campers ages nine to twelve. The older
girls live on the other side of the camp. We will visit them
in time and they will visit us as well. In fact, we all eat

together in the main house, which is about a ten-minute walk down the road. The pool is there with the tennis court, swings, and all the other goodies. Let's see . . ." she paused. "Oh yes. Miss Jeanette and I also sleep here; I don't know if you noticed, but there is another entrance to the cottage; that is our entrance only. O.K.?" She waited, then asked, "Now, Jeanette, you wanna say something?"

"Yes," Miss Jeanette smiled. "We hope to really have a good time here. You all might complain about our early bedtime . . . seven-thirty we get ready."

"Awww. . . ." "Nawww," the girls complained.

"By eight o'clock we should be in bed," Miss Jeanette went on, smiling.

"Nooo. . . . Awww." "Awwww," the girls responded.

"You will be so tired," Miss Jeanette went on talking, "that you will be glad to get to bed when we finish with you." She paused and smiled. "You'll see." She laughed. "Anyway—" The girls interrupted, giggling and protesting. "Shhhh . . . shhhh." She continued, "Now listen, you all have two pink jumpsuits. They will be what you are going to wear most of the time that you are here. Just put on a pair of clean panties and your jumpsuits. At the end of the day you can put them in the large laundry cart in the shower room. Now, they will be laundered; you will always have a clean jumpsuit to wear. In the morning someone will put all the suits and panties on one camper's bunk. She will look at the name tags and distribute them. Every day another camper will distribute the jumpsuits, so that everyone will take a turn, rotating . . . ummm . . . and . . ." Looking at Miss Rachel, she asked, "What else, Rachel?"

"Oh well, we will make a list of chores for everyone. Every day each camper has a special chore to do. We will alternate the work."

"Too bad." "Yeah." "Aw shucks," said some of the girls.

Miss Rachel smiled. "Never mind; everybody works. Here we make our own beds and keep our cottage clean, as well as help in the dining room at mealtime, and so on." Pausing, she asked, "Who's hungry?"

"Meeeee." "Me." "I'm starving," the girls yelled.

"O.K.," she said, "get your things put away and then wash up and make sure you all go to the toilet. Now, as soon as we finish, we go eat. All right? Make it snappy then," Miss Jeanette said.

"Wait, let's introduce ourselves."

"Oh, of course!" Miss Rachel looked around and said, "O.K., let's start." Pointing at Nilda, she said, "Your name is Nilda? Right? Tell us your full name."

"Nilda Ramírez," she said.

"Bernice White."

"Josie Forest."

"Evelyn Daniels."

"Stella Pappas." All the other girls called out their names.

Both women left the room and the girls started to put their things away. Nilda opened her suitcase and put her things away in the drawers. Then she set her bureau with her toothbrush, toothpaste, hairbrush, and comb. She picked up a pad of plain unlined paper and a small box of crayons, a present from Aunt Delia. She carefully wrote her name on them and placed them inside the top drawer.

All finished, she looked around at the other girls. She smiled at the girl in the next bunk.

The girl, smiling back, said, "Hello."

"Hi," said Nilda. "What's your name again?"

"Josie. What's yours?"

"Nilda. You been here before?"

"No. I've never been to camp before at all. This is my first time."

"Oh well," said Nilda, "I been to camp before. Not here, in another place, but I didn't like it; they were too strict." Looking around at the room she added, "This looks nice, don't it?"

"Yes," said Josie smiling. Some of the other girls were going off to the bathroom. "I guess we'd better wash up if we wanna eat. You wanna come, Nilda?"

"O.K." Nilda walked along with Josie into a large bathroom with several sinks and toilets. There were clean towels and soap set out. Nilda saw that the toilets had doors. Good, she thought, I can make alone. She washed up and waited her turn to sit on the toilet.

Outside the sun was still out and the trees cast long shadows on the fields. She walked with the group, looking around her at the quiet woods. They walked along the road until they came to a large white two-story wood-frame house. A sign was over the entrance; gold letters trimmed in white on a black background read, BARD MANOR CAMP FOR GIRLS. Nilda saw a lot of outdoor equipment, swings, climbing bars, a tennis court, and a large swimming pool. There were also several small wood-framed buildings near the main house.

They went into a large dining room set with long

149

tables and wooden folding chairs. Nilda saw that the chairs were exactly like the ones in Benji's church. Oh man, she thought. Turning to comment, she realized that there was no one who would know what she was talking about. Miss Rachel led them to a table set for ten persons and they sat down. The table was covered with a clean white tablecloth.

"Today we'll be served, but tomorrow we serve our-selves, as well as clear the table! So enjoy the service, ladies," she smiled.

They were served a vegetable soup, breaded chicken cutlets, carrots, hash brown potatoes, and a green salad. A large platter of bread with butter, dishes of jam, and pitchers of milk were on the table. Everyone passed them around. Dessert was an apple cake, which Nilda enjoyed. She ate everything.

The girls played outdoors for a little while after supper, running, and climbing on the equipment. Nilda began to play with a few of the girls in her group, chasing each other and tossing a large rubber ball around. Someone blew a whistle and the girls lined up.

As they walked back to their cottage, Nilda was feeling tired already. The counselors began to sing songs. At first, she barely opened her mouth, but then slowly she began to mouth a chorus, getting louder and louder. She heard herself singing clearly just like the rest of the girls.

That night in bed, Nilda pulled the covers around her, tucking in her feet. It was dark and quiet, except for the sound of the crickets. She could not fall asleep although she felt very tired. She thought of home again and the sounds and smells, so different. Sounds and smells she could understand. Footsteps on the hard sidewalk. A

150

woman's high heels clicking, or a man's heavy shoes slapping the concrete as he ran to catch the bus late at night. Someone coughing. Someone whistling. All the traffic whizzing by. Summertime, everybody outside. The radios playing, people talking. Her mother making fresh coffee with boiled milk. The smell of the heat. Sometimes when it got unbearably hot, her mother let her sit on the fire escape with her pillow and blanket.

Suddenly the silence scared her and she wanted her mother; she wanted to go home. Nilda began to sob quietly and heard some of the other girls crying. She thought, They are crying too? Surprised, she listened to them cry for a little while, then remembered that tomorrow they were going to use the swimming pool. She had never been in a pool before. I wonder what that's gonna be like, she thought.

Everyone had stopped crying and she heard the heavy breathing of the girls fast asleep in the silent room. Outside the crickets continued chirping, occasionally changing their rhythm patterns slightly. Slowly Nilda became used to the new melody of sounds surrounding her.

July 14, 1942.

Dear Mami,

I am fine. I'm haveing a real good time. I passed my swimming test. I am now advance beginner insted of only beginner that is a higher thing to be. We do a lot of art and crafts I am makeing you something and something

151

for Papa. I received you letter. I told everybody about Victor that he is in Fort Bragg North Carolina. We had a cook out that is where you make a fire and cook the food outside and it tasted real good. We ate hot dogs and hamburgers and milk and juice. We also toasted marshmellos. I like Miss Jenete she is really nice to me she is my counselor. I seen a lot of flowers like you told me about when you live in Puerto Rico. I hope you are fine and haveing a good time. Tell Titi Delia I made some drawings of the camp so she could see what it looks like here. I learn some songs. we really have a lot of fun it is swell here.

Well that is it. Mami I love you and Papa and Aunt Delia and everybody. Bendicion Mama.

Love
Nilda xxxxx

P.S. my friend Josie is
    nice and so is Stella they
    live in another state.

Nilda read the letter she had just written to her mother and, satisfied, folded it and put it inside an envelope. This was free time and she had finally decided that she had better answer her mother's letter. Most of the girls in her group were either writing, reading, or just sitting around. Getting up from her bunk, she decided to walk to the main house and put the letter in the mail basket. Looking for her two friends, she realized that they were probably at the main house anyway. Nilda started walking down the road; in the past two weeks she had gotten to know the camp quite well. She loved being able to recognize a large oak tree or a clump of bushes, a certain curve in the earth, a gentle slope in the horizon. All these familiar landmarks gave her a sense of security.

Nilda passed a trail off the side of the main road. They had all hiked through there one day; it was thick with trees and bushes. Stopping for a moment, she took the trail and started walking into the woods. She came to a fork in the trail. Taking the path on the right that seemed to climb, she continued along and came to a clearing where the landscape opened up into wide fields covered with wild flowers. The white Queen Anne's lace covered most of the fields, which were sprinkled with yellow goldenrod and clumps of tiny orange and purple flowers. The sky overhead was bright with the sun. Large white clouds glistened, rapidly moving across the horizon and out of sight.

Nilda remembered her mother's description of Puerto Rico's beautiful mountainous countryside covered with bright flowers and red flamboyant trees.

"There it was a different world from Central Park and New York City, Nilda," she could hear her mother saying. Looking ahead, she saw miles and miles of land and not a single sign promising to arrest her for any number of reasons. Signs had always been part of her life:

> DO NOT WALK ON THE GRASS. . . .
> DO NOT PICK THE FLOWERS. . . .
> NO SPITTING ALLOWED. . . .
> NO BALL PLAYING ALLOWED. . . .
> VIOLATORS WILL BE PROSECUTED.

No dog shit on my shoes, she laughed. And Mama always telling me to watch out for the broken pieces of whiskey bottles in the bushes. No matter where she was in Central Park, she could always see part of a tall building and hear the traffic.

Here there was not a building anywhere, she thought, no traffic and no streets to cross. She became aware of the silence again. The world of the Barrio and the crowds was someplace else far away, and it was all right. Miles and miles away someplace, but she could still be here at the same time; that could really happen. Yes, it's true, she smiled to herself. She felt the letter to her mother still in her pocket.

Nilda went back towards the main road, drinking in the sweet and pungent smells of the woods. She listened to the quiet buzzing of insects and the rustling of the bushes as small animals rushed through, sometimes appearing and disappearing within a split second. She noticed that off to the side of the trail a few feet away was a thick wall of bushes. Curious, Nilda went towards it and started to push her way through. Struggling, she pushed away the bushes with her arms and legs and stepped into an opening of yards and yards of roses delicately tinted with pink. The roses were scattered, growing wildly on the shrubs. The sun came through the leaves, stems, and petals, streaming down like rows of bright ribbons landing on the dark green earth.

Breathless, she stared at the flowers, almost unbelieving for a moment, thinking that she might be in a movie theater waiting for the hard, flat, blank screen to appear, putting an end to a manufactured fantasy which had engrossed and possessed her so completely. Nilda walked over to the flowers and touched them. Inhaling the sweet

154

fragrance, she felt slightly dizzy, almost reeling. She sat down on the dark earth and felt the sun on her face, slipping down her body and over to the shrubs covered with roses. The bright sash of warm sunlight enveloped her and the flowers; she was part of them; they were part of her.

She took off her socks and sneakers, and dug her feet into the earth like the roots of the shrubs. Shutting her eyes, Nilda sat there for a long time, eyes closed, feeling a sense of pure happiness; no one had given her anything or spoken a word to her. The happiness was inside, a new feeling, and although it was intense, Nilda accepted it as part of a life that now belonged to her.

After supper that evening, Nilda's group received a visit from the older girls. They wore jumpsuits as well, yellow with a brown trim, styled differently. Nilda was sitting alone at the side of the hill opposite the cottages. She was barefoot, reading a book. A tall dark-haired girl approached her. She was about fourteen or fifteen years old. Smiling, she looked at Nilda and asked, "Are you Nilda?"

"Yes," Nilda said, returning her smile.

"What's your last name?"

"Ramírez, Nilda Ramírez."

"Hi," she said, sitting down comfortably next to Nilda. "I'm Olga. Olga Rodríguez. This is my third summer here." Nilda nodded, impressed with the older girl. "Somebody told me about you. They said you are Spanish. Do you speak it?"

"Yes!" said Nilda. "I speak it at home to my mother sometimes, and all the time to my aunt; she don't speak English at all."

"O.K. then," said Olga, "let's talk. How are you?" she asked in Spanish, and continued, "How do you like camp? Tell me, how long have you been here?"

"Oh," Nilda responded excitedly in Spanish, "I been here since like about two weeks already. But I will be here a whole month. I like it very much here."

"Where do you live? In New York City?" asked Olga.

"Yes. I live near Central Park right off Madison Avenue—"

"In the Barrio?" interrupted Olga.

"Yes! Do you know it? Do you live there too? Maybe you go to my brother Frankie's school."

"I don't live in the Barrio," Olga answered. "I live downtown, on 14th Street between Seventh and Eighth Avenues."

"Oh, my mother took me there once. Is that where there is a big church? Our Lady of Guadalupe, I think. My mother and me took a subway there. That is a great big church."

"Yes, that is our church," responded Olga. In English she asked Nilda, "You are Puerto Rican, ain't you?"

"Yes," Nilda answered, reverting back to English.

"You know Puerto Ricans ain't really Spanish. You shouldn't say that. That you are Spanish. I can't even understand you when you talk." Surprised, Nilda realized the older girl was cross. "It's very hard to understand what you say . . . like when you say . . . say the number five in Spanish." Olga paused. "Go on, say it; say five in Spanish."

"Five," Nilda said clearly in Spanish.

"There, that's all wrong! You are saying it all wrong! What kind of accent is that? In Spain they talk Castilian. That's what my parents talk at home. You probably never even heard of that," Olga said angrily. Nilda did not know what to say and looked at Olga. "Say shoes," Olga went on. "Go ahead, I'll prove it again; say the word 'shoes.' "

Nilda wanted to say something. She thought, perhaps I should tell her about Papa. He speaks like that. He sounds like her and he comes from Spain, so he must speak like she says. But the older girl's angry face left Nilda mute. She said nothing.

"Go on," Olga insisted. "Say shoes. I'm waiting."

"Say shoes!" Nilda repeated in English.

"Very funny," Olga said. "Well that proves what you speak is a dialect." Getting up, she went on, "Don't let me hear you calling yourself Spanish around here when you can't even talk it properly, stupid."

"You're stupid," Nilda answered.

"I'm leaving," Olga said. "We don't bother with your kind. You give us all a bad name."

Nilda watched Olga turn away and disappear over the next mound of grass. Picking up a single green blade, she popped it in her mouth and began to chew. It had a bitter taste at first, then she got used to it and she chewed slowly, imitating some of the cows she had seen eating in the countryside. She lay back, digging her heels into the soft ground, thinking about the older girl and what had just happened. Nilda stuck out her tongue, then looked at the sky, the trees, and the small birds that flew overhead. At that moment she wanted to absorb all that was around

157

her. Quickly, she began to let her body roll down the hill; faster and faster she went until her weight carried her to a full stop. Jumping up, she ran back to get her sneakers and her book. She didn't care about being Spanish; she didn't know exactly what that meant, except that it had nothing to do with her happiness.

Nilda promised to take her two friends to her secret garden today. A few days after she had discovered the garden, she had told them all about it. Josie and Stella had been excited about going and, after much debating, Nilda had finally agreed to take them. She waited by her bunk for the other girls. They were going to meet in the dormitory and leave together.

"Hi, Nilda." Josie walked in and went over to her own bunk. She took her plaid cardboard suitcase and placed it on her bunk. The suitcase was a present from Miss Rachel and Miss Jeanette. Opening it, she began to re-arrange the contents, taking things out and then putting them back inside. At least once a day, Josie would take out her suitcase and go through this ritual. She was the only girl in the group who had come to camp with her clothes in a cardboard box tied with twine. The other girls had laughed and made fun of her. Josie began to brag that she was rich and lived in a mansion with a swimming pool, but her parents were separated and she was staying with some people for a little while. She had been sent to camp from a foster home and nobody be-lieved her. Nilda remembered Josie's reaction to the girls' laughing and teasing. "You won't laugh when you see what my parents are going to send me. They ordered a very special suitcase for me; it has my initials on it and they are J.F., which stands for Josie Forest. It is probably on its way to camp right now."

Nilda sat on her bunk and watched as Josie carefully busied herself with the suitcase. She's always fussing with that thing, she thought. Nilda recalled that when they had been in camp just a few days, she had entered the dormitory with Josie and found her large cardboard box sitting on her bunk. It was battered and had marks and words written all over it: JOSIE STINKS! JOSIE LIVES IN A GARBAGE CAN. JOSIE FOREST IS FULL OF BUGS. J.F. EATS WORMS! HA HA . . . HEE HEE . . . TAKE A BATH POOR LITTLE RICH GIRL. Bursting into tears when she saw the box, Josie quickly ran out of the cottage. Nilda saw a few of the girls look at her, then at one another, and begin to giggle. "I'm telling Miss Rachel and Miss Jeanette!" she had heard herself screaming at them. Running inside to the counselors' quarters, she knocked loudly on the door.

"Yes, come in," Miss Rachel said.

Nilda walked in and, before anyone had a chance to ask her anything, she blurted, "It's Josie, they took her cardboard box and marked it with things about her and then they tore it and broke some of it. Now she left crying. She ran out and—"

"What? Wait a minute," interrupted Miss Rachel.

"Inside. In the dormitory on her bunk. You'll see it; it's all marked up and everything," Nilda said.

Both women followed Nilda into the dormitory and saw the box on the bed. "All right," said Miss Rachel, "who did this? Come on now!" No one said anything.

"I'll go look for Josie, Rachel," said Jeanette.

159

"Miss Jeanette is going to find Josie. When she returns, I want a full apology from all of you. Personally to Josie, or we will have to take this matter a lot further. Maybe your parents would like to hear about this." Walking around the room, Miss Rachel looked at the girls and asked, "Did you take part in this? How about you? Nobody? You ought to be ashamed! How would any of you feel if someone made fun of you because you couldn't afford to have what other people are fortunate enough to have?" She marched up and down the room. "What did she do? What? To make you behave like this? I'm ashamed just looking at this!" she said, gesturing towards the cardboard box.

"They did it, Miss Rachel."

Everyone turned to see Stella, who pointed to two girls. "They took it and then they passed it around and everyone did something to the box, wrote on it or broke it, or marked on it or something."

"Did you write something or do something too?" Miss Rachel asked.

"No," said Stella. "I didn't."

"Josie brags too much, Miss Rachel! She has a big mouth." A girl with straight bangs and long braids spoke. Everyone looked at her, and she continued, "Always talking about her mansion and her clothes and her this and that. And a whole bunch of lies!"

"That's no reason to take what doesn't belong to you and destroy or damage it, Evelyn," Miss Rachel said, and walked over to the girl.

Looking at Miss Rachel defiantly, Evelyn said, "It will teach her a lesson. Not to be a liar!"

"How dare you!" said Miss Rachel. "Evelyn Daniels, who do you think you are? You are nobody special around here to decide who needs a lesson. That was a very cruel thing to do!"

Evelyn began to shake and cry. She opened her mouth and tried to speak, breathing hard. "She hasn't any parents!" she sobbed. "I'll bet she doesn't even have parents. She doesn't." Coughing and screaming she yelled, "She's lying . . . she is . . . she better just . . ." Almost incoherent, she tried to talk, sobbing and crying. "Ah . . . Ahhh . . ." she gasped.

"Stop it! Stop it!" said Miss Rachel. Evelyn opened her mouth and began to shriek. Miss Rachel grabbed her by the shoulders and began to shake her. "Stop that, I said. Evelyn Daniels, you will please stop it. Get hold of yourself. Right now! Do you hear!" Evelyn stopped screaming and sat down on her bunk, crying quietly. "Come inside with me," Miss Rachel said, pointing to the other girls. "We all have to straighten this thing out. We have to talk about this and what has happened. Evelyn, come on. We are all going inside." Evelyn did not move. Miss Rachel took her arm and gently pulled her towards her. "Please, Evelyn, you must come inside with us; we are going to work this out." Miss Rachel had not asked Stella or Nilda to come inside with them.

Later, when Miss Jeanette returned with Josie, they went inside with the others and were gone for a long while. Miss Rachel came out and removed the cardboard box. The next day it had been replaced by a plaid cardboard suitcase. It was green Scotch-plaid with a grey background. No one ever mentioned the incident again.

From that time on, Stella, Josie, and Nilda became a trio; they did almost everything together, except go to church on Sunday. Josie went to the First Methodist Church. Nilda and Stella went to the Roman Catholic Church. Stella was a Greek Orthodox, but there was no church available for her so she went with the group of Roman Catholic girls for Sunday services.

Josie had finally stopped rearranging things in her suitcase and had put it under her bunk. "Where's Stella?" she asked.

"I don't know, but she should be here already," said Nilda. "Before you know it our free time will be over."

"Let's wait outside," said Josie. The two girls walked outdoors and sat near the cottage. They saw Stella rushing towards them.

"Hi. I had to finish gluing something I'm making for my parents at arts and crafts," said Stella. "Let's go."

The girls followed as Nilda led the way down the road. She took the side trail, then the path to the right, and came up to the thick wall of bushes. "Just follow me. You're gonna have to push the bushes and branches out of the way." They made their way through the thick shrubbery until they were inside the clearing. "Well?" Nilda said. "Here it is."

"Oh . . . this is really pretty," said Stella.

"Look at all them flowers," said Josie. "With the sun coming in over there like that, it looks like church."

"Let's sit down," Nilda said, pleased with their reactions. They began to talk about camp and going back home. They were all leaving by the end of the week.

"That's only three days," said Josie. "But you can all

162

come to visit me, just as soon as my parents get together again. My dad is getting a new job and he's going to get our house back in Elmira, with the swimming pool and all. He and my mother are going to come and get me at the place where I am now. That's only temporary, you know."

Stella and Nilda looked at each other but said nothing.

Looking a little worried, Stella said, "I'll ask my father and mother and they will probably make room, so you can sleep with me in my bed. Except, the only thing is I gotta help out every day at the diner." Stella's parents owned a roadside diner outside Lancaster, Pennsylvania. She was one of twelve children. Everyone was obligated to help at the diner after school, and weekends as well.

"We can help you when we visit," said Josie. "Can't we, Nilda?"

"Sure we can!" agreed Nilda.

"Hey!" said Stella. "I'll tell them that; they will probably say yes. I'm sure."

"You can visit me. I'll ask my mother," Nilda said. "She won't mind. We can do a lotta things in Manhattan. We can go to Central Park and play and you can ride the subways. We can sneak in; I'll show you how. We don't have to pay."

"Oh!" "Wow!" said the girls, impressed.

"We can go to a lotta places, but we have to watch out for those tough kids, man!" Nilda loved telling stories about New York City to her two friends because they had never been there.

"Do they really carry knives, like you said?" asked Josie.

163

"Sure," Nilda nodded her head emphatically, "and guns and everything. They are real tough. You musta seen it in the movies. Didn't you?"

"Sure," said Josie.

"I did," said Stella.

"But I still would be scared," said Josie. "I've never been to a place like that."

"Don't be scared; I'll be with you and I know just what to do and . . ."

"Were you ever attacked?" asked Stella.

"Not exactly, but I seen a man knifed. Yes I did. He was bleeding and holding his stomach and everything."

"You seen it? The whole thing I mean?" asked Josie.

"What happened? Oh, Nilda, tell us," said Stella.

"Well," Nilda said excitedly, "I didn't see the whole thing exactly, but I was playing and then I saw this big fight. People—men—were pushing and beating each other up and everything. Then they ran. One of them had a gun . . ." she paused, "but he ran away. Then the man that was hurt ran into the hallway. I went in to help him and then we called the police and they brought an ambulance."

"Weren't you scared all alone?" asked Josie.

"Well, my mother was there with someone and they actually called the police."

"How come your mother was there?" asked Stella.

"She was just walking by, that's all. And she heard the commotion. So, she called the police," Nilda said.

"Did he die, Nilda?" asked Josie.

"No, he lived. When he left, I saw him stretched out and he looked like he was going to get better. . . ." Nilda continued to talk and the girls listened, enjoying what she had to say. They remained in the clearing for quite a while, talking and making plans to visit each other.

"Hey, we better get back before it gets past supper-time," said Stella.

"Oh yeah, we better go," Nilda agreed. "Well I'm glad you finally came to see it."

"It's beautiful."

"Just like you said it was, Nilda."

Quickly, Nilda led the way back through the thick bushes, out to the trail, and onto the main road. She had come to her secret garden as often as she could and knew the path even without looking.

They all hurried back to the cottage to wash up for supper. Nilda could not imagine not being in camp any more, or not seeing her secret garden. Well, she thought, we still got three days and that is a long time.

Some of the girls cried when they said good-bye. Nilda exchanged addresses with Stella and Josie. She wrote them down in her book of drawings, which was in her suitcase. The train ride seemed to go by quickly, and she was hardly aware of just when the tall buildings came into view. The Park Avenue Marketa appeared and the train moved on rapidly underground. They had said that they would see her again next year. Nilda thought about her garden and wondered if it would be there next year and still look the same. Would she be in the same cottage? And get her old bunk again? Her thoughts were interrupted by the excitement of Grand Central Station.

She stepped off the train with the other girls and saw her mother waving to her.

"Mami. Mamita, over here!" she yelled. Other children called out to their parents. There were lots of people and children with suitcases, duffle bags, and backpacks.

After lining up her group, the counselor began to discharge the children to the adults who waited nearby.

"Mrs. Ramírez, please!" Her mother came forward and Nilda jumped up to greet her. "Good-bye, Nilda. Mrs. Ramírez, it was so nice having her. We hope to see her again next year," the counselor said.

"Thank you very much. Good-bye. Thank you for everything," her mother said.

"Good-bye," Nilda said as she walked away, her arm around her mother. They hugged and kissed each other.

"My goodness. Dios mío. Look at you. My nena has grown almost like a señorita, so big."

"I made something for you and Papa, Mami. It's in my suitcase."

"Did you? Oh, well, I can't wait to see it. When we get home I make you such a good lunch, you will see."

"What, Mami? Plátanos?" Her mother nodded. "Oh boy, I haven't had them in a whole month."

"I'll make everything you like," her mother smiled.

They walked quickly over to the IRT Lexington Avenue line and boarded a local train, rushing to get seats next to each other. The warm stagnant air in the subway, the vibrations of the moving car, combined with the noise of the train passing over the tracks, placed Nilda in a familiar setting, one that she had known all her life. She leaned her head on her mother's shoulder and looked up at the advertising signs that were on the wall above the windows. Under almost every advertisement were the words:

BUY AN EXTRA WAR BOND.
YOU'LL BE GLAD YOU DID.

All the advertisements seemed to have something about the war. She read a bus company's ad:

HIGHWAYS WILL BE HAPPY WAYS AGAIN
IF WE KEEP FAITH WITH OUR FIGHTING MEN.
BUY WAR BONDS.
Courtesy of the American Wings Bus Lines Corp.

On the ad was a lifelike drawing of a man, dressed in a bus driver's uniform, saying good-bye to his employer. In the next section, the same man was dressed as a soldier, saluting proudly.

SPAM

SO MANY WAYS
COLD AS A SANDWICH
HOT AS THE MAIN DISH
CUT INTO A SALAD
DELICIOUS BUT ALWAYS NUTRITIOUS

This advertisement had a picture of a family sitting down to eat Spam. Everyone was there except the father; his chair was empty. On the wall over his chair was a portrait of a Naval officer, smiling.

Nilda read all the signs; there had not been much mention of the war at camp.

167

"Here we are, Nilda, 103rd, our stop. Let's go, mi hijita," said her mother.

Nilda climbed the familiar steps of the subway station. Outside it was hot and humid, hardly a breeze. They walked along, stopping for traffic and passing familiar shops: bodegas, candy stores, dry cleaning and tailor shops. They turned into her street. A few children were out playing and waved to Nilda, exchanging greetings. She climbed the steps slowly, following her mother. The door was open in one apartment and the radio was playing loudly. In another apartment, she heard an argument. Nilda felt very warm and tired. The perspiration began to run down the sides of her face and, for a moment, she remembered camp, the trails, her garden, and the silence. That is happening, she thought, right now too, someplace real far, where I was this morning.

"You hungry, nena?" her mother asked, stopping before the door to the apartment to catch her breath.

"Yes, Mami."

"Good. We are home now."

April, 1943

"Nilda, bring the rest of the holy water here," her mother said. "Don't wake up your papa. You know how he feels; if he finds out, there's gonna be the very devil and all hell to pay." Her mother made the sign of the cross.

Nilda carefully brought in a jar filled with holy water. That afternoon, right after school, she had gone with her mother to St. Cecilia's. Cautiously she had watched, ready to give warning if anyone came by, while her mother quietly filled several glass jars with the holy water. She had scooped the water out of the marble fonts with a metal measuring cup. When she was all finished, she took a small piece of paper and read the prayer that was written on it, as she had been instructed to do by the spiritualist. After making the sign of the cross, they had left.

"I'm hiding the holy water there, way in back of the closet, and as soon as Doña Tiofila comes, we can get to work. I don't know if it will work, since he don't believe. . . ." Her mother paused and sighed, "But maybe, if we believe." She walked over to one of her portable altars, knelt down, and began to pray silently.

Nilda walked into her room and started to put her books away. When Victor had left for the Army, her mother had given Nilda a bedroom of her own. Her step-father had suffered another heart attack and had been sent home from the hospital with no chance of recovery. Nilda knew that he was very ill despite the fact that he was always making plans to go back to work. She thought about the time her mother had gone to see the spiritualist, determined to try in every way to help her husband recover his health. "There is something bad, something evil that has come into my home, Doña Tiofila." Nilda had sat and listened as the two women spoke; she was quite used to going with her mother to see Doña Tiofila. "It all started with Jimmy, you see, and now, it's Emilio," her mother had confided.

"Doña Lydia, tell me, have you noticed or found anything unusual in the apartment?" Doña Tiofila had asked.

"Well, only as I have told you—the chicken wishbone wrapped up in red ribbon. It was hidden way on top of the doorway at the entrance to our apartment. It had a lot of dust on it, very dirty, and looked old, like it had been there for a very long time. So I couldn't tell whether that was actually monkey turds wrapped inside."

Shaking her head, Doña Tiofila had said, "You should have brought it to me right away. Immediately!"

"I know. But I didn't think. I was so upset. So I threw it in the garbage can outside."

"Well, Doña Lydia, we must have a seance. It is the only way to get to the bottom of this. I will arrange one. There are several people who also need a seance. I'll let you know." Nilda had refused to go to the seance with her mother. She was too frightened. When her mother had returned, she told Nilda all about it.

"Nilda, por mi madre, it was just fantastic. You should

have gone with me to see. During the seance, the message was spoken by Doña Tiofila; it was the voice of my dead Aunt Saiyo. Remember? I told you about her, she is Titi Delia's older sister. I recognized her voice right away. She warned me, Nilda. It is my father. Yes, your grandfather, mi hijita! Dios mío. He did not receive the last rites. His last wife did not believe. She is Lutheran; she did not call a priest. So now his soul is wandering around with no place to go and he is restless, tired, and angry. My father is now mixing with some other lost souls. Bendito! Some of them are evil; they have been lost too long. They are up to no good and they are the ones entering my house. My father cannot stop them. It is understandable; he is too restless and angry." Her mother had taken out a written list of items. "You see, Nilda, we must make the sacrifices. I have to get these things; they are important. Look," she held out the list toward Nilda, "the white rooster, the holy water, the herbs, candles, and all that. This way Doña Tiofila can help me so we can be rid of the evil."

Doña Tiofila was due to arrive in a short while. Nilda's mother had already bought the live white rooster and given it to the spiritualist, who had made the sacrifice in Central Park the night before. Now, there were prayers to be recited and rituals to be performed in the apartment. Everyone knew about it except her stepfather.

Her mother had warned everyone. "Papa is not to be awakened. But if he should get up, I will just have to tell him, and that's that! It is too important."

Nilda heard voices. She went to see who it was. A small plump woman walked in; she was bundled up in a heavy

172

winter coat and had a kerchief wrapped around her head. She carried a large cloth shopping bag. The woman took off her coat and kerchief. She wore a housedress, no makeup, and solid comfortable shoes with laces. "It's another nasty day out. Looks like snow or rain," she said. "Winter is too long in this country. Well, thank God, in another couple weeks we have the springtime."

"Thank you for coming this cold wet day. Everything is ready. My husband is sleeping; I pray he does not wake up. He is not a believer," her mother said. Pausing, she added, "He can be very difficult."

"I know," said Doña Tiofila. "I have to deal with all kinds of people in my work. That's why the good Lord gives me my faith and my powers. To meet with all kinds of difficulty and doubt. But that never discourages me. Mira, Doña Lydia, I wish I could tell you how many people come to me now, who, at one time did not believe. But after what has happened to them through faith and belief, they now come to me and believe with all their hearts." Looking at Nilda, who was standing listening, she asked, "How are you, Nilda?"

"Fine, thank you."

The two women went into the kitchen where her mother began to make coffee. There, Doña Tiofila started to take things out of her shopping bag and discuss the ritual with her mother.

Nilda went back to her room and took out a drawing she was working on for Easter. She was not in the mood to work on it, and went over to her "box of things," examining the contents. Most of her cardboard cutouts had been made some time ago. Lately, she had lost interest

173

in her cutout projects. I have to start seeing what I need and don't need, she thought. She took out a paper cutout of a crib, and remembered Baby Jimmy. Well, he certainly won't know me now; Mama says he's almost a year and a half already, Nilda said to herself. She found herself angry at Jimmy and Sophie, feeling it was their fault that she couldn't see Baby Jimmy.

Looking further into the box, she took out another cardboard cutout of a statue of the Virgin Mary that she had made after she had gotten home from St. Anselm's Camp for Catholic Youth. Underneath the Virgin's feet she had printed in tiny letters, trying to imitate the script in church, "Thank you, oh blessed Virgin, for THE MIRACLE." Remembering the "miracle" and camp, she wondered if what took place today would somehow make her stepfather better.

"Nilda?" Nilda looked up and saw her mother whispering to her from outside her room. "Nilda, you have to come inside with us; we need you for a moment, please." Her mother spoke very softly. "Doña Tiofila says we must have the youngest and most innocent one in the family present." Nilda followed her, sulking. "Now look, Nilda, only for a moment."

"Yeah, that's what you always say and then I have to stay and say all them prayers too, I bet," Nilda said crossly.

"Shh. You have to help. Stop that nonsense! This woman is very good to come and help. So you just get another expression on your face. Right now! Or I'll put one there for you," her mother said angrily. They walked back to the kitchen, where Doña Tiofila was holding a jar of holy water.

174

"You must follow me and recite the prayers I gave you, as instructed, Doña Lydia." Doña Tiofila closed her eyes and continued, "First we recite one for your son Jimmy and his young family. If he is in trouble with the police, the Most Just Judge will stand behind him, and soon you shall have news of his whereabouts. Then we shall pray for Victor, as he fights for his country and all of us; may the enemies' bullets never find him. Finally, we shall reach your father, Doña Lydia. I have the blood of the sacrifice. He shall leave those evil souls he is hanging out with and go back to rest in peace. I will receive the illness and then I will rid myself of it." She started to walk, pouring the holy water on her hands and sprinkling it over the walls, woodwork, and floors, going into the hall and from room to room.

Nilda and her mother recited the prayers, whispering in Spanish. As they entered Aunt Delia's room, she was quietly reading the newspaper. When she saw Doña Tiofila, she nodded and kneeled before her small altar, silently praying. They went into her brothers' room; it was empty. Doña Tiofila continued to pray. They stood before her parents' bedroom. Her mother looked in and said in a barely audible voice, "He is fast asleep."

"I will go in and come out quickly," said Doña Tiofila and walked into the bedroom. Tiptoeing, she gently sprinkled the holy water as she walked all around the bed where Nilda's stepfather slept.

Nilda could see her stepfather stretched out and could hear him snoring as the woman moved her lips and made gestures.

Doña Tiofila stepped out. "All done," she said. Nilda's mother crossed herself with relief.

175

They walked back to the kitchen and Doña Tiofila reached into her shopping bag and took out candles, herbs, incense, and oil. She began to rub her hands together and whisper to the evil spirits. Nilda could not make out what the spiritualist said.

Nilda's mother watched anxiously as Doña Tiofila went into a trance. Finally, the spiritualist opened her eyes wide and said, "Ay, ayyy qué dolor! What pain! I feel the pain in my heart." Grabbing herself, she gasped, "I feel the spirit coming into my body. Yesss. Go . . . go away . . . go! Leave this house! Leave these people in peace! Go!"

Nilda watched, terrified, as the woman groaned and moaned, convulsed with pain.

Doña Tiofila collapsed in a heap in a chair. "I have to rest. Dios mío. My goodness. I have a heart condition now . . . you must light candles," she said, catching her breath. "Place the blood of the sacrifice on the altar and light your candles beside it. The evil spirits will leave your home and leave my body. But you . . . you must continue the prayers and lighting the candles for a period of . . ."

As her mother listened attentively to every word Doña Tiofila said, Nilda quietly slipped out of her chair and into the hallway. She walked into her room and sat on her bed, glad to be away from them. Nilda sat for a moment, thinking about what had happened, when suddenly she heard loud voices. She left her room and went towards the living room.

"What is all this?" her stepfather shouted. "You at it again? Look at the walls and the floor. The house is all wet, for Christ's sake. I almost tripped and broke my ass!

When are you gonna learn, Lydia? What is this gonna get you, eh?" he asked.

"You don't believe, Emilio? O.K. But don't interfere; never mind! It's my business then. O.K.?" her mother answered angrily.

"Your business? Some business all right. We can't afford to eat chicken, but your friend, the healer, can, eh?" he shouted. "She's the only person in the whole Barrio who eats chicken every day."

"Emilio, please, that is a terrible thing to say. She does not even charge. Each person gives only what they can," her mother said, outraged.

"Why should she charge? She only has to give a list of groceries with chicken every day. She keeps the chicken and we get one lousy ounce of blood. Don't tell me she don't eat it. Devil knows what else she orders for supper as well. Then, little by little, the idiots pay her rent. Between that crew at St. Cecilia's with their crap, and this basura, it's a miracle we can afford to eat Spam!"

Doña Tiofila had her coat on and the kerchief around her head. She was standing by the door, holding her cloth shopping bag, ready to leave.

"Ay, Doña Tiofila, please forgive him. I'm so ashamed for his behavior."

"Never mind, mi hija," Doña Tiofila said smiling. "I told you it doesn't matter. I understand. I will help you."

"Thank you, Doña Tiofila. You know how grateful I am, and I will pray for you and your goodness," her mother said.

"What is all this water on the floor? Did she pee here too? It's not enough with these fairy tales, she has to

177

come here to pee? She can't use the toilet? What do I have to look forward to next?"

"Ay, Emilio, please shut up. Basta ya! Virgen María, what language. Shame!" her mother said. Opening the door, she walked out with Doña Tiofila. "Por favor, Doña Tiofila. He is worse than ever. I think it's his illness . . ." Her voice trailed off.

Her stepfather was still muttering and complaining when her mother returned.

"You ought to be ashamed, Emilio! That woman is a saint. You embarrassed me."

"I didn't know saints ate chicken or wet the floors. Or . . ."

"Stop that!" interrupted her mother. "It is for your own good I do this, hombre! And for Victor and for Jimmy."

"Oh, I see. This woman is gonna bring back your precious son. From where? Not a word do we hear from Jimmy, in how long? A lousy postcard now and then, with no return address. Who knows what he is up to? We got a drawer full of letters from the draft board for him. They have come here, in person, to look for him. The United States Government cannot find him, but she's gonna do it? She ain't a saint, she's a magician!"

Nilda heard her parents arguing as she returned to her room. She thought, Boy am I glad that's over. She began to think about Doña Tiofila, who was Catholic and always wore religious medals around her neck. I wonder what that lady tells the priest at confession? she thought. At Catechism, she had been taught that all superstition was wrong. Was the ritual today superstition? she asked herself. Nilda remembered her own confessions guiltily.

178

She had made her First Holy Communion last October, feeling miserable since most of the kids were seven years old and Nilda was eleven. She still had not told the priest everything, like the time in church when she stole candles and lit them, or the time she received Communion without ever having been to confession, as well as other things. Her thoughts were interrupted by a knock on the door. "Yeah?" she asked.

The door opened and Paul walked in. "What's all the fussing about?" he asked.

"That lady Doña Tiofila, the espiritista, was here. And she did a lot of stuff. Then Papa woke up and he was yelling at her."

"Oh man," Paul laughed. "She was still here when he was yelling?"

"Yeah." Nilda started to laugh. "You shoulda heard all the things he said. Mama was so mad, I thought she was gonna punch Papa. The lady was shocked. You shoulda seen her face." They both began to giggle. After a while Nilda looked at Paul and asked, "Do you believe in that espiritismo stuff, Paul?"

"I don't know," he shrugged. "It can't hurt nobody anyway, I guess. Do you?"

"I don't know neither. Mama said that lady Doña Tiofila can talk to the dead." Paul made a skeptical face. "Honest, Paul, she said she heard her in a seance and everything."

"Probably some fakeria," said Paul.

Nilda looked at him, smiled and shrugged, "Well, that's what she said."

"Listen, Nilda. I'm gonna join the Navy."

"What?"

"Yeah, I'll be seventeen this year. I made up my mind, you know."

"Mama is not gonna let you, Paul. She's not gonna like it."

"Well, I'm gonna do it. I'll run away to another state if she don't. I'm gonna put it to her, ask her to sign."

"Ain't you scared, Paul?"

"Naw. I'm not scared. We gotta fight for our country, right? Look at Victor; he's doing his part, you know. Man, I'm gonna do mine. Mama is real proud of Victor. She got the American flag out on the window since he left for the Army, man. She ain't taken it down yet. And now she's sewing that red-white-and-blue thing you hang up. You know, made of material, with a star on it and his name, 'Victor.' " Pausing, he looked at Nilda, who said nothing. "Anyway, I'm failing all my grades. I hate that school. God damn teachers always picking on me. Look, Nilda, if I join the Navy, I can learn me a trade, man. You know. Be something, be somebody. And help Mama out and the family."

"Are you gonna wait until school finishes this June?"

"No! I made up my mind. I wanna split as soon as I can. I'm gonna be Seaman Paul Ortega." Jumping up and saluting, he said, "There you go, dadeeooo! You like the uniforms, Nilda?"

"Yeah, they are nice. It's gonna feel funny, you being a sailor, Paul," she said smiling.

"How about that?" In a more serious tone he said, "Please don't say nothing to nobody. I haven't told Frankie yet. O.K.? It's still a secret till I talk to Ma."

180

"Sure, I won't say nothing to nobody."

"You coming to the burning tonight?" he asked.

"What burning?"

"The effigies, of Hitler, Tojo, and Mussolini. Didn't you hear? Down around on 102nd Street. Man, the whole street is getting together. They got a whole bunch of crates to burn and they are setting up a platform for speakers. There's gonna be music and. . . ."

"What's an effi- effi-," Nilda interrupted.

"Effigy?"

"Yeah, what is that?"

"That's what they call a duplicate, like a doll or dummy that looks like the enemies. You remember we did that last year? Before Christmas up on 106th and Lexington Avenue? They burned them dummies."

"Oh yeah! That's right," Nilda said. "I remember. They had people speaking and music and all that."

"Well, tonight they are gonna have a big rally. To raise money, you know, war bonds and stamps. They made three dummies, real good, man. They look just like the Nazis and Japs, you know. Oh wait," Paul laughed. "They made Mussolini into a monkey, man! He got a tail and ears just like a monkey! You know Indio? Well, he is a really good artist, man. He painted the faces really good." Pausing, he smiled at Nilda and said, "He is almost as good an artist as you are, Nilda."

"Really? Aww!" she said.

"Honest, you are really good, Nilda. You are gonna be a real good artist someday, you'll see."

"Wow. Indio is bigger than I am. I'll bet he's way better than me," she said.

"No, he's not. He's good, but nobody beats you, Nilda. You can really draw."

Beaming, Nilda said, "I'll send you some drawings when you are in the Navy, Paul."

"Well, I gotta go. Can't wait till tonight. Everybody is gonna stomp on them dummies. Man, then a big blaze. Whoosh! . . . You coming tonight?"

"Yeah, I'm gonna tell Benji and Petra; maybe they don't know about it," she said.

Paul stood up to leave. "O.K.," he said. "I gotta go. Remember, don't say nothing about what I said. O.K.?"

"I won't, Paul, don't worry. I promise." Paul walked out of the room.

Nilda put her "box of things" away and opened her schoolbooks. Taking her English grammar, she started her homework assignment. She thought about the rally tonight and her friends. Petra was already in junior high school. Next term, Nilda was going to the same school and was excited about the change. She had spoken to Petra and asked her all about it. Her friend had already gotten her period and was beginning to develop. She has to wear a brassiere, Nilda thought, impressed. She wondered when she would get her period, and what it would feel like. The thought that she would have to bleed every month scared her. She had heard different stories about it from her friends in the street. One girl had told her that it was very painful, and another said that sometimes the blood ran down one's legs, leaving a trail on the sidewalk.

She shuddered, frightened by the whole idea. Her mother had assured her that it was a perfectly normal function in a woman's body, and not to pay attention to such nonsense, but she had her doubts. Trying not to think about this, Nilda concentrated on her homework and began to write her assignment.

April, 1943
The Same Night

It was cold out and Nilda stood apart from a larger group of people gathering near the platform. There were amplifiers being set up and signs posted all over the stand and on the sound truck:

WAR BOND RALLY. . . .
BUY A WAR BOND. . . .
SAVE A LIFE. BUY A WAR BOND. . . .
KEEP THEM WINNING. . . . KEEP AMERICA STRONG. . . .
BUY WAR BONDS AND STAMPS TODAY. . . .
SUPPORT OUR BOYS ALL THE WAY.

Snow flurries sprinkled wet snow on everything. Nilda stood by the fire burning in a large trash can. There were several kids who lived on the block standing with her. On her way to the rally, she had stopped to call for Benji and Petra, and they had told her they hoped to come. Now and then she looked eagerly towards Madison Avenue, hoping to see her friends. Music began to blare out; a chorus sang, "Praise the Lord and pass the ammunition, Praise the Lord and pass the ammunition, Praise . . ."

A tall dark-skinned boy walked up to Nilda; she recognized Indio. He was almost her brother Paul's age and she was surprised to see him approach her.

"Hi, Nilda," he said.

"Hi, Indio," Nilda smiled. "Those dummies are real good, Indio. You did a nice job."

"Oh, thanks," he said. "Hey, Nilda, you seen Petra? You know if she's coming tonight?"

"She said maybe she could come. But she didn't know for sure," Nilda answered.

"Oh. O.K., man." He paused. "Look," Indio lowered his voice, "if she comes by, tell her I wanna see her, O.K.?"

"Sure," she said. Indio turned and walked away. Nilda looked at him, bewildered. He likes Petra? she wondered. He is way older. Petra had not said anything about Indio, and Nilda did not know whether her friend liked Indio or not. Feeling hurt, she realized that her friend often had excuses about not being able to go out to play any more and, at times, Nilda felt that Petra was avoiding her and Benji.

Nilda shifted from one foot to the other, trying to keep warm near the fire. Some of the cold wet snow traveled swiftly into her nose and mouth, and she leaned forward toward the flames in the trash can, feeling a prickling sensation as the drops of snow melted and the warmth penetrated her face. The music continued and more people started to come into the street. A microphone was being set up.

"Don't sit under the apple tree with anyone else but me . . . anyone else but me . . . Oh . . . don't sit under

185

the apple tree with anyone . . ." The Andrews Sisters sang out over the loudspeakers.

A wooden scaffold had been built right next to the platform, and each dummy was suspended from a rope tied around its neck. There was a huge pile of old wooden crates, broken lumber, battered cardboard, and old newspapers, ready for burning. She saw Benji coming towards her.

"Hey Benji, over here!" she called.

"Nilda? Man, what a time I had getting out. You know how Papi is. But we convinced him it was for the war effort, so he let me go. I came with my brothers, Manuel and Chucho, over there," he pointed. "See? But he didn't let my sisters come out nohow. We have to be home in one hour anyway. I hope I don't have to miss anything."

"They are already getting everything for the burning. You won't miss it, Benji, don't worry. Did you see Petra?" she asked.

"No. Are they coming? Marge and her?"

"I told them on my way to here. She said she would try." Pausing, she whispered to Benji, "You know what? I think that guy Indio likes Petra."

"Yeah?"

"Yeah. He asked me to tell her, if she comes, that he wants to see her." Nilda nodded her head.

"Wow," Benji said, "he's way older, ain't he?"

"I know. Petra never told me nothing about him, and I'm her best friend," Nilda said.

"Maybe she don't even like him," Benji said. There was a long silence and he said, "It sure is cold. I wish it was summer again, Nilda. You?"

"Oh yeah, I wish it was too. I'm going back to that camp again, you know, Bard Manor." She had told Benji all about her secret garden and all about camp when she had returned home last summer. "I wish you could come with me, Benji; if it was a boys' camp, you would have a real good time. I swear."

"Don't matter anyway. What's the difference; the way Papi is, everything is a big sin all the time."

They saw Petra and Marge walking towards them. "Over here. Hey!" Nilda called out, waving her arms at the girls.

The two girls smiled. "Hi," they said. "What a freezing night," Marge said.

Nilda noticed that even though Marge's hair was getting darker, she still had it fixed with lots of curls covering her entire head. She don't look like Shirley Temple no more, Nilda thought. She looked at Petra and said, "Petra, I have something to tell you."

"What?" asked Petra.

"Over there; I'll tell you alone."

"Secrets, secrets," Marge said.

"Mind your own business," snapped Nilda.

"Who cares!" Marge said, shrugging her shoulders.

Nilda and Petra walked away from the group and stood by themselves. "What is it?" asked Petra.

"Well." Nilda paused. "That guy Indio came over to me before."

Petra's eyes widened. "Yeah?" she asked.

"He said that . . . to tell you he wants to see you."

"How long ago?" asked Petra.

"Oh, when I got here before."

"Where is he? Did he say where he would be?" she asked quickly.

"No, but he was over there near the platform." Petra turned quickly in that direction. "Petra!" Nilda called. "Do you like him?" she asked.

Petra looked at her. "He's my boyfriend, Nilda."

"He is? Since how long?"

Petra looked down at the ground shyly. "For a while now. But it is a secret; you know how strict my father is."

"I wouldn't say nothing," Nilda said.

"Well anyway, sooner or later I was gonna tell you."

"Ain't he way older than you?" asked Nilda.

"You see," Petra snapped. "That's what I mean! I'm not a baby any more, Nilda. You don't understand that. You and Benji still playing kids' games! And you, Nilda, you are such a tomboy!"

Nilda looked at Petra angrily. "Go ahead! What do I care? Be his girl. No skin off my nose. I'd rather be doing what I'm doing than be going with any of them guys."

The two girls stared at each other. Finally Petra lowered her eyes and said, "I'll see you, Nilda."

"See you," said Nilda, and she walked back to Benji. Marge had left with her sister.

People were beginning to gather in front of the platform. The speakers were beginning to climb onto the small stage. Local politicians were stepping out of their limousines. A voice over the loudspeaker said, "Testing, 1-2-3-4," and a loud whistling sounded as they adjusted the microphone. Nilda saw the most popular politician in the neighborhood step onto the platform. People began to clap.

188

"Hi, Vito. Here's Victory!" someone called out.

"Viva Vito y la patria! Arriba la libertad!" people yelled. Some held up their hands, making a fist; others extended their index and middle fingers, making the sign of V for Victory. The politician began to speak.

"Ladies and gentlemen, fellow Americans. We are fighting a war not just to defend our homeland, but to wipe out Fascism." People clapped and cheered. "We have to pull together and show the world that we care about ending this menace to all mankind. Buy a war bond! Make it a regular part of your life, every week at payday. Buy a war stamp—even twenty-five cents—anything. . . ."

He went on speaking and Nilda half listened. She thought, I don't care if I am a tomboy. I'd rather be that than go with any of them dopey guys. She remembered how some of the girls in her neighborhood became pregnant and had to leave school, and thought of her mother's constant lectures. "You wanna be grown-up and fool around with boyfriends, eh? Let me warn you. If you think it is hard now, Nilda, with the welfare people, ah hah! You don't like charity; you wish we didn't have to take that kinda treatment, do you? Just get yourself in trouble with one of those lazy guys, those títeres. Go ahead, get a big belly. And he goes off with another woman and leaves you. Or if he stays and tries, what can he make? What kinda job can be get? When he himself still has dirty underdrawers? Don't bother coming here for sympathy, Nilda, because you must go with your husband; that is your duty. Then he can order you around. You who complain about your brothers being bossy all the time, and about your rights! Some rights you're gonna get. Well, what you have here to complain about is nothing, Miss, because I am here to protect you. But you try that with one of those no-good bums! First one baby, then two, three, four, a whole bunch. Dios mío! I was stupid, Nilda. Ignorant! What did I know? I had no mother, only a mean stepmother who beat me. If I could have had your opportunity for school and your privileges, never—lo juro por mi madre—never in a million years would I have had so many kids."

"Sssss . . . Sssss."
"Boooo."
"Kill the Japs!"
"Dirty Nazis!"
"A slip of the lip will sink the ship."
"Ssssss . . . Mussolini the monkey . . . ha ha ha . . ."
The majority of the group were young people. "Kill, kill a Jap!" they called out. The politician and some of his men took large sticks and gave the effigies a few hard blows. A huge cheer and a roar resounded over the entire street. Everyone began to hit the effigies. They were hung high, about six feet off the ground, and people jumped up to reach them. Someone pulled off Mussolini's tail. The stuffing started to come out of the Hitler dummy.

Some teen-age boys finally tore the dummies down. Nilda watched, standing a bit of a distance away, afraid she might get hurt. Dummy limbs were tossed around, some of the heads rolled. Tojo's head burst, the stuffing coming out of his smile.

Finally, all the pieces were heaved onto the large pile

of wooden crates, cardboard, and paper, and the mountain of trash was set ablaze. The entire street lit up, casting an orange glow, silhouetting the people, cars, and buildings. The music started again and Kate Smith sang loudly, "God bless America, land that I . . ."

Trucks were parked along the street, selling war bonds and war stamps. Nilda wished she could buy a war stamp. She knew better than to ask her mother; they were still on public assistance. Her brother Victor was allowed to send only very little, or they would be taken off the welfare rolls. Some of her friends had war-stamp books. Each time they bought a war stamp, they pasted it in the book. A full book was worth as much as eighteen dollars and seventy-five cents, as much as a war bond.

"Nilda, hey Nilda? I gotta cut, man," Benji shouted.

"Can't you wait a little while more? I can walk home with you then," she said.

"No. Man, you know Papi. Besides, I gotta go home with my brothers. They are leaving now."

"All right," she said, walking over to Benji.

"Hey, ain't that man your uncle? Over there, Nilda." Benji pointed across the street.

Nilda turned and saw Leo. "Oh yeah, that's Leo. I'm going over there. See you, Benji."

"See you, Nilda," Benji said. Nilda walked over to the other side of the street. Leo was standing and looking at the truck selling the war bonds and war stamps.

Music was still blaring out. Patriotic tunes. The war-bond rally workers called out to the people in the street. "Come on, folks. Buy more war bonds and stamps! Help our fighting men. Make us stronger. Buy war bonds;

191

they identify you! Do your bit! Make 1943 the best year of all. Buy a war-stamp book! Buy war stamps, everyone; they identify you!"

"Leo?" she said, tapping him on the arm.

"Nilda? Hello, nena; what are you doing out so late? And by yourself?"

"It's O.K. Paul and Frankie are here somewhere and Mami gave me permission."

"Well, and where is my kiss, eh?" Nilda put her arms around Leo, giving him a hug and a kiss. "So tell me how you are?" he asked. She noticed that underneath his coat he still had his bartender's apron on.

"I'm O.K. I got almost all A's in my school this term."

"Did you now?" He smiled and shook his head, "Just like your mama, so smart. How's everybody? How is Emilio?"

"He's like the same. You know," she said. "All right, I guess."

"Victor? You hear from him?"

"Yes, once in a while. He is somewhere in North Africa, but we get mail and the return address is to Washington, D.C., so we don't know exactly where he is."

"He's a wonderful boy. We are all very proud of him," Leo said. "Listen, nena, I got something for you, wait. . . ." Reaching into his pocket, he pulled out a book. "This here is a war-stamp book. See?"

"Oh, Leo! Honest?" she yelled.

"Sure. Look, see?" he opened up the book. "I already got two dollars' worth of stamps in it. I just bought it for you. Right now. You have to keep it and, when you can, you buy a war stamp and you paste it in."

Jumping up, Nilda gave Leo a hug. She grabbed the

book. "Wow, thank you so much!" She smiled. "Wait till I show Mami."

"I have to go back to work at the bar. Listen, honey, I'll walk with you to the house; then I have to go. I only came out to see the rally and get the book of stamps."

They walked towards Madison Avenue. Nilda loved being with Leo. He never hollers at me or criticizes me like Mama, she thought.

"Why don't you come to see us? Concha and me, eh?" he asked. "We like to see you, and Concha always asks me how you are."

Nilda smiled and shrugged. Her mother had forbidden her to go to Leo's without permission. She knew her mother did not like Doña Concha, the woman Leo lived with.

"Nilda, tell your mama that I will be coming by soon to visit, and to see how she is, and how everyone is. All right?"

Nodding, Nilda asked, "When?"

"Soon. Pay my respects to Don Emilio. Anything that I can do that Lydia needs . . . never mind, I will tell her myself." They stood by the stoop of her building. "Go on upstairs; it's cold and I have to get back to work."

Nilda leaned forward and said, "Thanks a lot for the stamp book."

"Oh, well I'll give you some more money for stamps when I see you again. You know, Nilda, the value goes up and in seven years you get twenty-five dollars instead of eighteen." Bending over, he kissed her cheek. "Now, nena, don't forget to tell your mama I asked for everyone and that I send my respects. Yes?"

"O.K., I won't. Good-bye, Leo." She went into her

building, holding her book of stamps. Man, she thought, wait till I bring this to school tomorrow and show everybody. As she climbed up the steps, she remembered something was bothering her. Petra! she thought. Well, I don't care; let her hang out with who she likes. Annoyed at being called a tomboy, she said to herself, I'm proud to be a tomboy! She tried leaping three steps at a time instead of her usual two. "Made it!" she said out loud. And she went on to try several more times; each time she was able to jump up the three steps at once. She reached her landing and was glad to be home to show her mother her new war-stamp book.

"Don't forget, now, what I told you. Ten cents on the number 305 straight, and eighteen cents on the number 382 combination. And tell Don Jacinto that Aunt Delia will bring down her own list of numbers as usual. That she is a little late today; she had to go to the clinic. All right?"

"O.K., Mami," Nilda said.

"I have to mail this package for Jimmy today." Her mother worked quickly and quietly, putting some jars of food and candy, boxes of crackers and cookies, and small tins of sardines into a cardboard box. "He is getting better, thank the good Lord and my faith in God," her mother said, almost in tears. The package was being sent to Lexington, Kentucky, to a federal penal institution for the rehabilitation of criminal drug addicts. Jimmy had been there for three months, serving a prison sentence of not less than one year and one day and not more than five years. "I wish I could afford somehow to go and see my son. He was so sick and I never saw him. Maybe if we hit the numbers, I could make the trip," she said, almost to herself.

Nilda looked out of the kitchen window; hardly a

195

breeze. It was sticky and hot out. She had not gone to camp this summer; her mother had told her that things could not work out and that she would have to wait until next year. At first, Nilda sulked and was angry with her mother, but after receiving the news about Jimmy, she realized that there was no sense in even thinking about anything like camp.

They had first found out about Jimmy through a phone call from Sophie. Sophie had telephoned at Don Jacinto's store. Nilda's mother had returned in tears, almost incoherent, after the phone call. Nilda had to call in a neighbor. Through the efforts of her stepfather and some other people, her mother had finally calmed down and was put to bed. Nilda had heard them talking. Jimmy had been sentenced for grand larceny, from one to ten years. But because it was his first offense, and he had given himself up as a drug addict, his sentence had been reduced. He had been very sick, in critical condition, and so they had sent him to a drug rehabilitation program.

Later they had found out that Sophie, frightened of the police, had left Jimmy. He had threatened to find her and kill her. She had gotten in touch with a priest and her aunt. The aunt was persuaded to take Sophie and Baby Jimmy in to live with her. An older man, an immigrant from the Ukraine who had escaped Europe before the war, was boarding at her aunt's home. He married Sophie, and Nilda's family learned that Sophie was pregnant again, soon to give birth to another child.

"Next week I have to make a package for Victor, may the Lord keep, protect, and look after him at all times," her mother said, making the sign of the cross. "And may

196

the good Lord protect my Paul and maybe not send him overseas."

Paul was in boot camp; Nilda missed him very much and wrote to him as often as she could. She had a picture of him in his sailor suit; it was neatly framed and sat on her bureau.

"Nilda? When are you going down to Jacinto's with my numbers? Tomorrow?"

"Mami, can I have some money for an ice pop?"

"Now where am I gonna get money for an ice pop? You are already a señorita! Not a baby any more! Don't ask me silly questions."

Nilda made a face. Her mother looked at her. "Don't start with those faces like a monkey. Maybe when Papa gets better soon, I can go to work. I spoke to Doña Carmen and Doña Rosa; they are working over in the new defense factoría at 110th Street. Sewing parachutes; piecework, and the pay is good. Bueno. We'll see; maybe I can work something out when you go back to school. It's your papa I hate to leave. I'm afraid, but maybe if he keeps on the same, and does not get worse . . . Thank God he has not gotten any worse!" Pausing, she looked at Nilda. "Nilda, por favor, now will you do as you are told!"

"O.K., O.K. I'm going. Bendición, Mama."

"Dios te bendiga. Now don't forget: 305 straight for ten cents and 382 combination for eighteen. I will light the candles and pray that maybe the numbers come out. You never know and one has to believe. . . ."

Nilda heard her mother's voice trail off as she left the apartment. She walked down into the street, heading towards Don Jacinto's grocery, holding a Spalding ball.

197

She bounced it on the sidewalk. Nilda looked around her; it was hot and deserted in the street. Bored, she watched the way the ball hit the pavement—up! . . . and up! . . . and up!

She seldom saw Petra any more. And now that she had gotten her period, her mother frowned on the games she loved to play: ball, hide-and-go-seek, ringo-leevio-tap-tap-tap, hopscotch—all the games she played with the kids in the street.

"You are too old! A señorita does not behave like that!" her mother would say, or, "Nilda, come away. What are you doing with all those boys?" and "Don't sit with your knees apart. What kind of a way is that for a young lady to sit!" I don't feel all that different, Nilda thought. She hated it when her mother said those things and embarrassed her that way.

There was not much to do and so she looked forward to the new school and next term. Junior high. Wow, she thought. That gave her a real feeling of growing up.

December, 1943

Nilda knelt on the foot rail by the casket and said a few Hail Marys and Our Fathers. Making the sign of the cross, she stood up, closed her eyes, and, bending forward all the way, kissed her stepfather on the lips. His lips felt cold and hard, like the sidewalks she had touched as she played in the wintertime. She opened her eyes, startled by the impact, and looked at the cadaver. Up close, he had a purplish reddish hue, like someone had put dark makeup on him. Nilda checked an impulse to reach out and touch him, realizing that there were many people watching.

The dark somber funeral parlor was crowded with people. There were three chapels, each occupied with a funeral party. Nilda had gone to see each one, and all three were identically decorated. None of the rooms had windows. A pink-and-maroon embossed wallpaper, soiled in spots, was interrupted by the dark brown woodwork. The floor was covered by a threadbare carpet with an Oriental design; throw rugs had been placed here and there to cover the worst areas. Large potted plants were placed at either side of the casket, which was covered and surrounded with floral wreaths.

TO OUR BELOVED FATHER AND HUSBAND
EMILIO RAMÍREZ
FROM HIS BEREAVED WIFE AND CHILDREN
LYDIA, JIMMY, VICTOR,
PAUL, FRANK, AND NILDA

COMRADE AND BROTHER
SINCERE CONDOLENCES TO THE RAMÍREZ FAMILY
FROM ALL OF US AT THE WORKERS CLUB OF 102ND STREET

REST IN PEACE
SINCERELY FROM LEO ORTIZ
AND CONCHA VELEZ AND FAMILY

OUR SINCEREST SYMPATHY
TO THE RAMÍREZ FAMILY
FROM THE NEIGHBORS AT 905 EAST 104 STREET

TO OUR DEAR SISTER AND FAMILY
IN HER HOUR OF NEED
EXPRESSING OUR CONDOLENCES
ROSARIO AND WILLIE JIMÉNEZ
AND CHILDREN ROBERTO AND CLAUDIA

There were all kinds of wreaths; some round, some heart-shaped, large ones, small ones. Nilda inhaled, and the sweet smell of the flowers and stale air made her nauseated. She recalled the overwhelming fragrance in her secret garden, fresh and clean, making her feel cool all over.

Nilda stepped down and stood aside. She looked at her mother who would be the last on line to say good-bye to her stepfather. Aunt Rosario sat with her mother, con-

200

soling her. Willie, her husband, sat apart with Aunt Rosario's two children.

Next to Willie sat Aunt Delia, crying quietly and nodding her head to anyone who spoke to her. Paul walked in; he had been home since yesterday, on special leave from the Naval base in California. Greeting everyone, he sat down next to his mother, taking his place as the oldest son present.

Nilda looked about her. It was quiet and people spoke in whispers. Leo sat off to the side with Doña Concha and her two married sons and their wives. All of Benji's family had come and they huddled together. Benji's father was dressed in his black suit and held his wide-brimmed fedora in his hands. His mother, also dressed in black, had lots of light powder all over her face. They look like they are dressed for a church service, thought Nilda. She looked at Benji and smiled, wishing he could sit with her. As if understanding, he returned Nilda's smile and looked towards his father. He wouldn't let him come over to me, she thought. Doña Tiofila sat in back with her eyes closed, quietly praying and occasionally making the sign of the cross.

Don Jacinto was there with his wife and three of his younger children. Other shopkeepers from the area and most of the neighbors were present. Nilda saw many union officials and members of the local Communist Party Club. She recognized them from the meetings she had attended with her stepfather.

Her stepfather had no living relatives in this country or in Spain. His people had been killed in 1936, in the Spanish Civil War, during a bombing raid which had almost totally annihilated his tiny village on the northern coast of Spain.

Nilda's mother had full intentions of giving her stepfather a proper Catholic funeral even though he had not received extreme unction. A priest had been sent for when it was apparent that her stepfather would not last the night. He had been under an oxygen tent when the priest arrived and began quietly praying and administering the last rites. It seemed the hospital staff had never heard such foul language and blasphemy from any dying patient as that from her stepfather when he awoke and began to yell. He tore down the tent and began attacking the priest. After they had calmed down the patient, the night nurse and attending doctor decided, despite her mother's protests, not to try that again.

Her mother had been upset, but felt that he was really in purgatory now, and that everyone had to pray for his soul. She had faith that someday his soul would be allowed to enter heaven. "I will not make the same mistake I made with my father. I will make sure that Emilio gets a proper burial," she had said.

Nilda waited apprehensively; they all had said their good-byes and it was time for her mother to finish. Then they would close the casket for the last time, go to church for Mass, and finally drive out to the cemetery in Queens.

"Nilda! Nilda!" someone called. It was Aunt Rosario. "You have to stand next to your mother with Frankie and Paul. What is the matter with you?" she said crossly.

Nilda had been trying to avoid this final scene somehow. Even though her stepfather's body had been in the chapel for five days, her mother had insisted that some member of the family always be there. She had kept Nilda home from school, restricting her either to the apartment or the chapel. Nilda had never seen her mother this way, so depressed and easily subject to crying and fits of hysteria. Very often she shouted at Nilda and Frankie, accusing them of bringing on her husband's death. Everyone had tried to console her and reason things out, but she continued to break down several times a day, sometimes refusing to leave the chapel even at closing time.

"Nilda! Here! Are you deaf, muchacha!" Rosario insisted. Nilda walked over to her mother and stood at some distance from her. Rosario grabbed her arm and placed her by her mother. Nilda began to feel unreal. Like a dream, she thought as she walked alongside her mother, who took short uncertain steps, moving slowly. They reached the casket and everything was perfectly still for a moment. Nilda watched as her mother suddenly lunged forward and began to scream. She jumped back in fear. Rosario and Paul grabbed her mother.

Leo came forward, trying to help. "Lydia," Leo said, "calm yourself."

"Mama, please," Paul said gently. "Mama, come on now."

"Ayyy-ay. I don't want to live. What for? What for? For more misery. More hardship. How much longer? God let me die . . . me! Emilio . . . me, I have to die!" her mother sobbed.

"Lydia, mi vida, por favor. Pull yourself together; you have young children. Please, honey," Rosario pleaded.

Her mother turned and looked at Rosario. "Yes . . .

children? Yes. Rosario? Remember? You remember when we were little girls in Ponce? Is that true? Was I a child once? Little Rosario . . . I remember, sometimes. I really do." Nodding her head and rocking gently, her mother began to sing a children's game song in Spanish. "Doña Ana no está aquí, está en su jardín . . . tendiendo las flores . . . y . . ."

Nilda could not control the tears welling up in her eyes, and she shook with fright at the enormous sense of pity she felt for her mother, who seemed like a stranger she hardly recognized.

"I wanna die. Help me. Emilio? Please help me, help me . . . help . . ." her mother began to cry more quietly. They were able to take her away quickly before the men in charge closed the casket.

Everyone began to leave the funeral parlor and head towards the church service.

At St. Cecilia's, the closed casket sat in front of the altar. An organ played, accompanying Father Shea's monotone voice as he said Mass. In English, Father Shea began to speak from the pulpit. "We are gathered here today, on a sad occasion, to pay tribute here today to a fine person. Although of no worldly fame or monumental achievements, he was, nonetheless, important as a father and husband. A simple hardworking person . . ."

Nilda was aware that no matter what Father Shea said, he always spoke in the same flat way. Even in Latin, when he says Mass, he sounds the same, thought Nilda. She remembered her stepfather's last days at home. "Nilda, when I die, don't go around weeping no stupid tears for me. Tell your mama not to give them damn priests no money to bury me. Don't be a sucketa! Be smart, Nilda.

204

Go to school; learn something important, no fairy tales. They mustn't take your mind and use you. Your mama, she is too far gone with that crap. But you, Nilda . . ."

"Emilio Ramírez," Father Shea continued, "was a good Catholic at heart, a believer in the word of Jesus, the Holy Trinity, Father, Son, and the Holy Ghost, the resurrection with life ever after. Amen."

"Using a pregnant woman and a poor Jew to turn people's heads," her stepfather had lectured. "They are a bunch of faggots, Nilda. No wonder they don't live normal lives. Look at that, men with men and women with women, a bunch of hypocrites! Them priests don't believe in birth control; they don't need it!"

"Although," the priest went on somberly, "Emilio Ramírez did not receive extreme unction, his soul is in purgatory and we must pray for its release into heaven. He was a good Catholic at heart. Let us pray. . . ."

"What kinda heaven and hell do they promise us?" She could almost hear him shouting. "Here on earth is heaven and hell, Nilda! Heaven for a few and hell for the rest of us!" Father Shea never even met Papa, she thought, and, looking at the closed casket, half expected her stepfather to jump out and begin to swear at the priest. He'd punch him right in the nose, she said to herself. She put her hand up to her mouth, suppressing a giggle at the thought of her stepfather listening to his eulogy by a priest. He's gonna be furious . . . and she became aware that he would not budge from the casket, that he was really dead. Gone forever. Everyone prayed and Nilda automatically made the sign of the cross and began to pray, feeling sad and tearful.

"Remember, Nilda, no crying? And no praying nonsense! Leave that to the ones that got no sense!" She remembered how he had smiled at her when he had left for the hospital. O.K., Papa. You don't want me to and I won't, she said to herself. Nilda sat there listening to the voices droning on in prayer and looked over at her mother. Her face was covered by a thin black veil and she prayed quietly.

For some time now, Nilda had experienced a feeling of helplessness gnawing at her insides. It began to bother her again; she wished there were something she could do to make things right for everybody. Everything seemed a lot simpler when she was younger, and she thought, Now things are getting too confused. Nilda continued to sit silently while the others prayed. She tried to make some decisions and understand what was going on, making an effort to avoid the feelings that upset her, but things became even more confused and muddled than before.

Mass was finished and everyone filed out to the parked cars. Nilda had never seen so many cars in her life.

"Nilda, come on over here! You ride with your mother and brothers," someone said. She stepped into the large black limousine and sat next to a window. It was early December. Outdoors it was balmy; most of the snow had melted and the streets were wet. As they drove out to Queens, they passed many small houses and trees. It almost feels like spring, Nilda thought.

January, 1944

"That was a mean thing she did, Nilda. Man, she had no right to say them things."

"I know, Sylvia." Nilda nodded her head in agreement. She was walking to school with her best friend. They had met this term in junior high school. It was an all-girls school, grades from seventh to ninth. Every morning they would meet halfway and walk to school. This way they could go through the dark tunnels on Park Avenue together, avoiding trouble and feeling less frightened.

"I'm glad she didn't leave me back," said Nilda. "When I got my report card, I was afraid to look at it or bring it home. I missed a lotta work, you know. I been catching up. I really appreciate your notes, Sylvia. Else, I woulda been up shit's creek."

"It's O.K.," Sylvia smiled. They walked along quickly, hugging their books as they fought the cold wind. Reaching the old school building, they rushed across the schoolyard and went inside. Nilda and Sylvia walked into their homeroom, put their coats away, and sat at their desks. Most of the students were already seated.

The morning bell rang and Mrs. Sheila Fortinash stopped putting things here and there, walked over to her desk, looked at her watch and then at the class. "Good morning, class."

"Good morning, Mrs. Fortinash."

"Your English assignment is on the blackboard." Looking at her watch again, she said, "Start! We will collect yesterday's homework papers now. Mary Gonzales, you may collect them and bring them to my desk."

Mrs. Fortinash had a habit of constantly looking at her watch. It always seems like we are late for something, Nilda thought, feeling uneasy. The new teacher appeared almost like a young girl the first time Nilda saw her; her yellow hair was cut short and straight, with bangs like Buster Brown. It had taken Nilda a while to get used to the teacher who never smiled despite her childlike looks.

"Today," Mrs. Fortinash said, "report cards are due. I hope you all have them here, signed by your parents. Remember what I said about lateness. There is never any excuse for lateness in this class. Mañana, mañana, is all right in another country, but not in America and not in my classroom."

Nilda had brought home her report card, relieved that she had not been left back, although she was just about failing in every subject. She had been out of school for more than two weeks when her stepfather died. A truant officer had been sent to her home, and finally Nilda got back to school. Her mother had seen her report card. "O.K. Nilda, I know you got an excuse," she had said, "but now I want to see these marks changed. You hear?" and signed the report card.

Her first day back in school had been an ordeal. Nilda

209

shuddered, remembering, and put it out of her mind as she waited to take up her report card.

"All right, you may all bring up your report cards now, one by one," Mrs. Fortinash said. Each girl walked up to the teacher's desk, handed her the card, and waited. Mrs. Fortinash would look at the report card, carefully inspecting it, and then, with a nod of her head, would dismiss the student. Nilda watched as Mrs. Fortinash raised her hand and called out, "Carmela!" A small girl who was returning to her seat turned around and looked at the teacher. "Carmela, please come back here and explain, if you will, what this is." Holding up a report card, Mrs. Fortinash gestured to the girl. "What am I supposed to do with this?" Carmela smiled timidly and shrugged her shoulders. "Answer me, please," Mrs. Fortinash insisted. "What is this?"

"That's my mother . . . who signed it."

"Signed it where?"

Pointing, Carmela put her finger on the report card. "There," she said.

"That's not a signature, my dear; that's an X. Can't your mother read or write?"

"No."

"I see," said Mrs. Fortinash. "How about your father?"

"My father don't live with us."

"How about your brothers; do you have any older brothers or sisters?"

Carmela shook her head. "They are all younger."

"How about somebody in the house who can read and write?"

"We got a boarder," Carmela said.

"Is this boarder related to you?" Mrs. Fortinash asked. There was a long pause and the room was silent.

"No," Carmela said. "He is just a boarder."

"Well, I'm going to have to talk to the Vice-Principal because I will not take the responsibility for accepting this. Anybody can make an X and imitate that!" Mrs. Fortinash looked at her wristwatch, shut her eyes, and shook her head. "Incredible," she whispered.

"My mother said that is her mark," Carmela said. "That is how she makes her mark all the time. She signs checks and everything like that." Several girls began to giggle; then everyone laughed.

"Shhh. Stop it, girls! Carmela, you will have to come with me to the office. You can tell them all about it." Carmela stood by and said nothing. "Well, go on. Go on, get to your seat."

Nilda remembered her own note, that first day back at school. Her mother had still been upset after the funeral, so Nilda had written the note herself, and her mother had signed it absentmindedly.

Dear Mrs. Fortinash,

Please excuse my daughter Nilda Ramírez for being absent from school. Her father died and she got lots of things to take care of at home. That is our custom. Thank you.

Very truly yours,
Lydia Ramírez

"What custom is that?" Mrs. Fortinash had asked. "How dare you return to class after almost three weeks

211

and hand me such a note! You just walk in, like it's nothing; perhaps you were away on a picnic!" Nilda had not known what to say or do, so she looked at the floor, avoiding the teacher. "You will just have to come with me to see Mr. Shultz. You people are the limit! No wonder you don't get anywhere or do anything worthwhile with these kinds of customs. People pass away every day—you are not the only ones, you know! That does not mean that one stops meeting responsibilities! Your mother will have to come in and explain that custom and what tribe you belong to!" Nilda felt the blood rushing to her face and the anger surging in her as Mrs. Fortinash went on talking. "Irresponsible, that's what you people are. Then you expect the rest of us here to make it easy for you. Well, you are not the first ones to be allowed into this country. It's bad enough we have to support strangers with our tax dollar; we are not going to put up with . . ." Mrs. Fortinash had turned beet red and was screaming. Nilda had looked up at her and felt herself shaking. "Don't you look at me like that! You should be ashamed!" Nilda thought, Dear God, make her stop! Please make her finish. "You come down with me right now. Follow me," she screamed.

Nilda waited on a bench at the office of Robert Shultz, Vice-Principal. Mr. Shultz opened the door. "Come in, Nilda," he said. She followed him into the office. "What about this note?" he asked. "Can you be more specific and explain what happened?" Mrs. Fortinash stood close by, looked at her watch and tapped her foot. Nilda was unable to answer; I will not cry in front of them, she thought. There was a long pause. "When you said custom," Mr. Shultz said, "did you mean that is the way things go in your family?"

"Yes," Nilda said softly.

"I see," Mr. Shultz said gently. "Go on."

"Yes." Nilda paused. "My mother was sick and so I had to do a lot of things and help. My older brothers, they are away in the service and so . . ." She hesitated, shrugged, and stopped talking.

"Well, I'll tell you what, Nilda. Could you manage to have your mother write another note, explaining a little better what happened?" Mr. Shultz paused. "O.K.?"

"Yes," Nilda said, "I'll tell her."

"That's all. Thank you. You can go back to class now."

Her mother had written a note, as requested, and had not been asked to come to school after all.

Now, Nilda watched Mrs. Fortinash and said to herself, "I hate her worse than Miss Langhorn almost." She felt a sense of relief when the bell rang sharply, and she could go on to her Spanish class.

A petite woman with silver hair, neatly done up in a permanent wave, greeted the class. "Buenos días, alumnas," she said in a thick American accent.

"Buenos días, Señorita Reilly."

"Today we are going to review chapters seven and eight in our Spanish grammar book. Turn to page forty-eight, girls." She spoke to the class in English most of the time. When she did speak Spanish, Miss Maureen Reilly's American accent was so thick that Nilda had a hard time understanding what she said. Most of the time the teacher spoke about her trips to the different Spanish-speaking countries around the world. Her favorite country was Spain, and today she spoke in English about Spain. "Now, of course, with this terrible war, there is no traveling. But I just can't wait for the war to end; I must go back to Spain and just listen to the way they speak. There they speak Castilian, the real Spanish, and I am determined, girls, that that is what we shall learn and speak in my class; nothing but the best! None of that dialect spoken here. If only you could hear yourselves chat chat chat! Like a bunch of Chinamen!" Pausing, she picked up her hands and brought them together, clasping her bosom. "Spanish is a language of drama . . . inspiration . . . love. Not to be slaughtered, young ladies, as some of you do to it!" As she went on talking, the girls looked at each other and giggled.

"She's got a boyfriend in Spain," someone whispered.

"She got the hots!" one of them almost shouted, and everyone began to laugh.

"Shhh," Miss Reilly said, annoyed. Very often she spent the entire lesson reminiscing about her trips to Europe and South America. Spain, however, was her very favorite. ". . . those wonderful bullfights. They are called corridas de toros. And the matadors. It is magnificent to see the pageantry and excitement that goes into a bullfight. The people cheering and the music playing. And the brave bulls. Olé! Olé! It is the culture, dear girls, the culture . . ."

Someone nudged Nilda; it was Sylvia. "Look, Nilda," she whispered, and pointed to the blackboard. Someone

214

had written something dirty in Spanish between the lines of the homework assignment: *Miss Reilly is in love with a Spanish matador who fucks with a Castilian accent!*

Nilda put her head on her desk to keep from bursting out in laughter. Very often one of the students would write profanities in Spanish on the blackboard, mostly about Miss Reilly. She often wondered if Miss Reilly knew what these dirty words meant. Maybe, Nilda said to herself, almost in disbelief, she don't really know that they are words.

Everyone began to laugh and point at the blackboard. "Shhh. Stop being silly," Miss Reilly said, and looked at the blackboard. She erased what was written in Spanish. "That's enough nonsense, girls. Always writing silly things, wasting your time. Now we must get to work. We will read and, remember, I want the correct accent on the words. Edna, read from paragraph one in section Roman numeral twelve. Accent! Remember, proper enunciation, diction . . ."

Nilda watched as Edna got up to read, straining to get the accent and trying to lisp in the right places. Edna was born in Puerto Rico and found it very difficult to speak Spanish with the accent Miss Reilly required. Nilda knew the girl was nervous because the teacher had given her a low mark on her report card. Edna read the Spanish newspapers and very often helped the other students with grammar, but she could not manage to imitate Miss Reilly's Castilian accent.

Edna finished reading and Miss Reilly smiled. "Very well, Edna, you are doing a little better. However, you must practice and stop speaking that dialect you speak at home; it is not helping you."

Nilda waited for the bell to ring. Only one more class, math, she thought, and then lunch.

"We mustn't forget," the teacher continued, "what the Spanish tradition is and means. A love of language . . . and pride. Yes, pride; those people have their pride."

February, 1944

"What's the name of your brother Frankie's club again?" asked Sylvia.

"The Lightnings. They used to be the Junior Lightnings, two clubs, but then Paul and some of the older guys went to the service, so now the younger guys took over the club. You know, they are like in charge, only one club, no more juniors."

"Well," Sylvia went on, "I heard that there is going to be a rumble between them, the Lightnings, and the others, the Barons."

"Really?" asked Nilda. "Where did you hear that?"

"Well, on my block lives a member of the Barons and he was bragging that they are going to fight the Lightnings and beat them. And that they got it in for Indio and Hector."

"When is this gonna be?"

"That I don't know. But soon," answered Sylvia. "Is your brother Frankie in charge of that gang?"

"No, Indio is. But Frankie took my brother Paul's place and he used to be Vice-President, but Frankie is too young so they made him like assistant something. But he is something, that I know." Nilda looked at Sylvia

217

and wondered if she liked her brother Frankie. She had never spoken to Nilda about it, but Nilda could tell from the way she acted in front of Frankie. She gets so nervous and looks so embarrassed every time she sees Frankie, thought Nilda. "Why are you always asking me about Frankie?" she asked, and smiled at Sylvia.

"I just asked about his club, that's all," Sylvia said.

"Do you like him?"

Sylvia stopped walking and looked at Nilda with surprise.

"It's all right. I don't care. Honest." Sylvia looked upset. Quickly Nilda said, "Look, if you like him, just say so. Really, honest, I won't say nothing to nobody. I promise."

"He doesn't even know I'm alive," said Sylvia.

"Maybe he does; how do you know?"

"He never even mentions me, I bet." Pausing, Sylvia asked, "Did he ever?"

"Well," Nilda answered, "he just never knew you liked him. Maybe if he knew about it, he could say something to you."

"Nilda!" Sylvia shouted. "You promised!"

"I didn't say nothing. I'm just telling you what I think. Honest, Sylvia, I won't say a word."

"Nilda, you better not . . . I'll die! I swear to you, really; I don't want him to know I like him. I mean it. If you say something, I'll never talk to you again, cross my heart and hope to die!"

"You don't have to worry," Nilda said. "I swear I won't. I promise. O.K.?" There was a long pause and both girls walked along silently. "Here we are," Nilda said. Sylvia looked at Nilda and they both smiled. "If Frankie says something, I will let you know."

"Nilda!" Sylvia screamed.

"If he says something! I won't say nothing. I said I promised. But just if he says something. O.K.?"

Sylvia giggled, "O.K." In a more sober tone she said, "He probably already got a girl."

"Uh uh, he don't," Nilda said emphatically. "That I surely know." Sylvia smiled at her, looking relieved. "Hey?" Nilda asked. "Why don't you come over tomorrow, if your mother lets you, and we can do our homework together?"

"I'll ask her, but she don't want me to walk home alone at night, when it gets dark, you know," Sylvia said.

"That's all right!" Nilda smiled and glanced at Sylvia knowingly. "Frankie can walk you back, and I can come along if you like."

"You think so?" Sylvia's eyes widened.

"Sure," Nilda said. "My mother will probably ask him to escort you and let me go too. I'll talk to my mother tonight, just in case you can come to my house tomorrow."

"Well." Sylvia bit her bottom lip and shut her eyes. "Oh, maybe I better not, Nilda," she said apprehensively.

"Why not? We'll just walk you to your stoop, that's all. No harm in that."

"O.K.," Sylvia nodded and began to walk away quietly, "I'll let you know by tomorrow." She called out, "See you."

"See you," Nilda yelled, almost giggling aloud. Uh huh, she said to herself, I just knew she liked him and I was right. Pleased with herself, she felt quite clever. She liked Sylvia; they were close friends. She never saw Petra any more, just Benji, now and then. In fact, the only one she saw all the time was Sylvia. Nilda began to think about Frankie: ever since her stepfather had died, they had gotten along much better and very seldom fought. She could never feel about Frankie the way she felt about Paul. She wrote to Paul and saved all the letters he wrote to her. She missed him very much. Not like Frankie, she thought. He's such a terrible pest; I wonder why Sylvia likes him?

Frankie walked alongside the two girls glumly. He had both hands in the pockets of his brand-new club jacket. It was black with bright gold trimming and stitching. His name was stitched on the front, FRANKIE. On the back, the word LIGHTNINGS was stitched, as well as the symbol for lightning in bright gold felt.

Nilda and Sylvia walked along; all three were silent. Frankie had refused to walk the girls, but Nilda's mother had insisted, losing her temper and threatening him. "Imagine!" her mother had shouted at Frankie. "Giving your mother such nonsense. At your age, your brothers would not dare to talk to me in that tone. And I just gave you some money for that club jacket. You must think I play all day at the factoría; caramba, sweating like an animal on that machine. Mira, Frankie, in Puerto Rico,

220

you know what a boy who is going to be sixteen is? A macho! Yes, and taking care of a whole family, not running around like everything is a party. They don't go to school and have your privileges. You get too smart with me, and you can come back and stay in all evening and not go to that meeting at all!"

Frankie was told to take Sylvia to her building and then bring Nilda back to the corner of their street. He had been furious with Nilda. "Why do you have to come?" he had protested. "Then I have to walk you all the way back, man, and really be late!"

"Just let me off at the corner," Nilda had insisted, and her mother, who was annoyed at Frankie, had let her go along as well.

As they walked, Sylvia said timidly, "Frankie, you don't have to take me, you know. I'll go home alone, really. Go on to your meeting."

"It's all right, Sylvia," he said. "Honest, I don't mind walking you; it's big-mouth here." Sylvia looked the other way, embarrassed. "Nilda," he said, annoyed, "you are going to make me real late to my meeting."

"You don't have to walk me back home, you know," Nilda said. "Just forget it; I'll get back by myself. Big deal!"

"Yeah," Frankie said, "then tell Mama and I get it. Tattletale!"

"I'm not gonna say nothing, Frankie!" Nilda yelled.

There was a long pause and Frankie stopped, then continued to walk a few paces ahead of them. Nilda stuck out her tongue and made a face at him.

221

"Honestly, Nilda, you are making it worse," Sylvia whispered.

Boy, some friend she is; thanks a lot! Nilda said to herself. They heard a shrill whistle.

"Hey man, Frankie!" someone shouted. Nilda turned and saw a tall boy, wearing the same kind of jacket that Frankie had, running towards them. Out of breath and wide-eyed, he said, "Frankie, man, you better split, split fast. Those motherfucker Barons, they raided us, down the basement in the clubhouse. They got Indio and Charley. They stomped the shit out of them. They had knives, sticks, and chains. Man, they dragged Mateo out and we don't know if he's alive!"

"When?" Frankie asked.

"Just before, during the meeting. We were planning the rumble and they attacked us—just like those Japs, man—sneaky, behind our backs. Maricones! They ain't no Americans, man; they're Japs!"

Nilda watched as the tall boy spoke. He had the name HECTOR stitched on the front of his jacket. His light brown skin was bright and flushed and his hair was mussed; some blood trickled down his nose and the right side of his mouth.

"A lot of us were able to get out. I fought a few of them and ducked down an alley. You was lucky you wasn't there."

"I got stuck; I had to walk my sister and her friend. Oh man, Hector, shit. I wish I coulda been there. I woulda stomped on their asses."

Hector had managed to stand inside the doorway of a small dry-goods shop that was closed. "Well, just split now, man," he said. "The Barons are after us and that bastard Pícalo got his knife. I don't know what they did to Mateo or where they took him. Man, I hope he is all right." With a worried look, Hector stretched and looked up and down the dark street. "But listen, the cops are after us too. Look, Frankie, get off the streets. You better walk back through the roofs and alleys, man. Get your ass home and keep cool; don't wear the jacket for a while. I'm cutting, man. See you, Frankie," and he walked away.

Nilda and Sylvia looked at each other and then at Frankie, who stood there confused. "Wait," he called out. "Man, wait, I'll go with you." Turning to the two girls, he said, "Look, I better cut."

"All right," Nilda interrupted him. "Go ahead, Frankie, split. We'll be O.K. I won't say nothing to Mama. Honest, go on!"

"You better go, Frankie," Sylvia said.

Frankie ran towards Hector and they both disappeared into a building.

"I told you, Nilda. Remember about the rumble?" Sylvia said.

"Maybe I should have told my brother," Nilda said, feeling miserable. "I'll walk you to your corner; we are almost there."

The two girls walked on quietly. "Here we are. Do you want to come up, Nilda? My father could take you back."

"No thanks, I better not. Else my mother would ask about Frankie. It's O.K."

"I'll see you tomorrow," Sylvia said.

223

"Good-bye. Please don't say nothing to nobody, or Frankie will think it's me who snitched. O.K.?"

"I won't. I won't say a word," Sylvia said, and pausing, she asked, "Nilda? Please tell me what happens."

"Of course," Nilda said. "So long." She started back down the avenue, heading for home.

"Nilda!" She heard someone calling her name and stopped to see who it was. It was Chucho, Benji's brother. "Hi, Nilda. What are you doing here?"

"Oh, hi, Chucho. I was walking my friend home."

"Wait, wait a minute. You going back home now?" he asked.

"Yes."

"O.K. Manuel is coming right down. We went to our aunt's house; you know Estelle, my mother's sister. We'll walk you back, Nilda."

"Sure," she said. "Will he be long? My mother is expecting me back right away."

"No, he'll be right back. As a matter of fact, we were outside in the street when Manuel remembered he forgot something and went back up." Chucho smiled. "Look, there he is. See?" and he pointed to a young boy who hurried towards them. He was younger than Chucho but almost the same height.

"Hi, Nilda. How are you?"

"Fine."

"Manuel, we'll take Nilda home; it will only be a minute out of our way."

"Sure, good," Manuel said.

The three young people walked silently for a while. It

224

was windy and cold out; they all walked quickly, trying to stay warm.

"Nilda," Chucho said, "we hardly see you any more. You don't come to services very often now, do you?" He added, "You are missed."

Oh, man, thought Nilda, annoyed. They are gonna start that business again. "Well, I been busy, you know. Now that Mami is working every day, I have to help out a lot," she said.

"This weekend, Nilda, try to come," Chucho said. "It is something special. We will have our meeting right on the corner of 116th Street and Lexington Avenue. You know, right by the subway station? The musicians will play and we will set up a platform and amplifiers. We would like you to come and be with us, Nilda."

"I'll try," she said timidly. She hated those street meetings and she knew Benji hated them. She remembered the last time she had been out in the street with them and how embarrassed she had been; she had wanted to cry. Everyone pointed and looked at you, she thought. The kids who recognized her had made fun of her, shouting remarks and making faces. She recalled how she had tried to leave but couldn't, because her group had been right in the middle where everyone could see them.

"Have you been reading the Bible we gave you and the word of Jesus?" Chucho asked.

"Yes," she said. I wish he'd stop preaching all the time, Nilda said to herself. Chucho was the most religious and the oldest of Benji's brothers.

Nilda heard a siren and saw a police car speeding

225

down the avenue. It passed them, stopped abruptly, and backed up. A police officer yelled out of the car window. "Hey, you! Wait a minute!" He stepped out of the car and ran across the avenue towards Nilda and the two boys. As he approached them, the patrol car made a U-turn and stopped in front of them. "Where you going?" the policeman asked. "What the hell are you doing hanging around the streets at night?"

Nilda, for a moment, could not believe that he was talking to them. Shocked and frightened, she looked at the large policeman as he spoke to Chucho. "Where do you live?" the policeman asked, and looked angrily at Chucho and Manuel, a nightstick grasped in his hand. As Chucho answered, the other policeman got out of the car and walked towards them. "That's quite a few blocks from here. What the hell are you doing way up here, God damn it!" the first cop said.

"We went to visit our aunt who lives two blocks up," Manuel answered.

"Shut your ass. I'm talking to him," he said, angrily pointing to Chucho.

"Yes, that is right, officer," Chucho said. "We just came to visit my aunt, that's all."

"How old are you?"

"Sixteen."

"And you?" the cop asked Manuel.

"Fourteen."

"Who is this girl?"

"She's a friend and we are walking her home," Chucho said.

The two policemen stared at the boys for a while. Then

226

the first policeman asked, "Where's the rest of you guys?"

Chucho looked, bewildered, at Manuel, who shook his head and shrugged his shoulders.

"Come on, cut the shit. We know all about the rumble between the Lightnings and the Barons." Nilda felt her insides begin to sink.

"We do not know, sir, who they are. We do not belong to any gangs," Chucho said.

Nilda did not know when or how it happened, but the first policeman held Chucho by the collar and up against the side of the building. "Look!" he shouted into Chucho's face. "Don't give me any shit, spick. I'm tired of this trouble. Now, either you tell me where you punks are, and quit lying, or I'm gonna smash your face."

"Officer, we don't know!" interrupted Manuel. He rushed to his brother, shouting, "We are of the Pentecostal faith. We do not believe . . ."

The policeman released his grip and let go of Chucho. He picked up his nightstick and swung hard at Manuel. Nilda heard a thud and saw blood coming down the side of Manuel's face as he reeled over.

"Stop! Stop!" Chucho shouted. "He's only a kid. Please, please." The policeman kept swinging his nightstick at Manuel.

"Hey, leave me alone. Stop, hey!" Manuel cried out, trying to duck the blows of the nightstick.

The second policeman leaped towards the first policeman and grabbed the nightstick. "Ned! Take it easy, for God's sake, Ned!" he shouted. "Hold it! Christ! Come on, hold it now."

"Manuel! Manuel!" Chucho yelled and grabbed his

227

brother, who was crying and wiping his face. His eyes, nose, mouth, and hair were full of blood. Manuel coughed and cried, clinging to Chucho.

The policeman had stopped using his nightstick and both men stood by, motionless, watching the two boys. Nilda had heard loud screams; only now, as she cried quietly, feeling the hoarseness in her throat, did she realize that it was she who had been screaming.

People started to appear; windows opened and some cars stopped to see what was going on. They gathered by the two boys and the policemen, asking questions. "What's happening? Look at that boy! He is bleeding." "Qué pasa aquí?" "Must be a fight. Officer? What happened?" "Look at those young kids in trouble."

"All right. Keep moving. Get outta here. Break it up," the policemen shouted at the onlookers. "O.K. now, we said beat it."

The policemen went up to the two boys. Manuel jumped back and whimpered. He clung to Chucho, who held him and wiped the wounds with a white handkerchief. "My brother is hurt," he said. "We need a doctor. Look," and he stepped back as if to show them Manuel. Manuel continued to cry, burying his face in Chucho's chest. Both policemen looked at each other but said nothing. Chucho continued to speak. "We are members of the Pentecostal Church on Lexington Avenue and 102nd Street, La Roca de San Sebastián. We do not believe in violence. Please," he pleaded, "take us to the hospital; my brother is hurt."

Nilda watched Manuel, who cried in pain, "Ay, man,

228

. . . qué dolor . . . it hurts, Chucho . . . it hurts too much . . . help me." Some of the blood was drying and Manuel's face began to swell and puff up. The wind blew his soft dark hair, which was covered with red blotches.

"All right, we'll drive you down to the emergency room at Flower Fifth, but next time stay off the streets or it will be worse. Now, we won't press charges, but we don't want any crap from you. O.K.?" the first policeman said.

"Please, sir!" Chucho said. "Just take us to a hospital. We don't want no trouble."

The second policeman looked at Nilda. "You get back home; a young girl like you should be off the streets. Where do you live?" he asked.

Nilda stared at him. "Not far; I can walk. It's only down a few blocks, that's all."

"All right, now get the hell off the streets and right home before we take you in."

"Yes," she said, frightened, "I'll go right home."

The policemen went to the patrol car and opened the back door. "Get in," the second policeman said, and looked at the brothers. "Go on, get in back; we'll drive you down to the hospital."

Nilda watched as Chucho almost carried Manuel to the back of the patrol car. Manuel breathed heavily and couldn't stop crying. "Don't worry, Manuel, we're going to the emergency room, man, to the hospital; hold on." The two boys disappeared into the car.

"Shit, Ned!" the second policeman said. "You oughta watch that temper."

229

"Bunch of bastards anyway. Spick got what he deserved," the first policeman said.

Most of the people had left, but a few still remained. "Hey, girlie," a man asked, "what happened? Are they friends of yours? Did they have a fight or something?"

Nilda looked at the man. "No," she said.

Several other persons gathered around her. "Was that kid shot?" "Was there a holdup? Hey, kid, what happened?" "Mira, nena, qué pasó?" Nilda watched the patrol car as it sped downtown and out of sight, and began to walk away, heading home. "Hey, kid!" someone called out to her. She quickened her pace, not looking back, and started to run until the voices faded and she couldn't hear anyone. She turned once to make sure that there was no one around to ask her anything, and stopped running.

As she walked briskly, she felt the blood flowing back into her limbs and had a sense of herself once more. Her legs felt ice cold, and she shivered. Reaching down, she touched her long wool stockings and realized they were wet; her panties were wet. Did I pee? she asked herself. Oh, man, I don't remember peeing, she thought, and reached down, touching her wet stockings. Then putting her hand to her nose, she inhaled. It was cold and she couldn't tell if it really smelled like urine. What else could it be? she reasoned, and a feeling of embarrassment and helplessness overcame her. Nilda began to cry again. What shall I tell Mama? And what about Frankie? Where is he? Mama will know he didn't walk me, and Benji's family will know. They will tell Mama anyway, she thought, feeling wretched. This was all my stupid idea to go and walk Sylvia, she thought, angry with herself. It was dark out and each time she saw someone, she prayed silently that it be no one she knew. Let me make it home, God, please, to my building, then I'll think of something. Nilda reached her stoop and hurried inside to the warm hallway, and over to the stairway.

"Psst, psst." Nilda jumped back in fear. "Nilda?" She heard a whisper. "Is it you?" She recognized Frankie's voice. "Behind the stairs; over here." Nilda followed the voice and found herself standing in the dark next to Frankie, behind the stairway. "Listen, Nilda, when we get upstairs, tell Mama I walked you; act natural. O.K.?" He paused. "What took you so long anyway? I been waiting here forever." He waited for an answer. "What's the matter with you?" he asked. Nilda opened her mouth and began to cry. "Hey, shh," he said. "What the hell is the matter, Nilda? You hurt, man?"

"Frankie," Nilda said, trying not to sob, "the cops, they beat up Manuel. You know, one of Benji's brothers."

"What?" Frankie said in disbelief. "Him? But why? Them people never do nothing."

"They were looking for the Lightnings and the Barons and they thought that they were them."

"Who was them?" Frankie asked. "Nilda, I don't know what you are talking about."

"Chucho and Manuel. I met them and they were walking me home." She began to cry again.

"Come on, Nilda," Frankie said, "tell me; what happened?"

"We were just walking, and a police car came and a policeman started to ask them about your club and the Barons, and Chucho couldn't answer, and then Manuel tried to talk, and then the cop hit him with the nightstick. Oh, it was horrible."

"Nilda, please stop it. Tell me what happened."

"He was bleeding and crying and that cop kept beating him with his nightstick and—"

"Who?" interrupted Frankie.

"Manuel! I'm telling you!" she snapped.

"Shhh. O.K., O.K. Go on."

"They took them to the hospital."

"Who took who to the hospital?"

"The cops, they finally took Chucho and Manuel to the hospital. Over to Flower Fifth emergency in their car," she said.

"Was Manuel badly hurt?"

"He was full of blood and his face was swollen and yes . . . he looked awful, Frankie. . . . He was crying and oh . . . it was just . . ."

"O.K., now take it easy. Calm down, Nilda. Did they take your name?"

"No, they just told me to get off the streets and go home. I split fast as I could," she said, aware once again of her wet stockings and feeling embarrassed. She hoped, at that moment, that Frankie could not smell anything.

"Good. Well, they don't know who you are. They didn't ask you nothing else? Are you sure, Nilda?"

"Yes, I'm sure. They only asked who I was and Chucho said a friend. That's all."

"Well, we gotta figure out a way not to tell Mama."

"How can we? Benji's family will tell her. I'm sure of that."

"Maybe," Frankie said, "but even if they do, they don't know every detail."

"I don't know, Frankie," Nilda said, shaking her head. "We better tell what . . ."

"Just let me think, Nilda, and do what I say." They stood silently for a while; then Frankie spoke. "Listen, we will tell Mama that I left you just for a moment and asked you to wait, but you was in a hurry to get back and do your homework. So, you left and met Chucho and Manuel, and then I went looking for you and found you after the cops left."

"First of all, I did my homework with Sylvia. Remember? Second, why did the cops hit Manuel and Chucho? She's gonna ask; you know Mama."

"All right, forget the homework. You don't have to say too much. Let me talk. O.K.?" Nilda looked at Frankie, making a gesture of annoyance, and turned her head. "Look, Nilda. Will you let me talk?"

"Suit yourself," she said, shrugging her shoulders.

"Maybe Mama won't ask anything. Go straight to your room and stay there tonight. O.K.?"

Nilda thought, I better wash my stockings and panties; that's what I better do. But she remained silent and followed Frankie up the steps and into their apartment.

Aunt Delia sat in the living room reading her paper. "Listen, Nilda?" she called out. "Come over here; I have something to show you, something important. Look, see what happened to a fourteen-year-old girl? She got attacked."

Nilda nodded her head. Oh damn, she thought, there she goes yelling. I hope Mama doesn't hear. She raised her hand, gesturing to Aunt Delia to wait.

"What? Nilda? No, listen, it's very important. Here in the paper, look at the picture! You better listen for your own good." Nilda walked quickly to her room, ignoring the old woman, anxious to get out of her wet stockings and underwear.

Once inside her room, she smelled the urine and began to undress rapidly, fearful that her mother might come in and see her. She put on her robe, went to the bathroom, and filled up the washbasin, dumping in her wet things, and began to scrub them with soap. As she washed her things she remembered the two brothers, and especially Manuel's crying and holding on to Chucho. Nilda began to cry again. Someone ought to tell Benji's parents about what had happened. Maybe they don't know, she thought. What if something worse happens to them? Nilda stood motionless; for the first time since she had left the two brothers, she worried about them. I have to tell Frankie, she said to herself, that we gotta tell Benji's family. They are my friends; they gotta know what happened to Manuel and Chucho . . . they gotta! She hung everything up to dry and carefully opened the bathroom door. Quietly she went to Frankie's room. "Frankie?" she whispered.

"Nilda? Mama's in her room; she's going to sleep. She told me that she gotta get up very early to work tomorrow, before us, and that we can make breakfast ourselves. What luck, man! Whew!"

"Frankie, we gotta tell Benji's family."

"What do you mean?"

"Maybe they don't know about it; we gotta . . . at least, to see if they know Manuel is hurt, and what happened to Chucho and Manuel. . . . It's only that maybe—"

"They probably know, man," Frankie interrupted. "Mind your own business!"

"What do you mean, Frankie? It is my business. I was there, right?"

"Yeah, but they didn't say nothing to you or bother you, so why do you have to get mixed up?"

"Frankie, I gotta tell Benji's family; you shoulda seen Manuel . . ." Nilda paused. "They are my friends, Frankie; we can just tell them what happened . . . and Mama will understand. . . ."

"No!" he snapped. "Why do you wanna be a big shot? Big-mouth, why don't you leave things right? Like they are."

Nilda stood up angrily. "You are so stupid, Frankie. They might just be hurt . . . and . . . they don't know . . . and . . ."

"They are probably home already, sleeping, and you are gonna bother them." Swiftly, Nilda left the room. Frankie followed her. "Wait a minute," he called. She continued to walk to her mother's room and Frankie reached out, grabbed her arm, and pinned her against the wall. "Lay off, Nilda," he said. "You are gonna get me in trouble!"

Nilda stared at Frankie for a while and neither of them spoke. "Let go, Frankie," Nilda said in a very quiet voice. "Let me go."

Frankie released his grip. "Troublemaker, blabbermouth," he said, and walked away.

235

Nilda went to her mother's bedroom. "Mama?" she said. "Mama?"

Her mother was lying in bed; she turned the lights on and looked at Nilda. "What is it?" her mother asked. "You been crying? What happened, chica?"

"Mama . . . something awful . . . Mami . . . just something awful. . . ."

June, 1944

Nilda looked out of her bedroom window; the clothes-lines were full of wash. The clean laundry hung limply, almost motionless; there was not a breeze. It was hot, and the sheets on her bed were wet and sticky with perspiration. Nilda had slept late; today was Saturday. Yawning, she stretched out her arms and thought about taking a cold shower. Instead, she continued to sit, looking out at a patch of bright blue sky just above the rooftop. A radio was playing music: the sound came from another apartment and traveled up the alleyway. "Say, it's only a paper moon, Shining over a cardboard sea, But it wouldn't be make-believe, If you believed in me. Without your love . . . It's a Barnum and Bailey world . . ."

"Umm . . . ummmm . . . um . . . mmmmm. . . ." Nilda began to hum along with the chorus as they continued to sing. The music stopped and she heard the disc jockey announcing a commercial. She put on her bathrobe and went into the kitchen, looking for her mother. "Mama! Mama!" she called out, and then remembered her mother was working half-day at the defense factory today. Frankie was working at the dry-cleaning store, delivering. Nilda went to look for Aunt Delia, but her room was empty.

237

Probably gone shopping, she said to herself. She was all alone in the apartment.

She went to the bathroom and dressed. Going back to the kitchen, Nilda started to make her own breakfast, singing, ". . . a paper moon, Shining over a cardboard sea, But it wouldn't be make-believe . . ." She began to think about camp. That was long ago, she thought, almost like make-believe. She wondered if she could ever go back to Bard Manor. Her mother had spoken to the Children's Aid Society about it this summer and had been informed that Bard Manor Camp for Girls had been shut down for the duration of the war. This year they had decided that they would do something for the servicemen and had discontinued the camp for girls.

It had been difficult for Nilda to hide her disappointment. Her mother had tried to cheer her up. "Listen, Nilda, I'll see if they got another nice camp for you to go to? Yes?"

"There's no other camp like that one, Mama; I just know it," she had replied.

"Let it go, then. You are a señorita now, and you must help me here at home. Anyway, it is better this way; maybe when I make the trip to see Jimmy in Lexington, Kentucky, you can come with me. How's that? I'm saving enough, and perhaps we can go together. Maybe that lawyer won't charge too much. Dios mío, in this country you cannot do nothing without a lawyer. We'll see," her mother had tried to console Nilda.

She began to eat her breakfast without much appetite; beads of perspiration gathered on her face. Maybe I can go back there when I'm grown up, she thought. And she began to see herself going back to Bard Manor. Nilda saw herself all dressed up in an outfit just like the one she had recently seen a starlet wearing in a war movie. A group of little girls, dressed in pink jumpsuits, were standing all around Nilda. I'll tell them what it was like there when I was a kid, she said to herself, and I'll take them to my secret garden. After all, I was the first to discover it. She saw herself walking down the familiar trail into the woods, and realized that she could not be dressed that way, with high heels and a long gown. Oh well, I'll wear something else . . . and she continued to drift, selecting the right outfit for her trip back to camp, when she heard a knocking. There was a heavy pounding on the door; Nilda jumped up and ran to the front door. "Who's there?"

"It's me—Benji!"

Opening the door, she said, "Benji? Come in."

"Man, Nilda, where was you? I been knocking forever."

"I was in the kitchen eating. Come on inside," she said.

"Jacinto sent me," he said, following Nilda to the kitchen.

"Jacinto? Why, Benji?"

"You better go and get your Aunt Delia; she's causing such a commotion. Man, she gave Jacinto a hard time. So he told me to get your mother to come and get your aunt and bring her upstairs."

"What happened?" asked Nilda.

"I don't know the whole thing. I just heard her screaming when I walked in to buy something for my mother. And she was cursing out Jacinto. She left in a huff. And he told me to go up and get somebody."

"What was she hollering about?" asked Nilda.

"Something about the numbers. You know, she said like he better take her bet because she been doing business there for a long time."

Nilda reached into a cabinet and grabbed a key. "O.K., Benji. Let's go."

On the window of Jacinto's grocery was a large white sign, and printed in bold black letters were the words:

THIS IS A RAIDED PREMISES
ENTER AT YOUR OWN RISK
Order of Police Dept.
NYC Borough of Manh.

Nilda saw the sign and remembered that Jacinto had been caught before, but this time her mother had said they were really after him and had threatened to close his bodega.

Jacinto was behind a counter, waiting on a customer. He looked up and saw her. "Nilda? Where's your mother?"

"She's working today."

"And Frankie?" he asked.

"He's working at Mr. Fox's."

"Listen, you know your aunt is nuts. She's causing me too much trouble," Jacinto said, shaking his head. "She comes in here with her list of numbers. Can you imagine? With that big sign outside!" Leaving the store, Jacinto went outside and pointed to the sign. Nilda followed him and listened as he continued to speak. "If they catch me at the bolita, they close me up! They gave me already fifty dollars' fine. I'm not a millionaire. They are gonna be after me. They are watching me." Jacinto took out a handkerchief and wiped his face. "She begins to holler at me. Threatening me. If I don't take her bet, she's gonna report me to the police! Can you imagine? Caramba, she's cuckoo, I tell her. It's the police that stop me in the first place. She says she knows her rights, calls me all kinds dirty names. I'm ashamed to hear such language; I gotta throw her out. So she leaves and threatens me! You better take her home, upstairs, keep her out of mischief."

"Where is she, Don Jacinto?" Nilda asked.

"I don't know. She just left in a big hurry, angry with me. I tell you . . ." he said, shaking his head.

"I'll go see if I can find her and bring her home," Nilda said. "My mother will be coming home soon anyway; she's only working till lunchtime."

"Hey, Nilda! Look, over there!" Benji said, and pointed to the corner.

Nilda saw Aunt Delia returning with two policemen. She could see Aunt Delia was busy talking and waving her arms. The policemen nodded their heads, looking confused as the old woman spoke excitedly in Spanish.

"Oh my God!" Jacinto gasped, and ran back into the store.

Nilda waited in front of the store and watched as the two policemen trailed behind the old woman. Aunt Delia came up to Nilda. "Nilda, I'm glad you are here. You are my witness to this ungrateful man in there. Explain, in English, to these two nice young policemen how long I been doing business here in this place. Go ahead!"

"Titi, come on upstairs. What are you doing?" Nilda yelled in her ear.

"Never mind," Aunt Delia said, and continued in Spanish. "Him; arrest him. You know how long I been playing the numbers here? Ten years! And now he don't want to take my business."

"What's going on here?" asked a policeman, looking at Jacinto. "What is this lady's complaint?" Jacinto stood wide-eyed and mute, unable to speak.

"Wait, look at this," said Aunt Delia, and turning away, hiding her bosom, she quickly unbuttoned her collar and reached inside her dress. She pulled out a long silver chain that hung around her neck. Attached to the end of the chain was a small black leather change purse; opening it, she carefully removed a long strip of paper with numbers listed on it. Holding up the list of numbers, she said to the policemen, "Here, see! My list, and he won't place my bet. That's some nerve. Since when? Eh? My money has always been good. I never play for credit." The policemen looked at the list and then at each other with complete disbelief. Aunt Delia handed one of them the list and, making an effort to speak in English, said "Play . . . el numbers . . . you do . . . him. Jacinto to play the bolita . . . me now! Sona man bitch!" she yelled. Nilda had never heard Aunt Delia speak so much English to anyone.

There was a complete silence. Nilda watched the policeman who held the list in his hand turn deep red. He looked at his partner and a smile of embarrassment crossed his face. The other policeman raised his hand and, covering his forehead, tried not to laugh out loud.

"All right now," the policeman holding the list asked, "what the hell is this all about?"

242

"She's crazy, officer," answered Jacinto. "She wants me to take her bet. I cannot do it. I don't take bets no more. You know that. I'm finished with all that."

Aunt Delia stood by, watching the men as they spoke, nodding her head emphatically. "Sí, sí," she said.

"Where does she live?" asked a policeman.

"Around the corner. This girl is her niece," Jacinto said, pointing to Nilda.

"Take your aunt home. And tell her she's not supposed to be doing something illegal. That she might get into trouble. And that she should keep out of mischief." Trying not to smile, the policeman gave the list of numbers back to Aunt Delia. Shaking his head and holding up his index finger, he said to her, "Mother, go home. Shame, shame, you don't do that. Now that is against the law."

"What? What? What did he say?" Aunt Delia asked, cupping her ear with her hand. Nilda went over and translated what the policeman had said to the old woman.

Aunt Delia listened attentively, sucking in her gums. She nodded her head and looked at the policemen and at Jacinto. Raising her hand and making a fist, Aunt Delia extended her middle finger at Jacinto and shouted, "Leprosy on your tongue," and turning to the policemen, she said, "You don't know how to enforce the law, only how to take away my rights. I know my rights; I am a citizen!"

"Titi, let's go upstairs. Mama is gonna be home. Come on!" Nilda spoke forcefully into Aunt Delia's ear and took her arm, leading her towards the door.

"Bunch of bastards. Jacinto, you are a hypocrite! I swear to you," Aunt Delia said, smacking her lips and

243

making the sign of the cross, "I will never play another number with you again."

Nilda led the old woman out of the store and into the street. "I don't want no trouble, officers," she heard Jacinto say as she started home.

Aunt Delia walked briskly and continued to speak. "If my number comes out, I will sue him. Yes, I will. He legally will owe me the money."

"Shh," Nilda said, annoyed, and put her finger up to her lips, looking crossly at Aunt Delia. Honestly, she said to herself, what a pest! Always embarrassing me. Several people looked at them and smiled, shaking their heads. Nilda halfheartedly returned their smiles and silent greetings by shrugging her shoulders. Everyone knew her Aunt Delia. The old woman continued to whisper, protesting, indignant and angry. Nilda ignored her as they walked to their building and finally reached the apartment. She walked in and heard her mother in the kitchen. "Mama?" she yelled.

"I'm in here, Nilda," her mother called out.

Aunt Delia ran into the kitchen and began telling her mother what had happened. ". . . and I will sue him, Lydia, if my number comes out. Yes, you give me the name of the lawyer you got for Jimmy. I will sue Jacinto."

Her mother looked at Aunt Delia and, closing her eyes, made the sign of the cross. "Nilda, did she really call the policía?"

"Yes, Mama, you shoulda seen it. I was so embarrassed. She was hollering at them and at Don Jacinto," Nilda said.

"At the police?" her mother asked incredulously.

"Yes," Nilda said, and couldn't help laughing. "Mami, she was trying to talk in English!" Her mother looked at Nilda and they both began to laugh. "She, she called him a son of a bitch. In English!"

Aunt Delia asked, "What? What did you say?" and looked at them as they both laughed.

"Delia!" her mother shouted. "What in heaven's name did you do? You know betting the numbers is not legal. How many times did I tell you already? Eh? You know very well that what you did was not right!" Aunt Delia listened and, looking at her mother, remained silent. Slowly, Aunt Delia began to smile and then to giggle; she looked at Nilda and her mother and started to laugh. After a while, all three burst out laughing. "Poor Jacinto," her mother said, laughing, "he's gonna lose what little hair he has on his head." Then, turning to the old woman, she continued in a more serious tone. "Delia, listen. You give me your list. Like I told you, and I will play them for you at my job in the factoría? O.K.?"

"I want to go myself," said Aunt Delia.

"You cannot! Until we get someone else that we know in the neighborhood, understand? If you do not give me your list, you will not get your bet placed. Now I am serious. Don't bother Jacinto again. No more! That's final!"

Aunt Delia nodded her head, looked away, and said, "Well, I have to read something very important now. Excuse me, but I have no time for this conversation." Quickly, the old woman left the kitchen.

"Mama, can I go out?" asked Nilda. "Sylvia's coming."

"Out to where?"

"Just around, outside. Maybe we'll go to the park, or walk around or something."

"Well, if you go to the park, who's going?" her mother asked anxiously. "I don't like you to go, just two girls alone, you and Sylvia!"

"If we go, it will probably be like a whole bunch of us. But we will just hang out."

"Who is a whole bunch?"

"Just some kids, Mama."

"O.K., but you must come home early, before supper; you have to help me. You are a señorita now, no more little kid running around."

I wish she would stop preaching at me all the time, thought Nilda. Out loud she said, "Fine, Ma, I'll be back early. I'm gonna wait for Sylvia downstairs, O.K.?" Her mother nodded her head. "Bendición, Mama," Nilda said, and left the kitchen.

"Dios te bendiga, Nilda. Don't forget what I told you."

"Hey, what kinda uniforms do you like the best?" asked Sylvia.

"I like the sailor uniforms the best. My brother Paul looks real good in it. I got a picture of him on my bureau." Nilda smiled and looked at the other girls. They were all seated on the stoop steps of Nilda's building.

"I love the Marines best," said Marge. "They all look so great in the dress uniforms. You know, the white hats and blue-and-red jackets, and that gold braid . . . real sharp." Marge's hair was now a bright yellow, and she wore it parted on the side and pulled up in two large pompadours. The roots at the part were a very dark brown.

"You know what I like best?" asked Petra. "The pilots; they have the greatest uniforms of all. I seen a picture last week with Alan Ladd, you know, and he gives his girl his wings. He is a bombardier and has to go out on dangerous missions. It was just terrific."

"I agree," said Sylvia. "The pilots look real neat in them uniforms. I saw that picture. Alan Ladd, man what a doll!"

"Did you see that movie, the one where they got all them lady movie stars? You know, Claudette Colbert, Veronica Lake, Lana Turner, Ann Sheridan, a whole bunch," Marge said, "and they are Wacs . . . I think they were . . . anyway, they are overseas in this combat zone . . . and they all got boyfriends . . . and . . ."

The girls continued to talk. It was hot and muggy. Nilda looked up and down the street; it was practically empty. She saw three boys coming towards them; she recognized Indio, Willie, and Hector. They looked disheveled, hot and sweaty. Indio had a white handkerchief tied around his forehead, keeping his straight black hair back. They carried a baseball glove and bat and their club jackets. She watched as they approached her stoop and was surprised as she saw Indio go into a strut and all three boys pass by without looking at the girls.

Nilda stared at them and said, "Hey . . . look . . . isn't that . . ."

Suddenly Indio made a sharp turn, went right up to Petra and, facing her, said with a smile, "Hi, ugly. I almost passed you by, but couldn't resist your charms."

Petra giggled and, raising her arm, gave him a polite punch on the shoulder. "Too bad," she said. "You shoulda kept right on going."

"I can't help myself," Indio responded.

Petra shut her eyes, shrugged her shoulders and, folding her arms, said, "Tough, boy. You just gotta suffer."

Nilda watched as everybody laughed; she felt her face flush. She had never seen Petra and Indio together like this before and couldn't help feeling embarrassed.

There was a short pause; then Willie said, "Man, we murdered them guys."

"Yeah, what a lousy shortstop they had. Next week we'll beat them worse," Hector said. "Especially if Frankie can play. Yeah . . . hey, where's your brother?" he asked Nilda.

"He's working. He's got a job delivering at Mr. Fox's, you know, the tailor's right around the corner."

"Man, that's a shame. He missed some good game. I hope he can play next week. He's the best second baseman we got," said Hector, and smiled at Nilda.

She returned his smile and shrugged her shoulders. "I don't know about that," she said.

Everyone was silent; they watched the traffic on the avenue go by. Music sounded from the tenements, bouncing onto the streets, several radios competing at once. A small group of children had gathered in the gutter and found a piece of shade where the black tar was not melting. They began to chalk out a large area, and then lined up to play hopscotch.

"Well?" Indio said, looking at Willie and Hector. "It's getting late. What do you say?"

"O.K., we got the money, man. Let's go," Willie answered. Hector nodded his head.

Indio looked at the girls and said, "Excuse me, misses," and bowed respectfully. "We gotta discuss something among us men." He gestured to Hector and Willie, and all three boys went over to the next stoop and began whispering.

Nilda and Sylvia looked at each other, perplexed, and then looked at Petra. Petra sat down next to her sister Marge and said nothing.

Nilda felt uncomfortable. "Two more weeks and school is over," she said.

"Yeah! No more Mrs. Fortinash," Sylvia responded.

"I'll be going to that school next year," Marge said. "I sure hope that I don't get her. Maybe I'll get Miss MacGavin; I heard she ain't too bad."

"I know somebody who's got her and she said she can be nice," Sylvia said.

The three boys returned and everyone was very quiet. After a short while, Indio said, "Listen, how would you girls like to go rowboating in the lake?"

"Oh great!" said Marge. "Huh, Petra?" Petra smiled and nodded.

Indio turned and looked at Hector. "Go on, man," he said softly.

"Nilda," Hector said, "would you like to come too? Rowboating?" Nilda felt her face burning up; she did not respond. "Sylvia, you are welcome to come also," said Hector.

"No!" Nilda said.

"I have to stay with Nilda," said Sylvia.

"Aw . . . come on, Nilda. Just for a little while," Marge coaxed. "We won't stay long. Come on, please."

"No," Nilda said sharply, "I have to go home soon and help my mother do something."

"O.K.," Hector said softly. "Another time then?"

"Another time," Nilda said, nodding her head and looking straight ahead, avoiding Hector's glance.

"Let's split, man," Indio said. "We're gonna miss the whole day, man, wasting time."

"Indio, you walk on ahead," said Petra. "We'll meet you at the entrance on 110th Street. Inside. O.K.? Don't wait outside, but like where the water fountain is, inside."

Indio nodded. "Make it snappy," he said.

The three boys started to walk away. Hector stopped and turned, facing Nilda. "Say hello to your brother for me, will you, Nilda? Tell him he missed a great game and that we murdered them creeps."

"Yes," Nilda said, looking at him, "I'll tell him." She wet her lips and swallowed, hoping she didn't look too embarrassed. The boys left and she heard their voices trailing off as they discussed their victory in today's ball game.

Marge and Petra stood up and looked at the boys as they disappeared from view. "Listen, Nilda . . . and you too, Sylvia. Please don't say nothing about this to nobody," said Petra. "Like if anybody asks, you know, where we went or anything."

"I won't say a word, Petra," Nilda said.

"Me too," Sylvia said.

251

"Thanks . . . it's just . . ." Petra hesitated. "Nilda, you know how my father is . . . well anyway, just don't mention nothing."

"Petra," Nilda said, "don't get into a sweat. I won't say nothing and neither will Sylvia. Right, Sylvia?" Sylvia nodded. "Go ahead, go on; I won't say nothing." She watched as the two sisters left, heading towards the park. Sylvia and Nilda sat for a while silently.

"Did you know Hector liked you?" asked Sylvia.

"I don't know that he likes me," Nilda said, looking away.

"Well, he asked you to go out with him, didn't he?"

"He just asked if I wanted to go rowboating, and he asked you too, didn't he?"

"Big deal!" Sylvia said. "He only asked me because we were together. Honest, come on, did you know? Do you like him, Nilda?"

Nilda looked directly at Sylvia and broke into a smile. "Sylvia, I don't even know him. Honest."

"But . . . do you like him?" Sylvia insisted.

Raising her hand to her mouth, Nilda began to giggle. "I don't know . . . honest! Really, Sylvia." She began to laugh; then both girls giggled.

"What do you think, huh, Nilda? Maybe you shoulda said yes and gone with them."

"Right away!" Nilda said. "My mother would only kill me into a thousand pieces, dead."

"He might ask you out again."

"Go on, Sylvia, don't be stupid."

"Well," Sylvia said, "he did say 'some other time' and you said 'yes.' "

"I did not!" snapped Nilda.

"Oh yes you did. I heard you. You said, 'some other time,' and even nodded your head," Sylvia said loudly.

"Shh . . . did I? Honest? Oh, my goodness," said Nilda, covering her face with both hands. "I'll die."

"Anyway, you are lucky. I wish Frankie would have been here," Sylvia said. "He never says one word to me. I don't think he likes me."

"You know what, Sylvia? We might have a party at my house this Christmas. My brother Paul might come home on a furlough. And my brother Victor may be coming home too; he got wounded and they gave him a medal. Well, because of all that, he is supposed to be discharged. My mother said she will give a big party, and I'll invite you. I'll ask her, and she won't mind. O.K.?"

"All right," Sylvia said dejectedly.

"Frankie will be at the party."

"He won't even notice me, I'll bet."

"Sure he will. There's gonna be dancing and everything."

"Will you say yes if Hector asks you out again, Nilda?"

"He won't ask," Nilda said. "Anyway, I don't care; I don't even know him." The two girls remained seated for a while longer. "I better go up, Sylvia; my mother says I have to help make some packages for my brothers."

"Walk me home, Nilda?"

"I'll walk you halfway. O.K.?"

"O.K."

They walked along the avenue; it was late in the afternoon and slightly cooler out. "Here we are, Sylvia. This is halfway."

253

"O.K. See you at school Monday."

"So long." Nilda started back home, walking slowly.

Every time she thought of Hector she felt embarrassed. He's way older; I'll bet he's almost fifteen, and he's Frankie's friend, she said to herself, and recalled that cold night last winter when she had seen Hector running away from the police with Frankie, and she had met Chucho and Manuel. I wish that had never happened, she said to herself. Manuel had been in and out of the hospital since then; he had lost almost all the vision in his left eye. He was going in again for a second operation. Nilda remembered when Manuel first came out with a black patch over his eye; everyone had said he looked just like a pirate in a movie. Her mother had been beside herself with anger. "They would have killed you, Frankie, if they had caught you!" She had yelled and screamed at Frankie. Nilda thought of her mother's constant lectures about boys, and decided that, at least for now, she would put this whole business out of her mind.

Early December, 1944

Nilda hurried all the way home. She couldn't believe what she had heard; and yet, everyone knew about it. At first she had been shocked, but now she felt a mixture of sadness and emptiness inside that she could not understand. Nilda felt sorry and frightened for Petra; she knew Petra's parents well, especially her father. He's so strict, thought Nilda. When Petra had stopped seeing her, Nilda had been heartsick and angry because they had been friends since kindergarten, but gradually she had become used to not seeing her friend.

Sylvia had been with her that afternoon when she had heard the news. "Nilda, you know what? Your old ace, Petra, got kicked outa school, man. I heard she's gonna have a baby!" Margarita Rojas had told her. "You know who it is, don't you? It's Indio. That's what everybody is saying. And you know he split; he joined the Navy."

"Are you sure you know what you are talking about, Margarita?" Nilda had protested. "I don't believe you."

"I don't care if you do or not. You used to be tight with her, her best friend, and you don't even know? I can't help it if you didn't even know about it. Go ask anybody you want. The whole school knows. Her father already came to school and signed her out and everything."

"That's right, Nilda," another girl had said. "She's

not jiving you. I heard all about it myself from Diana, who is in her class and lives on her block. Go ask her; she'll tell you."

Nilda had said nothing in reply, and had walked home with Sylvia, silent most of the way. Sylvia had tried to start a conversation a few times, but Nilda did not respond. Rushing up the steps, she thought, What's her father gonna do to her? She remembered that he used to beat his daughters. Nilda entered the apartment and went to her room, putting away her books. Then she went into the kitchen; her mother was home.

"Nilda? I left work a little early today; I had a lotta things to do and, at the factoría, things are a little slow this week. Anyway, I got bad news," she said, and held up a letter. "Look, can you imagine? I just received a letter from that place in Lexington, Kentucky. Your brother cannot come home yet for two months! When I made my visit in July, they told me he would be home for Christmas, that his parole was almost granted already. Here now, they tell me he has to wait!" She shut her eyes, and Nilda could see she was almost in tears. "Paul cannot make it either. I'm sure, because he said if he could come home for the holidays, he would write us last week, and he still did not send any word." She put down the letter. "I was hoping to have my family together this Christmas, at home and safe." Nilda did not know what to say, so she listened silently. "They don't tell nothing about Victor. At first they say he got enough points to come home. He was wounded in the shoulder and got a Purple Heart; that they tell me, but now I don't hear nothing. What am I supposed to think?"

"Mama, it's nothing bad . . . maybe he is just still getting better."

"Maybe," her mother said, shaking her head. "But I was planning something nice, something special. And now . . . some Christmas!"

"Is Victor's girl still coming for Christmas, Mama?"

"As far as I know, yes; that's what she says. I don't know any different, and I already wrote to her and her parents and told them that she will be looked after properly in my home. I have been waiting for an answer; maybe when she writes, she'll tell me something about my son."

Victor had written her mother that he had been corresponding, since he had left for the Army, with a girl he had dated in high school. All during his stay in the service she had written to him, even when her family had moved to Connecticut. They now planned to become engaged when he returned home. She was of German-Irish descent, and Nilda's mother had been worried about the girl's family and their attitude. "I hope them people don't start that business with us about us being Spanish, Puerto Rican, or whatever nonsense, because I will not put up with any of it." But so far the correspondence had been very friendly, and the young woman in Connecticut had sent a color photo of herself in her high-school-graduation cap and gown, signed: "To Victor's mother and family, With love from Amy Shuster."

"She's very pretty," her mother had said, showing the photo to Nilda. Nilda saw a smiling face with fair skin, pink cheeks, and light blue eyes. Her chestnut-brown hair was done up in a soft permanent wave and cut shoulder length. "I don't know, Nilda," her mother was saying, "somehow, this Christmas is important to me. One never knows if there is going to be another one."

"Mama!" Nilda said. "What's the matter?" Her mother looked at Nilda and quickly started to say something, then closed her lips tight and decided not to speak. "Mami?" Nilda said in a worried tone.

"Never mind, nena. It's nothing . . . it will be all right. What will be . . . well, we shall make the best of it. Like we always manage. O.K.?" Her mother smiled at her.

"O.K." Nilda returned her smile, relieved that her mother seemed less depressed. Then she thought about Petra. "Mama, something happened at school."

"What happened?"

"I heard something . . . something about Petra."

"Petra? What is the matter with her?"

"Well . . . they say . . ." Nilda hesitated. "They say she's gonna have a baby."

"A baby!" Her mother's eyes widened. "Petra? Pregnant? You are fooling me, Nilda!"

"No, Mama, that's what somebody told me and Sylvia this afternoon. They said her father signed her out."

"Who told you? Are you sure?"

"Everybody knows it, Mama. Believe me, I asked. And she is no longer in school."

"Do they know the boy that is responsible for this?" her mother asked angrily.

"They say it is Indio."

"Indio? From Frankie's club? Didn't that boy join the service, the Army or Navy?"

"Navy, Mama; he left in the summer. He didn't go

back to school; he quit. Like Paul. Remember you said, 'Just like Paul, he don't wanna finish school.'"

Her mother shook her head. "Poor Petra, poor fool. La pobrecita, bendito! If I know that rotten Jorge López, I don't know what he would do to that boy if he caught him. Maybe it is better for him that he is away in the service. Because that man would kill Indio for what he did to his daughter. He's so nasty and prejudice, he hates dark people, and that Indio is darker than Paul. Well, I know Indio's parents, the Carrions, and they are very nice people; maybe they can work it out so that their son will do right by this girl and protect her honor." Her mother made the sign of the cross. "What a disgrace that girl has brought to her family. What a shame!"

There was a short pause and Nilda wondered what she should say, perhaps in defense of Petra. Her mother's voice was sharp and angry. "Nilda! Look at me!" Nilda looked at her mother. Her mother walked up to her and, standing in front of her, shouted, "You don't disgrace me. You don't bring me shame. Nilda! When you want to fool around, think of that girl, think of Petra. What kind of life will she have? Finished, no more school, no more fun—no more nothing!"

Nilda continued to sit silently, frightened; she did not dare say a word. Her mother seemed very angry; she had stopped speaking and had sat down, covering her face with her hands. Nilda watched her and worried, wondering what her mother might be thinking. "Mami," she said softly, "are you all right?"

Without lifting her head, her mother said, "I'm all right, Nilda. Go do your homework; leave me; go on."

Nilda left the kitchen and entered her room. What's

she so mad about anyway, thought Nilda. Petra's gonna have a baby, not me! She thought of her friend. Wow, a baby! she whispered to herself. And for the first time in a very long while, she remembered Baby Jimmy. Once, about a year ago, she recalled that she had asked her mother if they would ever go to visit Baby Jimmy. "He is no longer ours, Nilda," her mother had said. "You must stop asking about him and thinking about him. Sophie is married to somebody else; Jimmy did not do right by that girl."

Nilda had never mentioned the baby again, and hardly thought about him any more. But now, this afternoon, she vividly recalled what he had looked like when she first saw him, and what it had felt like to say good-bye when her brother and Sophie had taken him away.

Nilda sat down and, opening her schoolbooks, stared at her homework assignment for a long while. She closed the books and took out a piece of white paper and a fountain pen, and began to write to her brother Paul.

Dear Paul,

How are you? I am fine. I hope you can come home for Christmas. Mama wants to have a party if you do. Maybe Victor can come too. So far we do not know for sure. Only what I wrote you last about him getting the medal and about him being wounded in the shoulder. Anyway, his girl is coming to stay here Christmas. She lives in Connecticut. Mama is going to ask her if she knows whether Victor will be coming home or not. She sent us a picture of her in a graduation cap and gown. She is very pretty. Mama says that they are very friendly. Her name is Amy Shuster. We are not really sure if she is coming here but we think so. I don't know about Jimmy's parole, but Mama said he will not be coming home for Christmas, that is definite. She got a letter from them. He is all cure from the drugs, and Mama says he will have a job and go back to school. Maybe drafting, you know he is good in math.

I heard some bad news and I feel sorry for Petra. You know Indio? Well they say Petra is going to have a baby and that it is Indio who is the father. I knew he was her boyfriend for a long time, and many times she had asked me not to say nothing. I never did because I was not going to snitch on nobody, especially if it is not my business. I told Mama about it and she starts to holler at me. Saying I should not do nothing wrong, and I don't even have a boyfriend even. Anyway she is very nervous. I hope she calms down and stops picking on me.

Aunt Delia is fine and still reading the newspapers and warning everybody in the whole neighborhood about murderers and getting attacked. Frankie quit his job at Mr. Fox's and is now working for Western Union, but Mami don't like it because he has to go out of the neighborhood. He is always talking about joining the Air Force, you know he loves airplanes. I sure hope you can come home for Christmas we all miss you. Mama wants to invite Aunt Rosario and her family. I like her except sometimes she is too bossy. Claudia is nice. This summer when I stay with her, (remember I told you when Mama went to that place in Lexinton, Kentucky to see Jimmy) she shared her things with me. But that Roberto thinks he is hot stuff and I think he just stinks. He is a spoil brat and I will tell his mother so if he gets smart next time with me, I am not scared of him one bit.

You ask me about school, well all I can say is I am doing alright. My teacher this year is a little bit better than the one I had last term, except she hollers too much. And I still have that dopey Miss Reilly for Spanish. I'm gonna take French if I have her again next year, I swear to you. Dont worry Paul, I will not leave school, and I am working on a drawing for you. When I finish it I will mail it out to you if you still want it. Well, that is it, I guess. Tell me how you liked that place Tiajuana in Mexico, if you did go there after all. Please take care of yourself. I miss you very much. If you can come home for Christmas, please write. I will invite my girlfriend Sylvia. I told you she's got a crush on Frankie still, but dont say nothing or she will never speak to me again. Send me more pictures of all the places you go to. I love to have them and show them off at school.

Well that is it. Love and kisses from me and Mama and Aunt Delia and love and hugs

> *Your loving sister,*
> *Nilda xxxxxxx*

P.S. Petra got kicked out of school, If you know where Indio is, since he is also in the Navy, maybe you can tell him.

> *Love N.*

April, 1945

She sat quietly, watching the buildings, shops, and crowded streets slip by as the bus moved steadily along. It was late in the afternoon and Nilda felt a warm breeze and bright sunlight coming in through the open window above her seat. She held on to a package in her lap; it was filled with a box of tissues, toilet water, and a jar of hard candy. These were the things she always brought to her mother. Nilda glanced at Aunt Rosario, who sat silently beside her. She was younger than her mother, a little bit taller, but she had the same coloring and a similar way of expressing herself. She's so bossy, Nilda said to herself. Always telling me what to do. I wish she would go back to the Bronx and leave me alone. Always acting like I'm a baby.

Her mother had been in and out of the hospital twice before in the past four months since Christmas. This time her mother had been in for almost three weeks. During that time Aunt Rosario had spent weekends at the apartment with Nilda, and many evenings as well. Now, Aunt Rosario had been with Nilda for the past three days.

Nilda thought about her mother and became frightened as she remembered what Aunt Rosario had told her when she returned from school this afternoon. Her manner towards Nilda had been soft-spoken and considerate. "Nilda, honey. We got a call this morning from the hospital, about your mama. She is very sick again. In fact, we had to send out telegrams to Paul and Victor; she might get worse." Aunt Rosario had put her arms around Nilda. Confused and upset, Nilda had not been able to respond. "Let us pray and hope that she pulls through. If she doesn't, then we must have a talk. Yes? You and me." Nilda had nodded, unable to answer her. "Get ready now; we have to go to the hospital right away. I have been waiting for you. I'll take Frankie tonight to see your mama. It's not visiting hours now, but Lydia is on the critical list; we got special permission to go anytime."

Aunt Rosario reached over and lightly tapped her arm. "We get off here, Nilda."

She was quite familiar with the hospital by now. The first time she had come to visit her mother, the nurse at the desk had asked her age. Aunt Rosario had answered loudly and sharply, saying Nilda was sixteen. "You have to come in to see your mother, Nilda," Aunt Rosario had said, determined. "You must attend to her needs. You are her only daughter; she has no one else. We cannot count on Delia."

They took the elevator up to the fourth floor and went down a long, narrow, windowless corridor, arriving at the very end at a set of double doors leading to a small ward. No one was about, and they walked swiftly inside. Her mother's bed was in the middle of the ward; Nilda saw heavy green cloth partitions near the sides of the bed.

Her mother lay back. Her long black hair had come

loose and fallen down over her shoulders, covering her breasts, barely touching her folded hands, which rested on her stomach. Her eyes were shut. Leaning over, Nilda gently kissed her mother on the forehead and, standing back, waited.

Her mother slowly opened her eyes and looked at her. Recognizing her and Aunt Rosario, she said, "Nilda? What are you doing here? Is it visiting time?"

"Lydia, how are you, eh?" Aunt Rosario said, and kissed her. "Nilda, give your mother the package." Nilda handed her mother the brown paper bag she had been carrying.

"Put it there on the table, nena," her mother said.

"I got them candies you like, Mama. Hard candy, you know, the round ones, different colors and flavors."

"Open it, honey . . . take some . . . go on." Nilda took out the jar of hard candy, opened it, and offered some to Aunt Rosario.

"No, thank you," she said.

"Mama?" Nilda asked, handing her the candy.

"No, honey . . . you take . . . go on." Nilda looked at the jar and took out one red and one yellow candy, popping them both into her mouth. She sucked the hard candy, and the sweetness melted in her mouth, down into her throat, helping to take away the dryness she felt.

"Do you want me to comb your hair, Lydia?" Aunt Rosario asked.

"Yes . . . Rosario, maybe you better. I feel like such a mess. The nurses have been busy and I hate to bother them to comb my hair. I feel too dizzy to do it myself. Braid it for me, will you? Just make two long braids, nice and tight, so that it will stay neat for a while." Aunt Rosario rearranged the pillows, and then began to comb her mother's hair. "How's Delia?"

"Ave María, Lydia," said Aunt Rosario. "She's wackier than ever. Now she's got it into her head that she don't trust the numbers man, and wants a receipt. She insists that he used to give you one! She's going to drive him crazy. The other day she followed him down the street, calling after him for a receipt."

Her mother smiled, shook her head, and said, "Jacinto has still not recovered from last summer." Both women laughed. "And my Frankie . . . is he going to school, or giving you a hard time?"

"No, he's a good boy, but all the time he talks about the Air Force and the airplanes. He gets together with my Roberto and they both start the business about joining the Air Force."

"Rosario, I hope this terrible war ends soon. Anyway, from what they say on the radio, we are winning, and maybe we will have peace soon."

Nilda heard the other patients coughing and clearing their throats. It was quiet at this time; visiting hours today were not until evening.

"Nilda," she heard Aunt Rosario say, "do me a favor, honey. Please take this pitcher of water outside to the nurse and ask for some fresh. Tell her it is full but not cold. It is warm. O.K.?"

Reluctantly, Nilda took the metal pitcher of water, annoyed that Aunt Rosario was again telling her what to do. She walked out into the hallway and went towards a desk that was placed outside a small examining room. The chair

267

at the desk was empty and there was no one in the corridor. She looked inside the examining room. A man dressed in white sat by a table, looking at a folder. Nilda cleared her throat. "Excuse me," she whispered, and waited. "Pardon?" she said a little louder.

"Yes?" the man said. "What do you want?"

"Some water, fresh water. My mother is in ward 4E, and my aunt sent me to see if I can get some more water. This water is too warm."

"Isn't there a nurse outside?" he asked.

"No."

"I don't know. You might try the water fountain down by the elevator."

"All right," Nilda said. "Thank you."

"Sure," the man said.

She walked out and headed down the corridor towards the elevator, looking for the water fountain.

"Hey! Psst, psst," someone called in a loud whisper. "Where are you going?" Nilda saw a nurse waving to her. "What are you doing here?" she asked irritably.

"I'm visiting my mother and I was going to get fresh water."

The nurse grabbed the pitcher out of Nilda's hands. She looked inside the pitcher and shook it. "What's the matter with this? It's full of water."

"It's too warm. My aunt said to get some that is cold."

"What are you doing here now anyway? It's not visiting hours till this evening."

"We got special permission to come," Nilda answered.

"What's your mother's name, and in what room is she?"

"Her name is Lydia Ramírez, and she is in ward 4E."

"Is she on the critical list?"

"Yes."

"All right, give me the pitcher; I'll take care of it for you. But in the future, you cannot walk around in the halls like this. You should call somebody. Your mother has a button on the wall over her bed; all she has to do is push it." She looked at Nilda and waited for an answer.

"Yes," Nilda said.

"All right then, go back to your mother and I'll take care of this."

Nilda returned to the ward. She saw that Aunt Rosario had been crying; she held a tissue up to her face, blowing her nose and wiping her eyes. Her mother's eyes were open wide, much wider than usual. Nilda wanted to tell her mother about the nasty nurse, but felt foolish for even thinking of complaining about anything. "The nurse took the pitcher and she said she's gonna bring it back with fresh water," she said.

"Good girl," her mother said, smiling. Her mother's hair was neatly parted in the middle and combed into two tight braids framing her face. With her hair fixed that way, Nilda noticed, for the first time, how much weight her mother had lost; her body seemed to disappear under the white hospital gown.

"Well, Lydia, I have to see the doctor now for a little while," Aunt Rosario said, quite composed. "Nilda, honey, you stay with your mama. I'll be back in a little while." She put her arm around Nilda and gave her a soft hug. "Lydia, now is the time to tell me about what you want. I can speak to the doctor personally. Besides more of the pills, anything else, Lydia? Eh?"

"Just to increase the pills, especially at night for the pain. Or maybe, Rosario, a sleeping tablet that is stronger . . . that's all."

"O.K.," Aunt Rosario said, "right away," and she left, walking out of the ward. Nilda took an empty chair and placed it next to her mother. She sat down, taking her mother's hand.

"Nilda," her mother said, "I have to talk to you, honey. Listen, I have to tell you something and you have to hear every word I say, O.K.?" Nilda looked at her mother, trying not to act too frightened, and nodded her head. "I may not get better . . . you have to think about that."

"No, Mama!" Nilda protested.

"Shh, you have to listen," her mother said seriously. "Now just in case . . . I have already talked to Rosario. She knows just what to do; you must listen to her." Nilda felt her face getting flushed, and she began to cry and shake her head. "Shhh . . . shh . . . Nilda, stop it! Now just cut that out. How am I gonna talk to you if you carry on like a baby? A big señorita like you should not act like this."

"I don't care," Nilda sobbed. "I don't feel like no big señorita anyway! And I don't like Aunt Rosario; she's always bossing me."

"Come on now, shh . . . honey." Her mother stroked her hair. "Now listen . . . if she bosses you it is for your good. She's wonderful and she loves you." Nilda shook her head furiously and sobbed quietly. "Never mind . . she does love you." Her mother waited and was silent for a moment. Nilda stopped sobbing and sat quietly. "Nilda," her mother continued, "if anything happens to me, you will go to live with her and you must be cooperative and listen to her; she has given me her promise and her solemn word that you will be to her as you are to me."

"Mama," Nilda cried, sobbing softly, "I don't wanna live with them . . . I wanna stay home . . . in my house with Aunt Delia and Frankie."

"You have to start to grow up, honey. If something happens to me, your home is with Rosario, and with no one else. Aunt Delia cannot take care of you! She cannot even care for herself; she has always been a worry to me and you know that. Frankie is going to leave; I know that as soon as he can, he will join the service, and you will be alone."

"What about Victor and Paul, Mama? I can live with Paul, and Jimmy is gonna come home, ain't he? Maybe if Jimmy gets a job, Aunt Delia and me, we can manage something."

"They are grown men with lives of their own. Victor will get married and have his family. Paul is in the Navy; I don't know when he will get out even. You have to go with Rosario. Jimmy is not even home yet. And he has his own problems; I cannot leave you in his care. I will not be here. Do you understand? Nilda?" Nilda was silent. "Your home is with Rosario and you will be a good daughter to her." Nilda remained silent. "Nilda?" her mother insisted, "You must promise me. I cannot die without your promise!"

"Mama! You are not gonna die! No!"

"Nilda, your promise," her mother said, determined. "I said your promise! Look at me." Nilda looked at her mother. "Go on, honey. I must know that you will be in good hands. She will be as your mother . . . you must promise."

"All right, Mama, I promise . . . if that's what you want," she said tearfully.

"Yes, Nilda, that is what I want."

Nilda put her head down on the bed next to her mother's shoulder, and they were both silent. After a while Nilda spoke. "Maybe you will get better? Right, Mama?" she asked hopefully.

"Maybe I will . . . you never know, nothing is for certain . . . so you must pray . . . and I will pray also. There is always hope. Right, honey?" Her mother seemed more cheerful; Nilda was relieved and became talkative, discussing school, her friend Sylvia, and their neighbors at home. Rosario returned and the three of them spoke a little longer.

A young nurse walked up to the bed. "Here's your water, Mrs. Ramírez," she said, smiling. "And it's time for your temperature and medicine."

"Lydia," Rosario said, standing. "I'm coming back tonight. Willie is bringing the kids. O.K.? We'll see you later. Don't forget I already talked to the doctor and he said he would increase the pills. So, let me know; anyway, you rest now." Nilda bent over, kissed her mother, and followed Aunt Rosario out of the ward.

Outside, it was still hot and humid. Traffic was heavy and people rushed back and forth. She walked quickly, beside Aunt Rosario, as they hurried to catch their bus back uptown.

Nilda waited in the corridor outside the ward, standing next to Victor, who was in uniform. He was to be discharged from the service in three weeks, but had arrived last night on special leave. Frankie walked back and forth nervously; once in a while he whispered something to Victor.

Everyone had been informed; telegrams had been sent to Jimmy and to Paul. Aunt Rosario had been at the hospital most of the night and, after going to the apartment briefly, had returned early this morning to summon a priest for Nilda's mother. Aunt Delia had not been allowed to come to the hospital this past week. Despite her persistent questioning, everyone had reassured the old woman that all was going well at the hospital.

Aunt Rosario stepped out of the ward, wiping her eyes. She looked at Nilda. "Nilda . . . go on inside now . . . but remember your mama is very, very sick, and I want you to try to compose yourself so that you don't make her too nervous." Aunt Rosario waited and Nilda did not move. "Go on . . . for heaven's sake," she said impatiently. "Lydia wants to see you alone for a little while . . . hurry up." Nilda nodded and slowly walked inside

273

the ward and over to her mother's bed. This time the heavy green cloth curtains were pulled around the sides and front of the bed. Nilda extended her arm and pushed a section of the curtains aside, looking in. Recognizing her mother, she stepped in all the way, closing the curtains behind her.

Her mother was lying back with her eyes shut, her head slightly tilted forward. For an instant she felt her insides jump. Is Mama dead? she thought. But then she looked up and saw a metal stand supporting a bottle which hung upside down. An invisible liquid flowed out of the bottle and into a long thin tube; the tube was attached to a needle that was taped into her mother's right forearm. She went closer to her mother and heard her breathing. Then raising her hand, she lightly touched her mother's arm.

Opening her eyes, she looked at Nilda and smiled faintly. "Nilda?" Her voice was very hoarse and just above a whisper.

"Mama, how are you?" Nilda said shyly. She had not been to see her mother for a few days.

"Nilda . . . I'm very sick, nena." She paused and breathed heavily. Looking down, Nilda began to cry. Her mother watched her and slowly shook her head. Nilda buried her face next to her mother's on the pillow and cried uncontrollably for what seemed a long time. After a while she raised her head. "Take a tissue," her mother said. Nilda picked up a tissue, blew her nose, and wiped her eyes. "How's school?" her mother asked.

"Fine, Mama."

"You still drawing those wonderful pictures?"

"Yes."

"You are gonna stay in school . . . like a good girl and finish?" Her mother spoke very slowly. "You are not gonna be foolish and quit?"

"No, Mama." Nilda sat on a chair and was very still, her eyes fixed on her mother.

"Nilda, you have to promise me that you will stay in school, and that you will listen to Rosario." Nilda nodded. "You eating all right?"

"Yes." There was a long silence. This morning, at home, Nilda had planned to ask her mother about a whole lot of things, and to talk about some of the things that bothered her. Now, as she sat close to her mother, she was very frightened and felt almost like a stranger. She did not know what to say or what to do. "Mama?" Her mother looked at her. "Petra had a baby girl last Sunday." Her mother smiled. "She had a little girl; she named her Marianne."

"Marianne? Do you know, Nilda, that was my mother's name. Mariana. Yes, your grandmother. That's a pretty name. Have you seen the baby yet?"

"No, I just heard about it. Maybe I'll go visit them next week."

"What about Indio? Nilda, did they get in touch with that boy?"

"Well, I heard he is coming home on leave, and that his father already gave Mr. López his word that Indio would marry Petra. Even though they are Lutheran, they said he will marry Petra in the Catholic Church. Anyway, that's what I heard."

"Nilda, you must never do anything foolish like that. Never. Don't have a bunch of babies and lose your life."

"You had children, Mama, and you love them and—"

"Nilda," her mother interrupted, and reaching out with her free hand, took both of Nilda's hands and held them tightly. "Listen to what I say. I love you, Nilda, and I love your brothers, all of you, regardless who the father was, I don't care . . . you are all . . . still mine." She paused and closed her eyes, remaining silent for a while. Nilda wondered if she had fallen asleep, but she opened her eyes again. "You are a woman, Nilda. You will have to bear the child; regardless of who planted the seed, they will be your children and no one else's. If a man is good, you are lucky; if he leaves you, or is cruel, so much the worse for you. . . . And then, if you have no money and little education, who will help you, Nilda? Another man? Yes, and another pregnancy. Welfare? Yes, and they will kill you in the process, slowly robbing you of your home, so that after a while it is no longer yours." She stopped speaking, and pushing her head back against the pillow, she stared at the ceiling, but continued to hold Nilda's hands.

"Mami?" Nilda whispered. "Aren't you happy? I love you, Mama. Aren't you happy with us? I want to be with you all the time, Mama."

Tightening her grip on Nilda's hands, and without looking away from the ceiling, her mother said, "I have no life of my own, Nilda." Her voice was very low and hoarse; Nilda had to lean closer to hear what she said. "I have never had a life of my own . . . yes, that's true, isn't it? No life, Nilda . . . nothing that is really only mine . . . that's not fair, is it? That's not right . . . I don't know what I want even. . . ."

She paused, and Nilda felt her mother's body shaking; she was laughing without making any sound. "Do you know if I were to get well tomorrow . . . what I would do? Nilda? . . . I would live for the children I bore . . . I guess . . . and nothing more. You see, I don't remember any more what I did want. . . . Sometimes when I am alone, here in the hospital, I remember a feeling I used to have when I was very young . . . it had only to do with me. Nobody else was included . . . just me, and I did exist so joyfully in that feeling; I was so nourished . . . thinking about it would make me so excited about life. . . . You know something? I don't even know what it was now. How is that possible? That there is this life I have made, Nilda, and I have nothing to do with it? How did it all happen anyway?

"Do you have that feeling, honey? That you have something all yours . . . you must . . . like when I see you drawing sometimes, I know you have something all yours. Keep it . . . hold on, guard it. Never give it to nobody . . . not to your lover, not to your kids . . . it don't belong to them . . . and . . . they have no right . . . no right to take it. We are all born alone . . . and we die all alone. And when I die, Nilda, I know I take nothing with me that is only mine." She paused and said, "You asked me something, didn't you? . . . oh yes. . . . Am I happy? . . . I don't know. . . . But if I cannot see who I am beyond the eyes of the children I bore . . . then . . ." turning her head, she looked directly at Nilda for a moment ". . . it was not worth the journey . . . and I might as well not have bothered at all." Shutting her eyes once more, she lay back against the pillow.

Nilda began to cry again, this time quietly. After a bit, she said, "Mama, I don't understand you."

"Someday you will, you know . . . yes. Hold on to

277

yourself, even if at times you have to let go some . . . but not all! No . . . Nilda . . . not ever. A little piece inside has to remain yours always; it's your right, you know. To give it all up . . . entonces, mi hijita . . . you will lose what is real inside you."

Opening her eyes, she turned and, smiling at Nilda, released her hands and stroked her hair. "My poor Nilda. I have nothing to leave you, nothing. I only know that you have a little more than I ever had, and that will have to be enough." Nilda watched as her mother breathed heavily; closing her eyes, she began to snore softly and evenly.

Nilda felt very confused. She had wanted to say so many things and had forgotten what they were. Watching her mother sleep, she remembered that she had wanted to ask permission to go to Leo's for a while. They had invited her, and Concha had said that she would be happy to have her the entire summer. She did not dare to wake her mother or ask her anything. She watched the bottle as it gulped bubbles of the invisible liquid into her mother, then glanced again at her mother, who seemed to sleep so peacefully. Nilda stood up and very carefully kissed her on the forehead, then walked past the curtains and out into the corridor, joining Aunt Rosario and her two brothers. They all looked at her anxiously.

"She's asleep . . . she . . ." Nilda hesitated and shrugged.

"O.K. Good, honey," Aunt Rosario said. "Did she talk long to you, honey? She wanted very badly to talk to you." Nilda nodded her head. "Good. Victor, the priest has already been here; now, do you want to stay, and shall I take Frankie and Nilda home for now? What do you think?"

278

"That's a good idea, Tía. Go on ahead. I will stay and find out what's happening. I don't think she should be alone now."

Aunt Rosario nodded and asked, "Will you come home for a bite to eat, Victor?"

"No, I'll grab something down in the hospital cafeteria. Go on, it's fine . . . now, if anything develops, I'll call Jacinto's grocery store. So don't worry . . . go ahead . . . you look tired, Titi Rosario, why don't you go on back and take a little nap yourself?"

"No, Victor. I'm O.K., and today is Thursday, so Willie is bringing Claudia and Roberto tomorrow. He has been a very big help to us." Victor nodded his head. "I'll see you this evening, Victor."

Nilda followed behind Aunt Rosario and Frankie. Outside it was hot and muggy; the streets were crowded with people.

"Let's walk to the subway, kids; it's faster," said Aunt Rosario. They walked along and Nilda glanced at the newspaper headlines as they passed the newsstand.

GERMANY TO SURRENDER
HITLER FLEES!
AXIS RETREATS
WAR TO END WITHIN 24 HOURS

A radio was blaring from an open lunch stand, and Nilda heard the newscaster talking about the end of the war and the signing of a peace treaty. She stepped down a stairway quickly, and all three headed for the subway train.

That night Nilda had a feeling of emptiness, making her exhausted. She felt that she would never see her mother again and that today was the last time they would ever speak. She had her window open and a cool breeze swept through the room. It had cooled down some, she thought, and remembered that tomorrow was school; she had an English test and she had not prepared for it. Too tired to really care, she fell asleep and dreamed she heard her mother calling her in a whisper.

"Nilda! . . . Nilda!"

She opened her eyes and felt someone's hand on her shoulder, gently shaking her. It was Victor. Sitting up, she looked at him.

"Nilda, wake up, honey," he said. "Mama is dead; she died this morning at two A.M."

Victor, Paul, and Jimmy greeted people at the door as they walked in to pay their respects. Aunt Rosario was busy mingling with everyone, making sure that each person was offered and given food. The apartment was crowded with friends and neighbors.

They had all worked, preparing lemonade, coffee, cocoa, and tea, and had set out an assortment of crackers, cheese, and cookies.

"Yes, thank you; it is a great loss to us all," Aunt Rosario said to a neighbor.

"She was so young," said an older woman dressed in black.

"Yes," added another woman, "and she looked so beautiful laid out in the coffin, just like in real life; it is amazing how they can do that." Nilda listened to the conversation as she helped to clear up the dirty cups, spoons, and dishes.

"It has cooled down," said Aunt Rosario.

"The rain is good for something," said a man who was sipping a cup of coffee. "It has cooled down things, so now it's not too hot."

"Yes indeed."

"Uh huh," they all agreed.

"That was a lovely funeral, Rosario," said a neighbor. "All those flowers. And they do a lovely job at that place; I had my uncle buried through them and they did a fine job."

"Well, we did the best we could, you know," Aunt Rosario answered.

Nilda walked by them, her hands full of dirty dishes. She walked past Aunt Delia, who had placed herself in a large armchair in the middle of the living room, with her paper spread open, and read to herself, moving her lips and uttering shocking comments. She ignored people when they tried to greet her, and only when someone shouted in her ear did she acknowledge their presence with a polite nod. Nilda remembered what Aunt Delia had said. She had been furious with Aunt Rosario ever since her mother died. "I don't trust that Rosario," she had told Nilda. "She has always been rotten, even in Puerto Rico, when she was little. And I am going to get a big lock and shut up my room." That afternoon she had come into Nilda's room and shown her a padlock with a large key. "See, I am going to put this on my door, keep it locked; that way Rosario cannot come inside and take my things."

Nilda was still upset when she remembered that Aunt Delia would be going away and she would not live with her any more. "She cannot live with me, Nilda," Aunt Rosario had said. "She's too crazy. I am not Lydia. Only your mother could put up with her, because she was a saint! But not me! I don't want my marriage to be broken up by that crazy old woman. Now, I've got her a wonderful place in this Catholic home, where she has a room and everything, and the nuns can look after her. She's gonna stay with a family till September and then we can put her in; we are lucky to get such a place!" Victor and Aunt Rosario had made all the arrangements; despite her protests, Nilda realized that there was nothing she could do.

She walked out of the living room and headed towards the kitchen. "Nilda!" she heard someone call. Turning, she saw her brother Jimmy coming to her. "Come over here, baby." She walked over and he put his arm around her. "This here is my old buddy; I want you to meet him. Jojo, this here is my kid sister, the only girl in our tribe, man."

"Hello, Nilda, how you doing?" A tall man with a pencil-thin mustache smiled at her. He was dressed impeccably in a brand-new suit.

"Hi," Nilda said, feeling awkward as she held on to the pile of dirty dishes. He smelled heavily of toilet water and fresh-scented soap.

"He's gonna help me get started again, honey," Jimmy said. "Look, I got a little favor to ask. Can we use your room, baby? So we can discuss a little business and straighten out a few things. It's the only empty room now, and . . . do me a favor, don't come in for a while? If anybody wants to go in, tell them not to. All right?"

"Sure," Nilda said. Both men left, going down the long narrow hallway to her room. She had not heard Jimmy talk like that since he had gotten home. He had been quiet and withdrawn, mostly keeping to himself. He

284

sounds like he used to, thought Nilda. She walked into the kitchen. Claudia was by the sink, washing dishes.

Nilda began to pile the dirty dishes into the sink. "Want me to wash for a while, Claudia?" she asked.

"Yeah, thanks, Nilda," Claudia said. "I'll dry them."

Nilda turned on the water and began to wash the dishes. "I wonder where that Frankie is?" she asked.

"He left with Roberto to get some glue for his new model airplane," said Claudia.

"He never helps," said Nilda, annoyed.

"Forget my brother Roberto. Mama never asks him to do nothing. He's a spoiled brat. And they won't be back for a while, I bet you, leaving us the dirty work."

They worked quickly, washing and drying the dishes.

Paul walked in. "Whew," he said, "they are finally beginning to leave. Man, it was too packed in there. How are you two doing?"

"O.K.," said Nilda. "We got all the dishes done. But you know what, Paul? That Frankie didn't help; he left with Roberto!"

"You know he's a knucklehead anyway, don't you?" Paul said, smiling at her. "We doing all right without him. Right?"

She smiled at Paul; she had been much happier since he had come home. "Too bad you have to leave tomorrow, Paul," she said.

"I'm gonna be coming back sometime this summer. I told you, didn't I? We're gonna go to the movies. How's that?"

"Hey," asked Claudia, "who's that tall man dressed so sharp?"

"What man?" asked Paul.

"Oh," Nilda said, "he is with Jimmy, but we don't know him."

Aunt Rosario walked in. "I sent Willie for more cookies a long time ago, and when he gets here there's gonna be nobody. Everybody left. I wonder what happened to him? Probably got caught in the rain," she said, and began to fill a tray with cheese and crackers. "O.K., this should be the last of it," she said, walking out of the kitchen.

"Let's go see who is out there. We are finished here," Nilda said. Paul, Claudia, and Nilda walked into the living room.

Aunt Delia still sat in the armchair, reading to herself. Victor spoke to several neighbors who were getting ready to leave. Leo and Concha were standing off to the side, talking to Aunt Rosario. Nilda walked over to them and, tapping Leo on the arm, asked, "Did you ask her, Leo?" He looked at Nilda and then at Aunt Rosario.

"She's not going anywhere with you, at any time," Aunt Rosario said firmly, staring at Leo.

"Well, Rosario, if you change your mind—"

"I don't change my mind," she interrupted.

"Look, Rosario," Leo said, raising his voice slightly, "I'm not going to argue with you, but after all—"

"After all nothing!" Aunt Rosario shouted.

"I have a right to see her," he said loudly.

"You have a right to nothing here!" Aunt Rosario screamed. "You lost your rights. Don't talk to me about rights. Years ago you gave them all up. Lydia . . . Lydia knew that, and now I know that, Leo! No rights at all—none!" Victor left the people he was speaking to and

286

walked over to Rosario, putting his arm around her. Leo stared at Rosario angrily, then glanced at Victor and looked away. The room was silent; Nilda watched as Aunt Delia put down her papers. The neighbors stood by the entrance of the living room, looking her way.

"She'll come to me when she is older," Leo said very softly.

"One has to earn love in this world, Leo. You don't get anything for nothing," Aunt Rosario said quietly but firmly.

"You don't know what the circumstances were then, Rosario," Leo protested.

"But I know what they are now, don't I? Lydia died alone, Leo. And I know all about the circumstances now."

The front door opened abruptly and Willie, Rosario's husband, walked in, holding a paper shopping bag. "I'm soaking wet. It's raining very heavy outside," he said.

Going towards him and ignoring Leo and Concha, Aunt Rosario took the shopping bag. "Let's go to the kitchen, Willie. I'll make you some fresh coffee." She went to the neighbors and, smiling, said, "Stay and have some more coffee. Yes?"

"No, thank you. We have to leave."

"Nonsense, you stay," she said.

"No, thank you very much." They exchanged good-byes and left.

Nilda was standing and remained silent; she didn't know what to say to Leo and Concha. Claudia had left, following Rosario to the kitchen.

Victor spoke to them. "Tonight I go to Connecticut.

287

I have only three days' leave left; I'll be back day after tomorrow, then back to the base, and then back to civilian life again."

"Well, that's wonderful," said Concha. "Good luck to you and the very best. When you come back to the Barrio, you have to have supper with us and let us meet that beautiful girl of yours."

"All right," Victor said, smiling and blushing.

"Well, son," Leo said, extending his hand, "you know where I am. If you should need anything at any time, I will always be available." Turning towards Nilda, he said in a very low voice, "Nilda, listen, honey. I will see you soon. Your aunt is upset, but don't fight with her; after a while, she will let you come and visit us. So don't worry. Everything is all right and everything will be fine." Reaching into his trouser pocket, he pulled out a dollar bill. "Here, nena, buy yourself something from me." He put the paper money in her hand and kissed her on the cheek.

"Thank you, Leo," she said.

"O.K. Now, you be good and listen to your aunt." Turning to Concha, he said, "O.K., let's go."

Concha kissed Nilda. "Remember," she said, "you know where we are." Nilda nodded and watched as they left the apartment.

"Looks like everybody's left," Victor said. "I better get packed; I gotta catch the train out to Bridgeport."

"Victor! Come here and look at this," Aunt Delia called out. "You too, Nilda." She jumped out of her armchair and held out her newspaper. "Look, see what I told you? Here in this article, they explain it all. You can read, can't you? Right in a hospital in the City of

288

New York, in the United States of America, they gave this man the wrong operation and he died. Now you tell me nothing happened to Lydia? This is proof. I knew she was fine; there was nothing wrong with her. Only," and lowering her voice, shifting her head in the direction of the kitchen, she went on, "that woman Rosario would not tell me anything because she knew I would stop what they were doing."

"Mama was sick," Victor said.

"What? What did you say?" the old woman asked, cupping her ear.

"I said," Victor shouted in her ear, "Mama was sick and she had to go to the hospital."

"Oh no," Aunt Delia shook her head. "Nilda, you tell him because you know the truth. No sir! Indeed not! The enemy are everywhere . . . don't be so stupid."

Nilda looked at Victor and they both shrugged.

"I have to go to Connecticut, Titi Delia. I have to leave now."

"O.K., go ahead," Aunt Delia said indignantly.

"I'll see you day after tomorrow. I'll be back. Please don't fight with Rosario or anybody; please be good. O.K.? Give me a kiss." Aunt Delia smiled and gave him a loud kiss on the cheek. "No more fights, O.K.?"

"I only tell the truth," she said, and closing her newspaper, left the room, muttering to herself and shaking her head.

"You see, Nilda?" Victor said. "Now who is gonna put up with that? Nobody. In fact, I feel sorry for the nuns in that home; she's gonna drive them nuts." Nilda burst out laughing. Victor laughed too.

They heard someone at the front door and went to see who it was. Jimmy was standing with the door ajar and calling out, "I'll meet you on 110th Street, in the candy store on the corner, Jojo. Take care, man, and keep it cool . . . and thanks!" Closing the door, Jimmy saw Nilda and Victor. "Everybody left, I guess, huh?"

Before Nilda could answer, Victor took her arm and said, "Let's go to the kitchen, Nilda, and see where Aunt Rosario is." Nilda could see that Victor was angry.

Aunt Rosario, Claudia, Willie, and Paul were in the kitchen. "You leaving now, Victor?" asked Aunt Rosario.

"Soon. Anything you want me to do?"

"No. Victor, who was that man with Jimmy?" she asked. "That bird all dressed up like a movie star or something! I don't like his looks."

"I don't know and I don't care. Don't bother yourself about Jimmy. That's his affair, not ours," Victor said angrily.

"That boy is on parole," Aunt Rosario said, "and after what his mother went through getting a lawyer and going down to see him, I don't want him to get into trouble again. Especially with the drugs." She paused.

"Well, he's on his own," Victor said. "You worry about Nilda; we can take care of ourselves."

"Well," said Aunt Rosario, "I worry anyway. I know Frankie will join the Air Force after this term. He already promised me he would finish this year. But Jimmy . . . I don't know what I can do for him."

"Don't bother yourself about it, Titi Rosario," Victor said.

"I can only do the best I can, but after all," she said.

"Look," said Paul, "you do the best you can, Aunt Rosario; like Victor says, worry about Nilda. But don't be so hard on Jimmy. Especially you, Victor. Man, it must be hard to come back after such a long time, and be sick, and now the family is split up. Maybe you are all jumping to conclusions and—"

"I was away too," interrupted Victor, "and I was lucky to get back at all and in one piece. It's not easy for anyone; he's not the only one with problems."

"Man," Paul said softly. "Victor, take it easy on him."

"Like he took it easy on Mama!" Victor shouted. Everyone stared at Paul and Victor and said nothing.

After a while, Willie said, "Hey, Lady Rosario? Where's my fresh coffee? I have to have something to drink with all them cookies I got." He smiled and everyone laughed with relief.

"You are right," said Aunt Rosario. "Victor? Tell me what time you coming back here, because we gotta talk to the landlord of the building."

"As soon as I have the time schedule I'll let you know," Victor said.

"We already pay for this month's rent," Aunt Rosario said. "Nilda and Frankie only got a few weeks of school left, so I can take them out a little early, and meanwhile they can manage till then. Also, I got a moving company coming. You have to look for what you might need. Extra dishes, pots, linens, some of the things your mama had, because I don't need that much extra. And you will be setting up house in Connecticut, so maybe you can bring your girl . . ."

Nilda suddenly felt very tired; she slowly left the kitchen, going to her room.

"Where you going, Nilda?" she heard Claudia calling.

"To my room; I feel very tired."

"Can I come?"

"Sure, Claudia."

"You know what, Nilda?" Claudia said as she walked with Nilda into her room. "My mother said she's gonna get us matching bedspreads and curtains when you come to live with us, just like sisters."

"Really?" Nilda said. "That's nice."

"Oh, look at all those nice drawings, Nilda," Claudia said. "Maybe we can hang some of them up in our room too."

"You like them, Claudia?" Nilda asked.

"Oh, sure. I always wished I could draw like you, honest. You draw great," Claudia said, smiling. "Can I see some more?"

"Oh," Nilda said, "it's nothing really."

"Sure it is. Let me see some more," Claudia said.

"Well, if you really would like to see them, I got some older ones here," Nilda said happily. "Let me show you." Opening her closet door, she pulled out a large box and, digging inside, took out a drawing pad. "Now, these drawings are ones that I made when I was a little kid; they are of a camp I went to once." Holding up the pad excitedly, she pointed to the drawing on the page. "Here is the cabin where we all slept; there were eight of us. And that's the inside here; that's my bed, and," Nilda turned the page, "here is a special trail in the woods. You see how it winds . . . well, that trail leads to a secret garden."

Format by Anne E. Brown
Set in 11 pt. Times Roman
Composed by The Haddon Craftsmen, Inc.
Printed by The Murray Printing Co.
Bound by The Haddon Craftsmen, Inc.
HARPER & ROW, PUBLISHERS, INCORPORATED